FETCHING

Kiera Stewart

DISNEP • HYPERION BOOKS
NEW YORK

First Edition

3 5 7 9 10 8 6 4 2

G475-5664-5-12006

Printed in the United States of America

Designed by Marci Senders

Library of Congress Cataloging-in-Publication Data

Stewart, Kiera.

Fetching / Kiera Stewart.—1st ed.

p. cm.

Summary: Deeply humiliated by the leader of the popular crowd on the second
day of eighth grade, Olivia, who has lived with her grandmother since her mother
left the family, plots her revenge using dog training techniques.

ISBN-13: 978-1-4231-3845-7

ISBN-10: 1-4231-3845-7

[1. Middle schools—Fiction. 2. Schools—Fiction. 3. Dogs—Training—Fiction.
4. Grandmothers—Fiction. 5. Mothers—Fiction.] I. Title.

PZ7.S84935Fet 2011

[Fic]—dc22   2011006102

Reinforced binding

Visit www.disneyhyperionbooks.com

For Kylie, with lots of love.
You are a treat.

ONCE THE BELL *rings, look around. You may not have noticed them at first, not in the way you think, but they're everywhere. Racing down the halls, lapping up their lunches, lazing around the classrooms, playing fetch in the gym.*

There are the toy breeds, society's spoiled little darlings, and the terriers, who really sink their teeth into things. There are the working breeds, who let nothing get in the way of an A.

There are the sporting breeds, who are better on the field than in the classroom, and the non-sporters, who are still sniffing out their niches.

There are hounds, who can smell fear a mile away, and there are herders, who are always looking for a pack.

There are mad dogs and female dogs, pit bulls and bulldogs. There are lapdogs and pets, puppies and runts.

Dogs. Every middle school has them.

Welcome to mine.

A Dog of a Day

SO IT'S THE second day of eighth grade and I'm hearing people giggle and whisper things like "Oh my God" behind me. That part doesn't surprise me—it's happened a few times before. Usually it's because my jeans might be a couple of inches too short, or maybe I have dog hair stuck to the seat of my pants, or maybe I missed a belt loop or something unforgivable like that.

But never because of *this*.

Mr. Chang is at his desk at the front of the room when I walk into fifth period a good three minutes early. As I pass his desk, I hear a loud gasp, and then he starts to stutter. It takes me a minute to realize he's trying to say my name.

"Um, uh, uh, uh, Olivia?"

I turn my head. His face is red and pinched like he's in a lot of pain. Whatever's going on with him, he doesn't exactly look healthy.

"You okay?" I ask stupidly. Moronically. I wonder if he's having a heart attack or something.

"Yes, uh." His hand goes to his forehead. I look around

2

the room. Erin Monroe is at her desk, already immersed in her Spanish warm-up. Carson Winger is slumped over his desk, taking a nap. They are the only other people in the room, and neither of them looks like they know CPR.

"Come here, please," Mr. Chang says quietly. His eyes are squinted closed, and his thumb and forefinger are squeezing the bridge of his nose. This is what my mother used to do when she was getting a migraine. Probably still does; who knows?

I walk closer. "Um, Mr. Chang, are you okay?"

He doesn't open his eyes. He just mutters something to me about the nurse's office.

Oh, dear crap. His life is in my hands.

More people have come into the room, but no one seems concerned about Mr. Chang at all—and he's practically purple and could be *dying*. In fact, they're looking at me, smirking. I guess they don't think I can handle this type of emergency. My heart is pounding, and time is wasting, so I open my mouth and yell, "Someone call nine-one-one!"

"*What!?*" Mr. Chang's eyes snap wide open. "No!"

The class is filling up quickly, and people start roaring with laughter. Mr. Chang winces, cups his hands around his mouth, and whispers to me, "You've had an *accident*." He exhales, closes his eyes, and lets his hands drop to his desk. "Now, hurry," he tells me, jerking his head toward the door and avoiding my eyes.

I'm nearly frozen with terror. Somehow I thaw enough to move in the general direction of the door, but I bump into Tamberlin Ziff, who says, "Watch it, Kotex," and gives me an evil smile, and I think, Oh, no. Oh, no. Oh, no. Oh, please God. No.

3

It occurs to me on the long sideways crawl to the nurse's office that despite the red stain on my pants, it can't be *that* time of the month. There's no way it can be.

It also occurs to me that earlier today, when I was just about to sit down to lunch, the evil/popular/conniving Brynne Shawnson approached our table, whipped out a camera, and started shooting "first-week-of-school" photos for the yearbook committee. My best friend, Delia, and I tried the duck-and-cover approach; Phoebe declared it "unwelcome and cruel"; Mandy raised her pierced eyebrow and made some illegal gestures; and Joey polished off his Little Debbie and was too busy huffing the oatmeal scent on the wrapper to really care.

It occurs to me, now that I think of it, my seat felt a little slimy when I sat down. And if I hadn't been so busy trying to hide from the camera, I probably would have thought to investigate this slime.

It also occurs to me now that Brynne high-fived Tamberlin when she returned to her own lunch table. And that Brynne and Tamberlin and all the rest of that mean, beautiful group threw their heads back and laughed out loud.

And it occurs to me now that a flattened ketchup packet fell to the floor when I stood up.

And it occurs to me now that I'm a complete and utter idiot.

"Oh, *honey*," Mrs. Arafata gushes when she sees the seat of my khakis.

"It's not what it looks like," I tell her, every inch of my body burning with embarrassment. My face is probably about as red as the massive ketchup stain on my butt. "It's ketchup. Someone's idea of a joke."

She gives me a big fake smile. "Of course it is, dear. Now *this*"—she lays a pad roughly the size and shape of the state of Pennsylvania across my forearms—"should take care of your lady problem. And *this*"—she turns around, opens what appears to be a big black trash bag, and pulls out a crumpled pair of tan polyester pants—the kind great-grandmothers wear. She shakes them out and holds them up for display. "This should take care of everything else."

I stare at the pants, horrified. "There's no way I can wear those."

"Sure you can, dear." She pulls her hands apart, stretching the waistband between them. "They've got an elastic waist." Then she folds up the pants and places them on top of the pad I'm holding. I look down at the label. It reads "Sassie Lass™ Walking Slack. Color: Taupe. One Size Fits Most."

The backs of my eyes start to ache. I blink hard and look up at the ceiling tiles and will myself not to cry. "Can't I just"—I try to speak, but my throat keeps closing up. I take a breath and try to finish—"call my grandmother? To pick me up?" My grandmother, Cornelia, a.k.a. Corny, is volunteering at the dog pound today. She's teaching basic commands to a couple of strays, but I know she'll come get me if I ask her to. It's been more than a year since my mother took off, and Corny is still trying to make up for it. My mom's her kid, so I guess she feels a little responsible.

"Well, now, there's only two hours of school left. And once you get"—she pauses—"well, shall we say, *cleaned up*, you'll be as good as new." She opens the door of the small clinic bathroom with a flourish of her hand. I go in, defeated.

The door shuts behind me. "Take your time, dear," Mrs. Arafata says. I close the seat of the toilet and sit down. Giving up on my battle against the tears, I let myself wallow in the feeling of hate. Hate for Brynne Shawnson and all her friends. For middle school. For my life, at least today. My therapist would say hate is not a feeling—that it's the result of a lot of other feelings, like humiliation and disappointment and whatever else, but I say, so what? That's like saying you can't call bread *bread*—that you have to call it water and flour and yeast and all those other things that go into it. I mean, *seriously*.

A few minutes later, Mrs. Arafata knocks on the door. "Sorry to disrupt, but I didn't mean *this* much time," she says. She adds a little giggle, like this whole situation is just some type of funny inconvenience and not the absolute worst day of my life.

I take a deep breath and step into the very condemning pants, which sag in the crotch and are cropped just above my ankle, and say farewell to my very last shred of dignity.

Mrs. Arafata sends me back to class, but I head to the front office instead. I do this for two reasons. For one, the last thing I want to do at this moment is to be seen in these pants by anyone under the age of forty. And two, I'm about to do something I've thought about doing many, many times before. All through seventh grade, in fact. I just never had the guts to do it. Until now.

Mrs. Forester, the assistant to the assistant principal, is manning the desk. The glass door chimes when I open it, and although her fingers and eyes stay on her keyboard, the corners of her mouth form an automatic semi-smile. "Can I help you?" she asks, without looking at me.

"I'd like to file a complaint," I tell her, my voice quivering.

"A complaint?" She looks in my direction, drops her auto-smile, and adjusts her glasses. "What kind of complaint, hon?"

I'm not sure what to say. What kind of complaint would you make against someone who spreads rumors that you have fleas? Who once hooked a dog leash onto your back belt loop—which took you two hours to discover? Who takes a simple little fact about you—in my case, that dogs outnumber humans in my family—and turns it into endless entertainment for herself and her horrid little friends?

It's not like I'm the only target of Brynne and her cronies. All my friends—Delia, Mandy, Joey, and Phoebe—have suffered their wrath. In elementary school, before I got here, Brynne and Delia were best friends, but last year, Brynne smuggled Delia's bra out of the locker room and stuck it in Corbin Moon's backpack. Delia's mother had, unfortunately, sewn her name into it. For a whole month Delia had to endure the nickname "Triple A." And Tamberlin, whose heart has been surgically removed and replaced by a pebble, convinced the art teacher that Mandy was some crazy goth girl who should be kept away from blades. Mandy had to do her midterm collage project with safety scissors and a buddy. And I'm sure it was Corbin who secretly signed up Joey for the wrestling camp at the high school, where competitive sports are not only allowed, but strongly encouraged. When Coach Adams called him down for a weigh-in, Joey had a panic attack. The school janitor found him later, under the bleachers, curled into a fetal position.

And I can't forget the bottle of eau de toilette that Carolyn Quim gave to Phoebe in the Secret Santa swap last year. Which really *was* de toilet.

"Well, hon, what happened?" Mrs. Forester asks, a little impatiently.

"I guess you could say I was sort of attacked by Brynne Shawnson."

Her eyebrows lift, making thick pleats in her broad forehead. "Attacked? Are we talking assault or harassment?" Her thick fingers pick up a pen. This is all sounding so serious—so *Law & Order*. I am picturing Brynne Shawnson being handcuffed and taken to jail. I'm sure she won't look so pretty in her mug shot. "Well, hon, which was it? With words or fists?"

I take a breath and say, "With ketchup."

Her lips clamp together, and she lowers her glasses and peers over the lenses at me. "Ketchup," she says flatly. "So no one was hurt in this 'attack.'" She even makes little quotation marks in the air with her fingers when she says this.

Now it's my turn to be shocked. "Hurt?" I say, loudly. "No one was *hurt*? First she tricks me into sitting in ketchup so it looks like I got my period all over my pants, which is painful enough. And now, just look at what I have to wear!" I step back so Mrs. Forester can see the Sassie Lass "slacks" I've been sentenced to spend the rest of the day in. I mean, I'm no style icon, but even I know better. I grab the material at the hips and stretch it out so she can see their width. I snap the elastic waistband. I lift my ankle so she can witness the exposed stubble. "It's sheer torture."

She sits back, looking me up and down. "Well, Miss Albert, I'm sorry you're not happy with your outfit, but you look fine to me. Absolutely fine. Personally, I think those slacks are *darling*.

8

Now, would you like me to call in a peer mediator?"

I shake my head no. This is how clueless middle school administrators are. They send the nosiest, most gossipy kids in school out on a ropes course somewhere in the woods, maybe throw in a few trust falls, and then stick them right back into the center of everyone's private business. It's a known fact that behind every juicy Hubert C. Frost Middle School rumor stands a peer mediator with at least a couple of team-building awards to his or her name.

"Well, then, I suggest you get back to class and think about some ways that you girls can get along. Maybe there's a hobby you both enjoy—I bet you hadn't thought about that." She gives me a fingernails-on-chalkboard smile.

I slowly make my way backward to the door. She sighs, turns back to her computer, shakes her head, and mutters, "Honestly, *ketchup*," under her breath.

That's when I start to realize that if justice is ever going to be served, I'll have to do the serving.

2.

House Broken

ON THE BUS home, Brynne sits by a window, her knees bulging into the back of the seat in front of her. Next to her is minion Danny Pritchard, a former geek who is enjoying recent fame based on rumors that someone saw him driving a car to CVS. He's one of the ten thousand guys in school who is madly in love with Brynne. I mean, sure, she's beautiful. If I didn't know her, I would swear that she was a model for Abercrombie or something. She has this long, wavy auburn hair and these eyes that are so blue you kind of wish you had a gem of the same color so you could wear it as a necklace. The only thing that doesn't look exactly right on her is this scar along her chin. It's like someone was drawing her and got the chin-line wrong and went back to fix it, but forgot to erase the original line.

And it's not just the boys who flock to her—the girls do too. Even if you don't like her, you kind of have to be in awe of her. Not only because of the way she looks—she just has this air about her like she's scared of nothing and entitled to everything. It's like someone really *did* die and make her queen of the universe.

You'd think that someone who can be so mean would have trouble making friends, but unfortunately that's just not true. Brynne is sort of the middle school version of a fancy country club. If you can get her to like you, then everyone seems to think you must really be pretty cool. And there are two categories of people at Hubert C. Frost: 1. her friends and/or those trying to be, and 2. fair game.

As a prime example of "fair game," I duck my head and practically tiptoe down the aisle, but Brynne is too busy being annoyed by Danny to even look up and see me in my social-suicide Sassie Lasses. For that, I am thankful.

"Danny, move over!" she is saying.

"What?!" he says, pretending to be equally annoyed. But it's clear he really doesn't want to move another inch away from her.

"God. Your breath smells like fart," she says to him and her audience. Everyone but Danny laughs.

"You told me to save you a seat!" He's forcing himself to smile, but you can just hear the humiliation in his voice.

"*Please.* Aim away when you talk to me," she says, waving her hand in front of her nose. "When I told you to save me a seat, I didn't mean next to *you.*"

There's more laughing. I find an empty seat in the back, next to a kid who is so small that I didn't realize anyone was there until I was practically on top of him. He's got to be at least in seventh grade to be in our school, but his feet don't even touch the ground. He is reading *Car and Driver* magazine.

I pull out a piece of gum and stuff it in my mouth, which feels stale and sticky and like it might stink the way Danny's apparently does. I think of offering a piece to the kindergarten-looking kid, just to be nice, but when I glance over again, his pointer finger is about an inch into his nostril, so I just (very slowly) stick the package back into an outer pocket of my backpack and pretend not to notice. I spend the rest of the ride folding and refolding the foil wrapper into different shapes, and pretending that I'm some kind of origami artist and not just a humiliated middle schooler riding home in a loaner pair of elastic-waist pants. Every time the bus stops and one of *them* gets off, it feels a little less like a big fat lie.

After about a million years, the bus wheezes to a stop in front of the old farmhouse where I live with my grandmother, spits me out, and groans away. It's not a pretty house—it's supposed to be white, but it's gone kind of gray and flaky where paint is peeling off—but today I'm incredibly happy to see it.

Oomlot races toward me like a bolt of yellow-white lightning. I must reek of humiliation, because Oomlot licks my wrist so much that I have to dry it off on The Pants.

This is one of the things I've really learned to love about dogs—they are the exact opposite of middle schoolers. You can do everything you're supposed to do in school—smile at people, use deodorant, join clubs—and *still* most people will look at you like you've just pooped in the middle of the School Rules! Welcome Back assembly. And dogs, well, you *could actually* poop in the middle of a back-to-school assembly, and they'd probably love you even more because of it.

Ferrill, a Great Dane of gargantuan proportions, lumbers down the porch steps toward me and nuzzles my hand. The screen door squeaks open and Queso, our tiniest dog, follows Ferrill off the porch, yapping, until Corny slaps her hands together, meaning "stop" in their language. Then she waves at me from inside the screen door. I squat down to pet Queso. I am surrounded by dogs. Oomlot pushes in closer and leans against me, placing his front paw on my foot. I squeeze him into a hug. Even though his main ingredient is yellow Labrador retriever, it's whatever secret ingredients he has that make him especially cute. His coat is surprisingly soft and thick, and he's got a little white patch of fur over each eye, like those Swedish punctuation marks—that's why Corny named him Oomlot. After she got his dog tags made up, she found out it's supposed to be spelled *umlaut*, but she stuck with her version. With his big round eyes, the O's really suit him.

Corny walks out onto the porch, followed by our most polite and proper dog, Tess. Tess is a greyhound. She's smart and fast, but not fast enough. She was a race dog that never won any races, so now she's ours.

"Will you just look at this?" Corny says from the porch. "I keep saying I should take a picture."

"Well, take one if it makes you so happy," I say, revealing how incredibly cranky I am.

She gives me her little closed-mouth smile. That's one of the funny things about her. She's never liked her teeth—they're crooked and kind of gray. She says she was always teased about them when she was my age, and I guess that was before they had braces and white strips. You'd think by the time you're old and people stop expecting you to be pretty, you wouldn't care anymore. But I guess the things that happen to you in middle school stay with you basically forever. So I can just *imagine* what I have to look forward to.

"You know, I can't believe how scared you were of these dogs when you first moved here," she says now.

"They seemed so huge!" I say in my defense. Besides, that was a whole year ago. Yeah, I was afraid of them—okay, like deathly afraid. But at the time they seemed like a pack of hairy, salivating, fanged, bloodthirsty creatures. But that was all *before*. Before Corny sprained her ankle and I had to get over my fears just to help keep her business going. Before Oomlot claimed me as his favorite human. Before I got to cuddle a freshly born puppy.

"Yeah, that Queso is a monster," she says, with fake seriousness. Queso's a full-blooded Chihuahua who was given away because she wasn't perfect enough for the dog shows. Her ears were too floppy, and she was one pound heavier than she was allowed to be. Sometimes I wonder if the whole world is just some supersized version of Hubert C. Frost Middle School.

Queso hears her name and runs back onto the porch toward Corny, who scoops her up and tells me she has a T-R-E-A-T for me inside. She has to spell it out or the dogs will start spazzing, bowing and panting, practically doing pirouettes just to get a biscuit. But I follow her inside, stepping over Bella, our laziest dog—a hound mix who has the round shape and gray-brown coat of an Arctic seal—and find that Corny's actually baked me a cake.

"It's all for you. No bonemeal. No yeast," she says, over her shoulder. When Corny cooks, she likes to do it efficiently. In this house, that means using stuff that can be eaten by both species— canine and human. "Not even a drop of beef broth," she adds.

She turns around to hand me a knife. Then she almost drops it, finally seeing me at full-length. "Good God, Olivia. What are you wearing?"

I try not to break into tears as I explain what happened. And somehow I manage not to. Her wrinkled face gets even more wrinkled as I talk.

"I'm so sorry, Liv. I can't believe they put you through this. If only I had known—"

"It's okay," I say. Which it isn't, but still, it's not like it's *her* fault.

"I'm going to call that nurse lady and tell her, if anything like that ever happens again—"

"It won't," I reassure her. But inside, I'm not so sure.

"I don't care if they got a zillion sanitary napkins and a pair of gold-sequined pants worn by Elizabeth Taylor—"

She hugs me. It always surprises me how warm and soft her hugs are since she looks so old and bony.

The cake has white icing, and she's made little pink asterisk-looking things across the top with a tube of frosting. "Those are supposed to be flowers," she says.

"Thank you," I say, and mean it.

You know how sometimes you can be sad all day and not cry, but then someone does something nice for you, and it should make you really happy, but instead it turns you into a sobbing mess? Well, this is one of those times.

I call my dad after I eat a piece of the cake, which is surprisingly good, considering Corny's cooking habits. He asks me about school, which I don't want to talk about. Then I ask how things are going at work.

"Unfortunately, very well." He laughs apologetically.

My dad is supposed to be moving here with me and Corny when things start to slow down with his job. He's a carpenter, and his boss keeps promising to retire when the work stops coming in so quickly. But I guess everybody and their brother in Valleyhead, where I used to live, is building additions onto their houses, and my dad's boss keeps giving him more and more money to stick it out.

"Wish I had better news," he says.

Oomlot settles on the floor next to where I sit, and I reach out and ruffle his chest. Yellow-white fur floats into the air. A few years ago, Corny found Oomlot living behind the Food Lion. She took care of his worms and his fleas and his manners—but his shedding, it's the one thing she couldn't fix.

"It's okay," I lie. I don't bother telling my dad I miss him, because I think he already knows that. Plus I might cry all over again, and crying is one of my least favorite activities.

He says, "I'm glad you're okay with this," and I wonder if I'm becoming a better liar.

It's hard missing my dad. Just this past summer, I did have the chance to move back home with him. But I didn't. I loved my old cat Grey, but I couldn't see leaving the dogs for her. There's also another reason, a secret reason, I didn't go back home, and it's this: apparently, living people can have ghosts. Last time I was there, I could still smell the cinnamon my mom used to put in her coffee. I swear, one time after she left, I heard her goofy laugh coming in from the back porch. It's not like it was scary or anything—I mean, I loved her laugh—but still, it made me feel a little haunted.

But now, on the phone, my dad won't drop the school question. He comes right back to it and asks why I don't want to talk about it. So I have to say something. I don't tell him about the ketchup packet, but I do tell him about my new science teacher, Ms. Flamsteed, and how yesterday, the first day of school, she told us how proud she was of her last name because she comes from a long line of scientists, including the guy who first sighted Uranus.

He breaks into a monstrous laugh, just like we all did in class when she said it, despite the fact that she carefully pronounced it *YOUR-uh-nuss*. I say it the normal way when I tell him.

I'm glad he's not one of those adults, like Ms. Flamsteed, to use the word *inappropriate*. That word might not be dirty, but it sure can make someone feel that way.

It's good to hear him laugh. And it's good not to feel like crying.

Invisible Fences

IT'S BEEN LESS than twenty-four hours since the ketchup incident, but already Corny has washed and ironed the life out of the Sassie Lasses and folded them into a thick, tidy square. I'd tried to "forget" them this morning—and hopefully forever, actually—but Corny ran out to the bus stop, clutching them to her chest as if they were spun from gold or something, and made me promise to return them to Mrs. Arafata.

I find Delia at her locker before first period. "Can you go to the clinic with me?" I ask.

"Why? What happened?" She spins me around and examines the butt of my jeans.

"Nothing. Except, oh, *yesterday*," I say, turning back around quickly. "And now I have to turn the old-lady pants back in."

"But I'm supposed to get to Math five minutes early—I get extra credit for writing the warm-up on the board."

"Please? I *really* don't want to go alone. It's like reliving the whole humiliating event," I explain. "You're my best friend. I need you!"

It was just last week that these exact words were spoken, and that time, she was doing the pleading. Delia was worried she had a chronic foot-odor problem, so I had to take a whiff of three pairs of sneakers and some flip-flops and let her know if it was just her imagination. (It wasn't.) So we both know she owes me.

"Okay, you know I will."

We wind our way through the crowded hallways until we are close to the clinic. Then I brace myself and pick up my pace, and she follows me through the door.

"Oh, Olivia! Hi!" Mrs. Arafata says, way too loud, giving me the same wide-eyed, spacey smile that adults sometimes give to preschoolers.

"I'm supposed to give these back," I murmur, studying the floor tiles.

"Oh, honey," she says, extra-syrupy. "You didn't have to. Consider them a gift." I glance up just enough to see her looking very pleased with herself.

I try to stay polite. Maybe she's the type of person who would offer them as a gift to anyone. Maybe she secretly knows how horrible they are, and really doesn't want them back. Maybe. But then she lowers her voice to just above a whisper, and says, "And Olivia, you know you can let me know if you need anything else. I understand your *situation*."

My situation. That my own mom ran away from me. So it's perfectly clear. The pants are charity. She's judging me. It's not just girls like Brynne who see me as a reject; it's the whole freaking human world.

I want to throw the pants at her and run, but my arms seem stuck to my sides and my feet are like bricks. Luckily, Delia remains fairly pliable. She takes the pants from me. "She actually doesn't

19

need them," she says, and hands them over to Mrs. Arafata, who blinks and smiles.

And then Delia pulls me out of there.

"Thank you," I say as we walk down the hall together.

She puts her arm around my shoulder and gives me a little squeeze.

Then we spot Tamberlin Ziff and Carolyn Quim standing in the hall in front of us. I stare at the floor and concentrate on keeping my feet walking forward. As we pass through the cloud of Tamberlin's strawberry-scented perfume, I hear her say, "You think those two are a couple?"

"I know, *right*?" Carolyn screeches with laughter—a sound that feels like it will stay with me all day, like an annoying song you can't get out of your head.

After school, I summon Delia, Mandy, Joey, and Phoebe to an emergency session of the Bored Game Club.

Okay, so it's not actually spelled like that on the Hubert C. Frost Official List of Student Activities. It was just the backfire from one of Phoebe's brilliant ideas—the one part that stuck.

Halfway into seventh grade, she decided we needed some new members. We all spent a week designing flyers to advertise the Board Game Club—drawing squares around the borders with things written in them like (her idea), "You made a new friend! Advance three squares," and other things that make me cringe now. Two days after we got the flyers up, the Chess Club fired back, plastering the walls with their own "The 'King' of All Board Games" signs. And then—the nail in the coffin—by the end of the week, the Sudoku Club had managed to produce about two billion of their own full-sized neon-orange posters, which they used to cover every square inch of space in the math and science halls, and even the creative arts alcove, screaming in eight-inch letters, "Who needs BORED Games? Sudoku + U = Fun!"

The Sudoku Club recruited eleven new members. The Chess Club, a respectable seven. And us, well, we got Joey.

I've started rehashing the scandalous details of the ketchup incident when Mandy sighs and clunks her head down on her desk, revealing the blond roots in her jet-black hair, and says, "We're all a bunch of Marcies." This word—*Marcie*—may be by far the biggest contribution I've made to my group of friends. Marcie was the name of the head ribbon dancer of *The Great Me! Self-Esteem Tour*, which came to my elementary school every fall, so naturally, my then-best friend Rachel and I used this as a code word for "loser." Last year, I moved away from Rachel and left my old school, so this word is one of the few things left of my former life.

Joey twists up his face and says, "Shut up, Mandy. *Your mom's* a Marcie." This really has nothing to do with Mandy's mother at all, it's just Joey's way of saying he disagrees.

Phoebe's pale little eyes have been blinking wildly since I started talking. Now she turns to Mandy. "Excuse me, Mandy. Olivia just got attacked—in the worst way possible—and you call us all *Marcies*?"

Joey jumps in. "I don't think it was the worst way *possible*. It's not like she got mugged or anything."

"Joey, you don't understand. You're not a girl," I tell him, and immediately regret it. He is taking this as a compliment.

"What I mean," Mandy says, "is that we might as well all walk around with, like, bull's-eyes or something across our backs.

I can't stand it. Why does stuff like this keep happening? Why do they always make fun of us?"

"Well," Joey starts. He sucks in a breath like he's about to spew out a list.

"Don't answer that," Delia pleads.

We all sort of look around the table and answer it for ourselves.

Take Phoebe, for one. She's almost invisible. Not personality-wise, I mean. She's actually really outspoken, so it's not like you can ignore her. It's just that Phoebe is so pale she's almost see-through. Her eyes are the color of water in the shallow end of the pool, and her skin also has a watery quality, like skim milk. Her hair is long and white-blond, which kind of adds to her ghost-ish looks. She's also got some serious braces on her teeth, which gives her a smile about as pretty as a box of nails. But she's mostly serious and doesn't smile very often. It's almost like she got cheated out of the gene for humor—but if that's the case, she makes up for it with a double serving of brains. In fact, everyone seems to think that if it weren't for Phoebe, Mandy would have failed both the third and fifth grades. Or, as Mandy tells it, "I probably eventually would have been the only sixth grader with an assigned parking spot."

Not that Mandy's dumb. Not at all. Actually, most of the time she "gets" things that leave the rest of us clueless—jokes, people, that kind of thing. She's just not great with things you learn in a classroom. And people don't always "get" her. Mandy's what you might call emo. In some schools this would be cool, but Mandy, she takes it just a little past that point. She dyes her hair black and sometimes gray, and wears black Sharpie on her lips. Also, she has a pierced eyebrow, and it sometimes gets a little infected, so half the school calls her "Bubonic," and the other half is just afraid that she really is.

Joey's the only guy in our group. He's a full year younger than the rest of us (and acts it!) because he skipped fourth grade on account of being some weird type of math genius. He's kind of round and looks a little like the kid in the *Far Side* cartoons, which makes him a favorite target of ninety-nine point nine percent of all middle school boys. We've gotten used to Joey—he's obnoxious, but sometimes he can be pretty funny. Also he has the unique ability to keep score when we play board games without writing down any numbers at all, which is an added plus.

Delia is probably the most socially acceptable of us all. She's got these really pretty light brown eyes that remind me of root beer candies, and wavy black hair, and she's small and thin and wears good clothes. But her social problem is acne. Really bad acne. The skin on her arms and neck and hands is smooth and the color of, say, a Frappuccino, but her face is rough and blistery and different shades of red. Her mother won't let her wear makeup because she's afraid it'll make Delia's acne worse, so she just tries to hide it with her dark tumble of hair. I love Delia—she's my best friend out of all of them and the first friend I made when I moved here—but even I have to admit it's pretty bad. The worst thing about it is that it's made her shy—maybe not with us, but with the outside world. I hear that she used to be really outgoing and stuff in elementary school, but when she got zits, she crawled into her shell.

And then there's me. My outward defects are that I'm almost six feet tall and kind of scarecrowy in parts. If you took the word AWKWARD—with all those pointy A's and W's, and that unwieldy K—and made it into a person, that person would look a lot like me. My clothes fit me strange. I also have really frizzy dark brown hair. Actually, it's beyond frizz—it's more like fuzz. So sometimes I wear knit hats, even in August, when it's ninety degrees out, like today. My inward defects are that, thanks to a bunch of bad genes, I'm probably destined to a life of social problems and insanity. Also, thanks to Brynne Shawnson, people say I smell like dog. There may be some truth to that, since I live with a bunch of them, but I *do* bathe.

"Well, you know what?" I say now. "I'm tired of being picked on. We've got to do something about it. We need justice."

"Oh, so we're talking about revenge, right?" Joey leans forward. "Cool. What do we get to do?"

"Nothing," Phoebe says sternly. She puts her hands on the table. "Look, I don't want to get suspended or anything."

"Yeah, I don't either," Delia says. "I can't believe Brynne's like this now. We used to be such good friends."

"Yeah, in *fifth grade*!" Mandy says.

"Maybe you should just try to talk some sense into her," Phoebe suggests.

"Sometimes you're so naïve," Mandy tells Phoebe.

Delia shrugs. "I guess it's worth a try. She hasn't always been such a monster. I mean, she used to spend like every weekend at my house. We even played Scrabble together."

"Just because she used to play Scrabble with you doesn't make her a saint, you know," I remind Delia.

"Well, Clue too. She liked Clue," Delia adds. "And you know what? She actually used to let me win sometimes."

Something about her words makes me uneasy. Am I jealous maybe?

"Okay, fine. I don't care. That's settled. Now let's play Yahtzee," Joey says.

"No way. Scattergories," says Mandy, getting out the game. Delia rolls an *E*.

"How come we never play Yahtzee anymore?" Joey complains.

Just then, we hear "Did someone say 'Yahtzee'?" All of us—including our club sponsor, Ms. Greenwood, in the back of the room—look to the door to see her and her wavy auburn hair glide into the classroom. Brynne is here.

"I'm so sorry I'm late," she gushes, approaching the table.

"You're not here for the Bored Game Club," Mandy says. And then adds, "Are you?" Like it might, in some crazy parallel universe, be possible. She's usually a little smarter than this.

"Oh, well, I like games," Brynne answers, her blue eyes widening. Her head bobs as she rattles off her list. "I like Monopoly. And checkers. And cards."

Phoebe looks at her and back to us. "We like Boggle here," she says. I think she's falling for it. She is probably the smartest, most academically gifted person I know, *and yet*. I sigh.

"Oh, I love Boggle."

"You do?" Phoebe asks. Mandy gently puts her hand on top of Phoebe's, as if to try to bring her back to reality.

"Well, sure. And Clue. And Candy Land. And . . ."

I glance over at Delia, whose eyebrows are pulling together with concern. The Scattergories timer dings, but words beginning with *E* have been forgotten. There's only one word running through my mind. It, however, begins with a big fat *B*.

"You really like Yahtzee?" Joey asks, hopeful. Oh, no. Him too? "What about Stratego?"

25

"Straget . . . Strate . . ." Brynne tries. And then a laugh roars out of her, like a ripping lung, and she doubles over.

"Miss Shawnson!" Ms. Greenwood's voice belts out from the back of the room. "I suggest you. Get the heck. Out of here!"

"*Oh. Em. Gee.*" Brynne is still laughing as she stumbles to the door. "You all are such—*dweebs!*" There's a ripple of laughter outside the door from Brynne's portable, eavesdropping audience.

"Miss Shawnson!" Ms. Greenwood rips off her glasses and stands up. Her head wiggles like an angry bobblehead.

But Brynne's gone—we hear the scuttle of her and her fan base running down the hall.

"Never mind her," Ms. Greenwood says. She takes a deep breath, pulls a hand through her gray, fluffy hair, and sits down. "Carry on," she tells us with a flick of her hand. As if the whole incident was nothing more than an irritating mosquito.

We all look sunburned with embarrassment. Phoebe is nearly purple. Delia's eyes are wide with shock. Joey stares down at his blank list, biting his lower lip. And Mandy, whose words are dripping with sarcasm, says, "So, Delia. You still think a good talking-to will do it, huh? Maybe a nice heart-to-heart? Over some tea, perhaps?"

"Oh! I quite like tea," Phoebe says, unhelpfully.

Mandy lowers her face into her hands.

"I'm just saying. I could try. Anyone have any better ideas?" Delia asks, exasperated. She looks around at us. We're quiet. "I didn't think so." And then she picks up the letter die and rolls an *L*, and I set the timer. We drown our sorrows in the game until the bell finally rings.

I am heading down the hall with Mandy and Delia when the PA system screeches on and our principal, Mrs. Vander-Pecker, reminds us to "evacuate the building in an orderly fashion." Like it's a fire drill or something instead of a normal bell. She also reminds us that campaign parties for class president will be forming within the next few weeks and that all candidates will receive extra credit for Social Studies. "Remember, everyone has a shot at becoming the next class president. This means you," she says in her old-lady voice.

"Ha," Mandy says. "What a joke. Watch Brynne Shawnson become president again, for like the fifth year in a row."

"It's not like you'd ever *want* to be class president," I say.

"Oh, I don't know." She shrugs. "It's more like no one would ever vote for me."

"*We* would," Delia offers.

"Gee, thanks." She smiles. "Maybe in another lifetime."

A horn honks and I jump. Corny's waving wildly from the pickup. "Hurry up, Liv," she calls. "You've got an app—"

"Coming!" I yell, before she can blast the news that I've got to go see my therapist to the entire school. She might as well just hang a neon sign on me, announcing DAMAGED GOODS. "I better go. Dentist appointment," I say. Delia gives me a knowing look. She's the only one of my friends who knows that my own *mom* doesn't want to be with me. Lucky for me, I can trust Delia.

"Didn't you just have one last week?" Mandy asks. Which is why it's good to keep track of your lies.

"Cavities," Delia says, covering for me. "I keep telling her she's got to brush better."

Which is why it's good to have a best friend.

4.

The Dog Word I'm Not Allowed to Say

CORNY'S HAD ME in therapy since I came here to live with her. She says it helps to have someone to talk to, but I really think she's just worried that the crazy gene I'm carrying around, thanks to my mother, is going to rise up and do something awful. She shouldn't worry. Not that I don't have the crazy gene—everyone who knew my mom tells me how much I remind them of her, so I'm pretty sure I *do*. But the difference is that my mother's crazy gene made her run away and leave my dad and me, forcing me to move in with my grandmother, while my crazy gene will probably drive me to devote my life to watching *Full House* reruns and playing Scrabble. Alone. I think it probably makes you do whatever you would do if no one could tell you that you weren't allowed. So yeah, at least I don't expect my crazy gene to hurt anyone, but still, it's not exactly the path to social acceptability.

My therapist isn't an actual therapist—not yet. She's still in psycho school and I'm her guinea pig, so it's basically a discount version of the real thing. Sometimes my *whole life* feels like a discount version of the real thing. I mean, my family split at the seams like a cheap pair of underwear, and here I am hanging by a thread. If my life were, say, a sock, it would be the one stitched shut on both ends, with the heel halfway up the calf, selling for seventy-five percent off. At the dollar store.

Not that I talk about this with Moncherie. That's my therapist's name. She's not French, but her name sort of is, and whenever she says it, it sounds like she's got something stuck in her throat. Anyway, Moncherie may be twenty-six years old and well out of middle school, but still, sometimes I feel like she's going to laugh at me and spread rumors. So I have a policy. I don't tell her anything that I wouldn't want written on the bathroom walls.

Usually, that is.

But today, for maybe the first time ever, Moncherie hasn't brought up my mother, a topic that practically makes her salivate. Not even once. I mean, she seems to be listening to me and is completely ignoring her checklist of questions, which are: 1. How does that make you feel? 2. How do you feel about that? and 3. How would you describe what you are feeling?

In fact, she's acting so interested that I almost expect her to peel off her face and reveal a different identity. I find myself telling her about the ketchup packet. And not only that, but everything I can possibly think of about how Brynne and her friends have made my life miserable. I'd almost forgotten about the time last year, when I was new to the school and even more clueless, that Brynne and Tamberlin stopped me in the locker room to tell me there was a call from my grandmother. I started to worry, and asked if she was okay—I mean, she was old even *then*. And they said, yes, that she was fine, but she'd asked for her panties back.

Get it? *Granny panties*—which is what the cotton underwear I've always worn is called when you get to middle school. I don't know if grown-ups realize this, but being forced to take off your clothes in front of strangers is a serious form of abuse that wouldn't be tolerated in any other setting, except for maybe jail.

Today, Moncherie has on a boxy-looking yellow blazer that looks like it was pulled out of a time warp. She's got her notepad on her lap and her pen in her hand, but instead of taking notes, she's twirling the pen like a baton between her fingers, which are nicely painted in glittery blue. Her eyes are wide and her mouth hangs open a little as she listens.

"She sounds like a real you-know-what," she says, shaking her head.

I smile. "You can say it. Corny does. It's just means female dog."

She gives me this you-know-better-than-that kind of look. "Yes, well, Corny works with *dogs*. In the dog world, maybe it's not a dirty word. But in the human world, well, it's just not very nice."

The dog world *is* a strange world. Dog people get away with all sorts of shocking words that would land most kids my age in detention. If, for example, you were in school and were to even form your lips around the words *shih tzu*—which is just the name of a fancy-schmancy kind of dog you see in dog shows—a team of assistant principals would be circling you in no time.

"So," she says, clearing her throat, "speaking of dogs, how's the training been going?" She always likes to hear about the dogs we work with, the different problems they start out with. There was one dog, Cosmo, a German shepherd who would go into attack mode if he saw a tail wagging, even his own. Corny trained him

30

last year, and I helped. And then there was Dinah, the spoiled Chinese Crested that treated her owner like an indentured servant. And then there's Bella, who lives with us now. She used to be obsessed with wood. Her owners gave her up because she couldn't stop chewing on their doors and banisters. But I helped Corny train her, and she's been wood-free for almost six months.

I tell her about Loomis, the dog who gets majorly pissed off when he sees someone riding a bike, and how, as part of the training, I will have to do exactly that—*just so* he can get mad and Corny can correct him. Yeah, fun. And I tell her about Kisses, the dog that's afraid of grass—yes, *grass*! Corny and I are supposed to meet Kisses today, right after our session.

"Sounds like you're doing well with the training," Moncherie says, and gives me a huge smile. "Now if only school could be so easy. Too bad Brynne's not a dog, right?"

"Right," I say, and laugh. Even though she sort of is, just not the kind I'm allowed to say out loud.

Beware of Dog

WHEN CORNY TOLD me about a grass-fearing dog with a wimpy name like Kisses, this wasn't at all what I expected. But here we are, parked in a driveway, sitting inside the pickup, staring through the windshield because every few seconds a howling, pointy-eared, batlike creature pops into view over the hood.

"Are you sure that's a dog?" I ask Corny, as Kisses jumps into view again.

"Yep. A Mexican Hairless," she says over the weird creature's howling.

I snort. These dog breed names can get really ridiculous. Then it all becomes even funnier to me because a balding man who could be described as an American Hairless pokes his head out of the screen door and yells something at the dog, which we can't really hear over the howling.

"Poor Mr. Dewey," Corny says, waving to him. "He's got his hands full with this one."

But I'm thinking this Kisses is about the size of one of Ferrill's paws, so I'm wondering how much of a wuss this Mr.

Dewey is. "Shouldn't we get started?"

Corny puts her hand on my arm. "Don't let her size fool you, Olivia."

"Um, didn't you say this dog was scared of grass?"

"She was bitten by a snake a couple of months ago. Since then, she won't step foot anywhere near grass, and she's been using Mr. Dewey's carpet as her personal toilet," Corny explains. "She's really insecure. Remember what I told you about insecure dogs? You have to take them very seriously. If they sense weakness, they might attack. Understand?"

Weakness. Ugh. After a few days of middle school, I probably stink of it. But I say, "I know!" I mean, this dog's about the size of my thumb.

Corny takes a breath and opens her door just as Kisses howls again and pops back into sight. The dog sees the open door and makes a scrambling motion in midair. With the same frantic motion, she makes it past Corny, through the open truck door, and is a fraction of a second away from sinking her tiny but sharp-looking fangs into my bottom lip. Lucky for me, Corny is quicker than the evil Kisses. She scoops the dog away with one hand, managing to save my life. Or at least save me from several stitches and a tetanus shot.

You'd think this near-death experience would mean that my grandmother would call it a day, take me out for ice cream, and station me in front of the TV for the evening with a bell to ring when I want something.

Instead, we're still here in Mr. Dewey's driveway. He's sent the bat-dog inside, and I'm perched on the bumper of the pickup as Corny talks with him. Kisses wails from behind the storm door. It turns out that the near-attack on my bottom lip wasn't just a random thing—and neither is the name "Kisses." No. In fact, Kisses has "kissed" her owner a few times before. "But only one time required stitches," Mr. Dewey said earlier, in his dog's defense. I noticed a faint scar along the edge of his lip.

Corny is asking him questions. "What kind of rules do you have for her?"

"Rules?" Mr. Dewey looks confused. "Well, I'd prefer, of course, that she'd go outside to relieve herself."

I know Corny doesn't like that answer.

"And is she allowed to jump on the furniture?"

He laughs. "Allowed? Well, I don't *allow* it, really, but she has her own mind about that. But then, she's not a shedder, so it's not too big of a problem."

Mr. Dewey doesn't know it, but he's failing this interview. Miserably.

"How much exercise is she getting?"

He looks down again. "Well, I used to take her on walks, but now she's a lot more difficult to manage."

F, Mr. Dewey. *F*. You have officially earned an F on this interview. Even I can see that.

"Mealtimes?" Corny asks. "When are they?"

"Well, I just feed her when she's hungry. She gets a little antsy if she has to wait." He chuckles a little, but I notice his fingers go up to his lip scar.

I sort of wish I could stop him from talking now. It's like watching a train wreck happen. Thankfully, Corny stops questioning him. "The problem," she says, "is that Kisses thinks she's in charge."

"Well, that's just—" He puts his hands on his hips and shakes his head. "I mean, that just can't be. Look at her—she weighs twelve pounds."

"She could weigh twelve pounds or a hundred and twelve—it wouldn't matter," Corny says to him. "Look, I know you love your dog. But right now Kisses is in charge, and as bossy as she may get sometimes, she really doesn't want all that responsibility. Someone's got to be a pack leader—and if you won't take over that role, Kisses will, whether she wants to or not. It's instinct."

I think back to what Moncherie said, that it's too bad Brynne's not a dog. But isn't she acting just as mean and bossy as Kisses? Could this same thing be true about her?

Mr. Dewey takes off his glasses and rubs his eyes. "I appreciate your insight, but I actually called you here because of the grass problem. I have to walk her in the street. She's afraid of the lawn, she's terrified of the park, and my house—well, inside, it smells like a kennel. Most of my friends have stopped visiting, and the one or two who still do, Kisses does her best to scare off." He looks up at us, his frustration edging up his eyebrows.

Corny nods patiently. "Dogs are pack animals, and they need a pack leader, an alpha dog. Usually, in the case of pets, a human takes over that role and the dog can relax and just enjoy being part of the family, the pack. But when the owner doesn't take leadership—" Corny interrupts herself. "What kind of work do you do, Mr. Dewey?"

He looks confused, but he answers, "I'm a chef."

"Perfect," she says. "So when an owner doesn't take charge, it's like having a restaurant with no chef. Someone's got to do the cooking, right?"

"So, what are you saying? The dog—does the cooking?" Mr. Dewey asks carefully, looking at her sideways.

I imagine Oomlot standing on his hind legs, wearing a poufy white hat and an apron, stirring a pot of stew on the stove, and stealing all the little chunks of meat out of it, as I know he would.

"So to speak," Corny says. "Except the dog really doesn't want to do the cooking. It's a lot of responsibility, and it requires a lot of decision making. All that cooking is very stressful for the dog."

In my mind, Oomlot rips off the apron and storms out of the kitchen. The situation is made funnier to me by the serious looks on Corny's and Mr. Dewey's faces.

"So," Corny continues, "the dog starts to snap at people. She growls. She doesn't know what to do, and no one wants to tell her what to do because, frankly, they're getting a little scared of her."

Mr. Dewey nods slowly, still serious.

"And things set her off. Say one day a plate falls on her toe. She's so anxious and insecure that she starts to develop a fear. It may be irrational, but that's what the dog feels."

Mr. Dewey is hanging on Corny's every word, and something about their seriousness makes a laugh bubble up in me. It comes out as a snort.

Corny turns. "Olivia, are you okay?"

"Sorry, just thinking. Fear of plates," I mutter. *Snort, snort.*

Mr. Dewey glances over at me like he's almost forgotten that I'm here. "No, actually, I think your grandmother means the fear of grass. She was just using plates as an example," he tells me, like

I'm stupid. I fight the urge to ask whether that means dogs don't really cook either.

Corny shoots me an *I know, I know* look and pats the back of my hand.

"So where do we start?" Mr. Dewey asks.

"With body language," Corny tells him. "We're also going to let her work some of that energy off. You're going to take her for a walk."

His eyebrows raise. "Oh, I don't know about that. She doesn't listen. Last time I tried, she wore me out."

"Actually," Corny says carefully, "last time you tried, I'm sure she took *you* for a walk. This time, you're the pack leader."

He scratches his bald head and squints a little.

"Let's take a deep breath," she tells him. He inhales.

"Now, stand up tall. Really tall," she says. He laughs like it's silly, but straightens up, and seems to grow an inch or two.

"Think about relaxing your face. Your doubts are showing."

His eyebrows even out.

"Great," she says. "Now think confidence. Think dignity. Think calm, cool, collected."

"I'm trying," he says.

"Now. She walks right next to you. If she gets ahead, you stop. If she howls, you stop. *You* are in charge." She smiles at him. "*You* are the chef."

He opens the door, sweeps up Kisses, and carries her back out like a football. The dog gives me a dirty look as she's carted by. I think about how she bypassed Corny to try to attack me when we first arrived, and I wonder what that says about me and my own place in this world. So un-alpha. And I realize that I've been letting Brynne and her groupies lie all over my furniture and pee all over my carpets. It has to stop.

I watch Mr. Dewey and Kisses walk—if you can call it that—along the pavement, far away from the grass. He steps, she runs ahead, he stops, her harness pulls her back. This is repeated over and over. Even though it's probably the most awkward dog-walk ever, I can already see a little change take place. It's becoming slowly believable that Kisses may be just a strange little dog and not a direct descendant of the devil. Maybe just a third cousin, tops. And Mr. Dewey is becoming a taller, smarter, calmer version of himself.

You know, it's funny how many things your body can say about you, even when your mouth is completely shut.

And I begin to think that Moncherie might have actually, for the very first time ever, given me a good idea.

Perhaps even a great one.

6.

Such Dogs

THE NEXT DAY, Thursday, the five of us are hunkered down at our lunch table, ready to fend off ketchup packets and year-book committee members, when I ask, "What are you guys doing tonight?"

"I am *not* coming over for another *Full House* marathon," Phoebe says.

I narrow my eyes at her.

"Yeah, your popcorn sucked," Joey adds.

"Come on, guys. *Full House* is a classic. I'll bring the pop-corn," Delia offers.

"I can't even *think* about eating popcorn," Phoebe says, point-ing to her braces. "Count me out."

"This isn't about *Full House*. Or popcorn. This is about us not taking any more crap from anyone." I look around at them, but no one will meet my eyes. "Aren't you guys sick of being picked on? Aren't you sick of being treated like dorks?"

"I've got karate tonight," Joey says, pronouncing it *kar-a-TAY*. Mandy karate-chops him on the forearm on behalf of all of us.

39

"Joey, are you really ever going to be a black belt?"

"*Yeah*," he says, scrunching his face up like he's offended I asked.

"When?"

"Like next year." He shrugs and stuffs a Ding Dong into his mouth.

"So one night won't matter," I tell him.

Now I turn to Mandy. "And *you*," I say. "Remember what you said to me yesterday?"

"Like what? I'm sure I said a lot of things."

"*Remember*? In the *hall*? You revealed *something* to me?"

She tenses her forehead. "I was joking, Olivia. There's no such thing as a wedgie that has to be surgically removed. It was just a little uncomfortable."

"That's not what I'm talking about." I turn to our friends. "Yesterday, on our way to the buses, our Mandy here—who we all *think* we know so well—said she wanted to be class president."

"That's right! She did!" Delia jumps in. "I heard her, too!"

Phoebe and Joey turn and give Mandy pop-eyed stares.

She shifts her gaze toward her lap and smirks. "Well, I just meant—okay, they're offering extra credit to anyone who tries. I can always use extra credit. You guys know that."

"If you need tutoring," Phoebe offers, "remember, all you have to do is ask."

"I know, I know," Mandy says, twirling a strand of her dark hair and studying its split ends. "You always bail me out, Pheeb."

"You got to be kidding me," Joey says. "Mandy Freaking Champlain wants to be class president."

Mandy shrugs. "Okay, so what if I do?" This is a passionate *yes* in emo language. She looks at me. Then her face twists up

40

like it's trying to fight back a smile, and a gust of a laugh escapes through her nose. "Okay, okay," she finally says. "I know it's stupid and I'll probably regret saying this, but yes. I do."

I give her a big smile back.

"Okay, everyone," I tell them. "Tonight. My house. Seven o'clock. No excuses."

The bell rings and we head to our classes, and I'm already starting to feel a little like a pack leader.

We're all in my room. Delia and Phoebe sit on my bed—well, my mother's bed, really, from when she was about my age—with Queso curled up between them. Joey's on the floor, trying to unbraid the braided rug. Mandy leans her back against the side of my bed, throwing a Raggedy Ann doll from one hand to another (also my mom's; I'm *so* not a doll person!). I'm sitting cross-legged on the rug so I have a lap ready for Oomlot to lay his head on. He keeps trying to come into the room, but every time he shows his face, Delia and Mandy squeal about how cute he is, which scares him off. So for now, my lap is empty.

Phoebe looks around my room slowly. "Does it ever make you feel kind of weird? That she slept here?" She's talking about my mother.

"She's not dead, you idiot," Mandy says to her. "She's just— you know, traveling."

That's what I've told people. It's not exactly true, but Mandy doesn't know that. Neither does Phoebe or Joey. In fact, Delia's the only one in school who knows what's *really* happened with my mother—and all the big gut-punching words that go along with it, like *depression* and *abandonment* and *treatment*—and she kind of shushes Mandy, since I get nervous when the subject comes up. They don't think I notice, because I'm leafing through my dog-breed book.

It used to be that I didn't know where my mother was. Some days it was Las Vegas, others it was San Francisco. One time it was Des Moines. But now she's supposedly "stable," as they call it, which means that she sees her *own* therapist and lives in some special type of place in Spokane, Washington, where they give her drugs. I know, I know. I always thought drugs were bad too, but I guess these are supposed to be helping her somehow. She can't call or e-mail very often, but she does send letters every now and then. That's supposed to be a good thing, but I don't really know. A couple of months ago, she wrote to me about her new *friend* named Darren, so I haven't opened one since. I mean, *yuck*.

They're all looking at me expectantly. "Here it is," I say, turning to a page in the book Corny gave me when I moved here and started helping her with the training. "'The seven standard dog-breed groups,'" I read out loud.

"Uh," Joey interrupts.

"What?" I look up.

"My mom's picking me up in an hour," he says. "And I really don't want to sit around here for that hour talking about dogs."

I sigh and look around. They all have these blank looks about them. "I know you guys don't get it right now, but just listen to me," I tell them. "Okay, Joey. Let's start with you. You're probably a non-sporter."

"What? I do sports. Hello? I'm a martial artist," he argues, angling his hands as if to prove it.

"'In the past, non-sporting dogs were bred to perform specific

42

jobs or tasks, like vermin hunting,'" I read out loud, and then say to him, "Or in your case, kicking." His father was the most celebrated football kicker in his high school's history, and his grandfather was a kicker in one of the pro football leagues. But the only kicking Joey's good for is the kind that involves a surprise sideways heel into someone's butt cheek, usually Phoebe's. "'In general, these dogs'—meaning you, Joey—'can be aimless and difficult to control without proper and consistent training.'" I look up at him. "That's the polite way to say 'annoying.'"

He rips the book from my hands and looks at one of the pictures next to his breed. "Oh, great. Like a poodle. You're insane."

Mandy grabs the book from him. She looks at the page and breaks into a laugh. "You know what else is a non-sporter? A bichon frise," she says, pointing to a photo of a small cottonbally dog. It's supposed to be pronounced like *bee-shon free-zay*, but she doesn't say it that way. At all. She says it in a way that makes Phoebe suck in air and makes the rest of us laugh.

"I'm not a poodle," says Joey. "And I'm definitely not one of *those*. This is just crap." He starts kicking at the book in Mandy's hands. She lifts it higher than he can kick, and he gives up easily. She hands the book back to me as Joey says to her, "You're probably a pit bull."

"Actually, you're kind of right, Joey," I say. "They're basically terriers, and Mandy probably is too."

Joey makes a sound like *ooooh*, lifts his right hand, looks around expectantly, and ends up high-fiving himself with his left.

I turn back to the book. "'Determined but not easily controlled. They can be spirited and courageous, but also combative and aggressive.'"

"Ouch," Mandy says. "I sound like a delinquent."

Delia stares down at the book in my lap. "I want to be like that dog." She points toward a photo of an Australian terrier. "It's so cute." Phoebe glances down at the book and hums in agreement.

"Well, Delia, I'd say you're more of a herder, like Lassie and those German shepherd police dogs. Very smart, but can be suspicious of strangers and sometimes territorial. But the good news is that herders are usually pretty easy to train."

"Oh, great. Wonderful," she says.

"Phoebe, you're in the working group. Totally goal-oriented," I say, and read from the book. "'With proper training, they are dignified and devoted companions. Without it, they can be belligerent and high-strung.'"

"Let me see that," she says, scooping the book out of my hands. She scans the page. "So this says Great Danes are in the working group. Your dog Ferrill is a Great Dane, right?"

"Right."

She shrugs. "Well, it's just that I've never seen him working."

"He used to," I explain to her. "This rich guy bought him when he was a puppy. He was supposed to be a guard dog. But it turned out he wasn't mean enough for the job, so the guy just left him at the pound. So now, I guess you could say he's retired." I think about our sweet, gigantic dog who is probably asleep in his favorite spot on the porch right now. Even though he wouldn't hurt a fly (I really mean this—they land on him all the time and *I* end up shooing them off), his humongous size alone is enough to scare some people. So maybe in his mind, he's still working.

"What are you?" Delia asks me.

"Probably a hound. Like Tess." It's pathetic, but my keen sense of smell and decent eyesight may very well be my strongest character traits. Secretly, I would probably—okay, *gladly*—trade

44

them in for things like popularity and good looks.

"Hey, no fair," Mandy says. "Wasn't Snoopy also a hound? Hounds are cool."

Delia leans over toward Phoebe and glances at the book. "Oh, yeah. And those little wiener dogs, too. Dachshunds."

"You said *wiener*." Joey laughs. Alone.

"Listen," Phoebe says, pointing to the description in the book and reading aloud. "'Hounds can be stubborn, territorially aggressive, and prone to destructive behaviors,'" she says, and points to my hands. "Just look at her cuticles!"

I ball up my hands so no one can see how true it is.

"Look, the point is that we're all like dogs—different kinds of dogs, but still dogs," I say. "Everyone's got different good points and bad points, and the bad points can get out of control if things aren't right. Which is the case of Brynne Shawnson and Corbin Moon and Tamberlin Ziff and all the others. Bad training!"

The door squeaks open. Oomlot is giving us another chance. "No squealing. You'll scare him away," I warn my friends. Bella follows Oomlot into the room. The two dogs plop down on the wood floor, which creaks under Bella's weight.

I continue. "And you know what? Any dog can be trained."

"So what are you saying, Liv?" Delia asks.

"I'm saying that if we use dog training on everyone at school, secretly, of course, we can be the top dogs. Instead of the underdogs."

They're all quiet for a moment, staring at me, until Mandy says, "I kind of like this idea."

"I don't know," Phoebe says. "It sounds complicated. This whole thing would be a lot easier if Brynne had just listened to Delia." Then Phoebe's eyes go suddenly wide. "Whoops."

"What?" I turn to Delia. "You talked to Brynne?"

"Yeah, well, I tried," she says, shrugging and giving me an apologetic smile. She stares at the rug. "I told her the ketchup thing was over the line and I asked her to leave you—all of us, actually—alone. But it was a total waste of time."

"When did this happen?"

"After school," Phoebe answers. Delia shoots her an annoyed look.

I feel like I just got socked in the stomach. "So everyone knows but me?"

"Sorry, Liv. They rode over here with me, and I told them in the car. You knew I was going to try to talk to her," Delia says, wrinkling her forehead.

"Yeah, but—" I'm not sure what to say. "Did you talk to her face-to-face?"

"No, I just called her at home. I didn't really want all her friends around. But like I said, it was a waste of breath."

"But, what do you mean? Did she say anything at all?"

"Not really."

"Come on! Like, *nothing*?"

"Well, she was like, 'Whatever.' And then we hung up. I seriously wish I didn't even try. It was a stupid idea."

"Jeez," I say. "Next time *tell* me when you consort with the enemy. Like, a lot sooner."

"Okay. Sorry," Delia says, her root-beer eyes looking soft and sincere.

"If it makes you feel any better, Liv, I never thought it would work anyway," Mandy chimes in. "Your idea is much better. I think it's the only way we have a shot at changing our rank at school."

"Yeah, and maybe even winning the elections," Delia says. "Mandy for president!"

Mandy turns to Delia and smiles. "You are such a herder—of *course* you're going to try to push us all in that direction."

Delia looks a little baffled. "Oh. Weird."

Phoebe sighs. "You know everyone always votes for Brynne."

"Exactly," I say, still slightly annoyed. "Because they've never been trained *not* to."

Phoebe looks skeptical. "Well, how are we planning to do this? I'd need a step one."

"You are *so* obviously working group," Mandy tells her.

"You got anything to eat?" Joey interrupts. He's playing with an unbraided thread that he managed to cut loose from the rug with his teeth.

"Non-sporter alert," Phoebe says, pointing to him. "'Aimless and difficult to control without proper and consistent training,'" she recites, which makes the rest of us laugh. She remains serious. "Okay, how do we do this?"

I take a breath and look at Delia. She gives me a gentle little smile, and I breathe out. It's hard to stay mad at her.

"Okay, first, let's get a couple of things clear," I say, in a hushed tone that makes me sound very important. "No one at school can know that Mandy's running for president yet. We have to be well on our way to being pack leaders before we announce this, okay?"

They all look at each other and nod.

"And second, and this is extremely important." I emphasize every word. "*No one* can know that we're using dog training. If they know they're being trained, it won't work. The whole plan will fall apart. It's got to stay top secret."

Phoebe starts to look a little panicky. "But we've only got a little more than two months until elections."

"I think we can do it," I say. And then I add, "If we stick together."

"You'll be my campaign manager, right?" Mandy asks me.

"Me?" I ask.

"Well, this is your idea. Plus you're the only one who knows how to train anything. I mean, yet."

She looks so excited, so utterly un-emo (despite the gray she recently dyed into her hair), that I can't say no. "Sure."

"Seriously, guys," Joey says. "My stomach's aching from hunger." Then he spots something under the dresser and reaches for it. It's an old Mento. "Ooh," he says. "Can I have it?"

"Go ahead," I say, like a quiet dare. Delia, Mandy, and Phoebe start screaming about how gross it is. The dogs look up with interest. Joey pops it into his mouth and smiles, apparently thrilled with his power to disgust everyone around him.

Corny knocks on the door and pops her head in. "Well, I've been calling you all, but you can't hear me," she says. "Johnny's mom's here."

Delia, Mandy, and I laugh. But Joey just looks confused.

"She's not any good with names," Delia tells him quietly.

"It's *Joey*, Grandma," I correct her. I roll my eyes and tell her we'll be right down.

Mandy waits for the door to close. "You haven't said what type of dog Brynne is." Then she smiles. "Besides the obvious, I mean."

"I bet Brynne's a sporter," Joey says. "Spiritleader and all." He makes this little snooty look when he says this. I know the word *Spiritleader* sounds all Native American and mystical, but it's nothing like that. Spiritleaders are the Hubert C. Frost Middle

48

School version of cheerleaders, if you take away the short pleated skirts and replace them with blue spandex unitards, and if you also take away competitive sports and replace them with safer, seated activities.

Spiritleaders serve two purposes. One is to cheer on the major clubs at our school, such as the Anime Club and the Mathalicious Team, and *of course* the Chess Club. To be considered "major" you have to have an enrollment of ten or more students, so the Bored Game Club isn't considered major in any way. The second purpose is to try to make everyone feel some vague emotion called "school spirit," which someone high up and suffering from dementia must think is best achieved by sending Spiritleaders through the halls chanting and attempting acrobatic stunts named after things that are cold. Get it? Hubert C. Frost equals just frost, which equals snow and ice and winter, and is best represented by blue. Blue spandex unitards, that is.

"She's definitely competitive, but I don't think she's attentive or loyal enough to be a sporter," I say. I reach down to pet my own little loyal and attentive sporter, Oomlot. I mean, he's no athlete, but put some food in front of him—any kind of food—and you get the idea that he'd make a really great competitive eater.

"So what is Brynne, then?" Delia asks. "A toy?"

"Toys are too sweet. They live for affection, like Queso there," I say. Queso has inched her way into Delia's lap. "I'd say Brynne's a hound, like me and Tess. Just a poorly trained one."

"You're nothing like her," Delia says, trying to comfort me. I give her a thank-you smile, although a little part of me wonders what it would be like to be. You know, to be popular, accepted. Beautiful. Well, our plan may not make me any prettier, but hopefully it will put an end to the teasing, at least.

"When do we start?" Phoebe asks.

"Tomorrow," I tell them. "Remember, we've got to keep this secret. Not a word to anyone."

They start making cross gestures over their hearts (and Joey mimics sticking a needle in his eye, along with the accompanying pain), and we file downstairs to wait for the other moms.

"You all look a little hungry," Corny says, and starts offering around snacks—"special crackers," as she calls them. I spot Tess gnawing on one in the corner, so before anyone can accept, even Joey, I tell Corny we're all fine. ("Stale," I mouth to them.) The fact that Corny doesn't really do a good job of differentiating between dog and people food—well, that's just another embarrassing thing about my family that my friends don't need to know.

At the Starting Gait

IT'S THE NEXT day—day one of the plan—and I'm carrying my tray to the lunch table, concentrating on walking with dignity. I set my tray down and find Mandy staring at me. "Why are you walking like you're squeezing a quarter between your butt cheeks?" she asks.

"Shhh," I say, and feel myself slacken a little, ashamed. I slump into my seat and open my milk carton. But my friends are still looking at me, waiting for an explanation. "Is that really how it looked?" I finally ask.

Delia nods like it hurts. Joey asks if I'm wearing a thong or something.

My earlobes start to burn a little. "Okay, okay, I'll work on it," I say, already feeling like a balloon with a slow leak. Deflated. And these are my *friends*! "I was kind of working some body language there. It's the first part of the plan," I explain. I get confused stares. "Don't you guys understand what body language is?"

"I totally understand the concept of body language," Phoebe says. "But what that walk just said was *bathroom emergency*."

"Yeah, I totally understand the concept of body language too," says Joey. He raises his eyebrows, cocks his head, holds up an index finger, and says, in a fake foreign accent, "Please to witness." Then his eyes roll toward the ceiling and he slowly pushes a table-shaking, Dorito-scented, foghornlike belch through his gaping mouth.

"Joey!" Delia whisper-yells, hiding her face from the disgusted glares of onlookers, who act like such a thing is *so far* beneath them—onlookers who are only slightly higher up from us on the Hubert C. Frost Middle School food chain. Onlookers who have loogie-hocking contests.

"Oh, *good Lord*," Mandy says, and really does seem to be making a plea to God.

"I can't live this way," says Phoebe. She also seems to mean it.

"Are you done?" I ask him.

"Here, give me another one—you're right, it could be better," he says, but I grab the Dorito bag away from him and basketball-throw it into the overly stuffed mouth of the massive, sour-milk-scented trash can at the end of our table.

"Keep it up and I'll have some more body language for you," Mandy warns him. "My fist may want to say hello to your face."

Joey laughs. "Good one," he says to her. She fights back a proud smile.

"We've gotten off track, guys. *Way* off track," Delia says. "If we're going to do this, we need to focus. Olivia was trying to explain something." I'm starting to realize this is one of the wonderful things about having a herder as a best friend.

"One of the first things you learn when you're training dogs is that you have to have good body language," I tell them. "No dog's going to give you any respect if you don't. And if you think about it, people are the same way. I mean, look around. You can tell who's an alpha dog just by their body language."

Max Marshall walks in our direction. He looks completely at ease with himself even though he is carrying a container of green Jell-O, which is the most made-fun-of food in middle school history. He eats a spoonful while walking, and doesn't even look stupid doing it. "Alpha." I nod my head in his direction.

Across the cafeteria, Brynne and the rest of the Spiritleaders swarm their table, wearing pajamas. Instead of their standard-issue tight-fitting jeans and camis, they're covered in pink fleece and striped flannel and long cottony robes—and there's nothing weird about it. It's just another Spirit Dress-Up Day, one of those days when the Spiritleaders all dress up in some sort of outlandish theme to try to bring even more attention to themselves.

I hear a peal of laughter come out of Brynne. She's showing her friends pictures on her digital camera, and they're all laughing too. "Also alpha," I say. "Unfortunately."

"You know who else is an alpha?" Phoebe says. You can almost hear her heartbeat quickening. *"Him."* She is staring a hole through the Robert Pattinson of Hubert C. Frost Middle School, Brant Farad. "Just look at him. He moves like the ocean," she says.

"Someone kill me now," Joey pleads.

"What? All I'm saying is that he's got good body language. The way he walks, the way he talks. He eats very nicely too. Like a *gentleman.*" She turns to Joey and narrows her eyes at him pointedly, before continuing. "And he keeps his locker very neat, which is a plus. And have you ever seen him comb—" Joey's booming "POW," a sound he makes while pulling the trigger of his finger, which is pressed up next to his temple, interrupts her. He closes his eyes and lets the side of his head fall to the table in slow motion. His tongue, Dorito-orange, hangs out of the corner of his mouth.

"Anyway," Phoebe says, stiffening, as the rest of us try to hold back our laughs. We have a hard time doing this. Finally, Phoebe, who has become a color best described as *salmon*, says huffily, "Are we going to get anything done today or are we just going to sit around acting like idiots?"

Joey raises his hand.

"Yes, Mr. Spagnoli?" Mandy says. It just makes us laugh more.

"I'm voting," he says, "for sitting around and acting like idiots."

Phoebe flares her nostrils and vacuums a full lungful of air through them, her pinkish color reddening. "I've had enough!" she yells, and starts to stand.

With her usual calm, Delia reaches for her wrist and pulls her back to sitting. "We're sorry, Pheeb," she says. "Aren't we, guys?" We nod and murmur apologies. "Let's finish talking about body language," Delia says to me.

"Yes, *please*. We don't have all day," Phoebe says.

"Okay, you're right," I say. I think about Kisses, and Mr. Dewey, and everything I've learned from Corny. "Basically, the way you walk and stand and talk tells everyone how you feel about yourself. It can say that you're in charge and you know what you're doing, or it can say 'loser.'"

"Well, I don't know about the rest of you, but I'm fine . . ." Joey drops his gaze and starts to draw circles in the unnaturally orange crumbs on the table in front of him. "You know, with myself."

"No you aren't. You can barely even say it," Mandy tells him.

"Well, *you're* all hunched over," he says back to her.

"That's because I have a *condition*," she says. At one point in her life she was told she had a mild spine disorder, but the only time you hear about it is when she's getting out of something in P.E.

"Yeah, your condition's called being a Marcie," he says.

"Stop!" Delia shouts. "That's not helping. How are we supposed to start acting like we have any confidence at all when we keep taking it away from each other? And anyway, if anyone has a 'condition' at this table, it's me. *Cystic acne.*"

"All right, look," I say, trying to rein them all in. "We all have stuff wrong with us. So does everyone else in this cafeteria. Brynne Shawnson included."

"You wouldn't know it to look at her, though," Phoebe says quietly.

"Who cares if she's pretty?" Mandy says. "I'd rather have a smart friend like you any day, Pheeb." It's not really the comfort Phoebe's looking for.

"Okay, this sucks," Joey says. "I'm going for a Nutty Buddy."

"Sit down, *please*, Joey," Delia pleads. "Everyone, let's just listen to Olivia, okay?"

I look at the clock. Lunch is almost over. And I'm starting to wonder if the plan might as well be too. But I take a deep breath and continue, as hard as it is. I'd expected a little more enthusiasm. Right now, the whole thing just seems a little impossible. It's so much easier to stay on the bottom of the ladder. We only have four more years of school ahead of us anyway. That's not so bad. And I always hear that Marcies like us do so much better socially in college anyway.

But Delia nods at me. "Go ahead, Olivia."

"Yeah," Mandy says, and sweeps her hair back from her face. "Sorry. We're listening."

And Phoebe says, "We really do want to do this." Her light blue eyes go round with sincerity, and I feel a pang of appreciation for her.

Even Joey's looking at me. Which probably means some of my Hot Pocket is stuck in my teeth, but at least I've got everyone's attention.

"Okay, okay." I take a breath. "The thing with dogs is that they have to have a pack leader. And if you look around at all the cliques here, it's pretty obvious they do too. But before we can become pack leaders, we have to think like pack leaders, act like pack leaders. Become alpha dogs."

"But I'm still waiting on the how," Phoebe says.

"At first you'll probably have to fake it. That means you walk tall, you hold your head up high, you make sure your shoulders don't slump and your feet don't shuffle on the ground. When you talk, you talk clearly—not too loud, but loud enough so people can hear you."

"Yes, hello there, Mrs. Appleton. How, may I ask, are you today?" Joey says, in his finest impersonation of a complete fool.

I ignore him. "Delia, you can't hide your face any longer," I tell her. "Start wearing your hair back."

Her eyes go wide with alarm.

"So you have a few zits. Big deal," I say.

"It *is* a big deal—it's gross and humiliating and ugly."

"And you tell yourself that every day, don't you?" I ask.

She looks away. I feel smart.

"Fine," she says. "But that means you have to stop wearing a hat."

She reaches over and pulls it off of my head. My hair springs free. I'm sure I look like I've been electrocuted. But I say, "Okay. Fine."

I turn to Mandy. "No more slumping."

"I'll try not to, okay?" She sounds a little annoyed.

"Pheeb—" I start.

She cuts me off. "I don't have a problem with confidence."

Mandy jumps in. "Yes, you do. That's why you act like you're smarter than everyone."

"Who *are* you?" Phoebe says to Mandy. "Dr. Phil?"

"Your *mom's* Dr. Phil," Joey says, to anyone within earshot.

"Joey, you need to learn to zip it," Mandy says.

"If you were just *half* the gentleman that Brant is—" Phoebe starts.

But the bell rings, which means lunch is officially over, and everyone slinks away to fourth period all wrong. Mandy's remembered the shoulders-back part, but forgotten to stand up straight, so her neck tilts forward like a giraffe's. Phoebe is not shuffling her feet, which would be good if she wasn't marching like some sort of robot soldier. Delia is walking like her spine was replaced with a metal rod. And Joey just looks like he sat on a tack—I can't explain that one.

I, on the other hand, am walking with maturity and dignity. My shoulders are back, my head high, and my buttocks completely unclenched. This last part I make sure of.

Me and my very confident body language walk into fourth period English.

"Olivia?" Mr. Renaldi says as I pass his desk. "Are you okay?"

Everyone in the class stops talking. Their stares burn into me. I try not to let my posture slip. "I'm fine," I say, and tall-walk to my desk.

Alpha dog Max Marshall, who sits in front of me, twists around. "Did you get in an accident or something?" Max, who has never spoken to me before in the full year that I have been at this school, actually looks interested.

I try to smile at him. "No, but thanks for—" I don't finish, because he's clearly disappointed and has already turned back around. Out of the corner of my eye, I see Janie Lindy, who sits to my right, looking at me. I turn toward her and she gives me a sympathetic smile. Then she slowly pulls up the back of her shirt to reveal some type of flat brace on her back. "Gymnastics injury," she whispers. Her smile broadens like we have something in common.

Okay, I get it. More practice needed.

The Almost-Hot Dog

AFTER WALKING OOMLOT, and then Tess, and then Ferrill up and down our road again and again over the weekend, I feel like I've almost got it down by Monday. My walk is more of a stride, I've decided. I try to pretend like I'm proud of my height, and I glide down the hall with my shoulders back and gaze ahead of me. I start to feel so much less invisible. Maybe it's because I actually *am* a couple of inches taller. I usually think grown-ups are just trying to be nice when they tell me being tall is a good thing, but today it's starting to feel like it could really be true.

But it all falls apart in P.E. My group is playing volleyball, and over in the corner of the monstrous gym, another group is forming teams for a relay. Brynne is in that group, and I watch with envy as she is one of the first people snatched up by a team. And then she watches with amusement as I get a volleyball assault to the forehead for being so extra tall now that I'm actually an obstruction to the game.

My forehead turns magenta. In between sixth and seventh periods, Delia tells me it doesn't look that bad, but fishes a Steelers cap out of the bowels of her locker anyway. It feels good to have something on my head again—I've really missed that. So I don't say anything to Delia when she lets her hair fall down over her face. She looks like she's got a bad breakout coming on anyway.

Phoebe asks who's up for Monopoly. Joey moans. Delia asks, "Do we still play games in this club?"

Phoebe glances around at the group of us and says, "Maybe Brynne's right. Maybe you guys are hopeless."

"What's the matter with you?" I ask, annoyed.

"Me? What's the matter with you guys? Olivia, you're the one who thought this whole dog-training thing up, and you're probably the worst off right now." She reaches over and rips the cap from my head.

"But my *forehead*," I hear myself whine.

"No excuses," Phoebe says. Then she turns to Delia. "And you."

Delia says nothing, but starts gathering her hair back into a ponytail. Mandy pulls a rubber band out of her backpack and hands it to her.

"Well," Phoebe says, putting the Monopoly box down, "just so you know. It's already working for *me*."

Delia and I exchange confused looks. It can't be working—it's way too early. "What are you talking about, Pheeb?" I ask.

It's one of those rare moments where she looks almost happy. Not smiling, really, but close. "I've been asked to the dance," Phoebe announces. She quickly glances around for our reactions, then starts rooting through the Monopoly box for the little shoe game piece.

She's talking about the Fall Ball, which takes place in six weeks. None of us has ever gone to anything like this. None of us has ever been *invited* to anything like this.

"By who?" Joey asks, suspiciously.

"By Brant Farad," she says.

I shoot a panicked look to Delia, who returns it with even more alarm. This *has* to be a prank that Phoebe's fallen for.

"Brant Farad?" I ask. "Are you sure?"

Phoebe nods.

Delia just looks terrified.

"No *way*," Mandy says.

"I *know*," Phoebe adds, another almost-smile flickering on her face. "I can barely believe it!"

Neither can we.

Seriously.

"But Pheeb," Delia says, looking around at us for support. "You can't be thinking of actually *going*."

"Well, duh. It's *Brant Farad*. Of course I'm going." Her forehead starts to crinkle up. "Why? What's the problem?"

"Brant Farad is, like, *so* out of our league," Mandy says.

"You ever seen the movie *Carrie*?" Joey asks. "Might sound familiar. You know, loser girl gets asked to the prom and ends up soaked in pig blood. It's a classic."

"Just shut up!" Phoebe yells. She pushes back from the table, throws the little shoe back toward the box—and misses—and storms out of the room.

Ms. Greenwood glances up from her papers. "Anyone hurt?" she asks. When we say no, she adjusts her glasses and goes back to her reading.

"Maybe we shouldn't have said anything," Delia says, her voice quiet, her body stiff. "It's got to be some kind of joke. Maybe she'll figure it out."

"Maybe," I mumble. Mandy is as still as a statue.

"Cool. I wanted the shoe," Joey says, and begins to set up for Monopoly.

A few minutes later, Phoebe comes back in. She grabs the shoe from Joey and stuffs the wheelbarrow into his hand. Then they start arguing about who lost the dog game piece, which has been missing since last year.

Phoebe: "*You* lost it!"

Joey: "No I didn't, *you* did!"

Phoebe: "*You* did! You're an idiot!"

Joey: "Your *boyfriend's* an idiot!"

"I can't listen to this," Delia says, over the yelling.

"Me either," I agree.

Mandy stands up. "Come on, you guys," she says to me and Delia. We leave Phoebe and Joey to their spat and follow Mandy to the bathroom. She opens her backpack and takes out a pencil pouch. "I've got a ton of makeup. Let's cover up that volleyball bruise," she tells me. I get a little nervous, because I start to wonder if by "cover" it up, she means scribble over it with her beloved Sharpie.

But she unzips the pouch and pulls out a little tube of concealer. "Is that going to work?" I ask. Mandy has me sit down on the radiator and dabs the little spongy tip of the stick on my forehead. As she rubs it over the bruise, being extra gentle, Delia stares at me with big eyes.

"It's a little lighter than your skin tone, so it's not perfect," Mandy explains. "But it's like way better than it was. And if you just part your hair on the side and sweep it over a little, you can't even really see it."

I get up and look in the mirror. She's right. Under the bright buzzing fluorescent lights of the bathroom, where every flaw can enjoy its own very special moment in the spotlight, I only see a slightly raised, slightly pink circle. "That's pretty incredible," I say.

"I want some," Delia says. She grabs the concealer—almost hungrily—from Mandy and starts dabbing little spots all over her zits before Mandy can stop her. In the seconds it takes her to finish, she looks like she's got a reverse case of chicken pox.

"Uh, Dee . . ." Mandy starts.

Delia is now rubbing the dots in frantically, making little chalky spots over her cheeks and forehead. The faster she goes, the worse it looks.

"Uh, it's really not the right color for you," Mandy tells her. "If you want some, we'll go shopping this weekend."

Delia stops and sighs. "You're right. I look like crap," she says into the mirror. Then she bends over the sink and begins washing it off.

"Just be glad you don't need any of the rest of this stuff," Mandy says, reaching into her bag and pulling out a little yellow tube of mascara. I watch her put it on. She blinks in the mirror, wipes away a few specks, and then sees me watching her. "Want to try some?" she offers.

I've only worn mascara once in my life, and that was when my ex-best-friend Rachel and I went through her mother's makeup drawer. That day, I wound up with a black gooey mess that cemented my upper and lower eyelids together, and three days after that, I wound up on antibiotics. My mom didn't get mad or anything, but something about it seemed to make her a little sad. I still remember what she said to me. *You don't really want to grow up, Olivia. Believe me, you don't.*

"I'm not sure how to do it," I admit now, to Mandy.

Thankfully, she doesn't laugh. Instead she sits me back down and puts it on my lashes herself, and when I get up again to see myself in the mirror, I say it's an improvement. Inside, however, I'm *shocked*. I had no idea my eyes could look so good.

"You look so pretty, Liv!" Delia says. "Your eyes—they're *so* green."

"They are," Mandy agrees. "They're kind of bluish-green. Like that really pretty ocean."

"Oooh! Yeah!" Delia says. "Like the Caribbean!"

"That's it! Caribbean green!" Mandy smiles proudly. I guess I'm not going on and on enough about how wonderful my eyes look, not out loud, at least, because she says, "Don't you like it?"

"Well, yeah," I say. I'm actually embarrassed by how much I do. It catches me a little off guard. I don't even look like myself, not really. "It's just weird."

"What else do you have in that bag?" Delia asks her.

"Oh, the usual. Eyeliner, lip gloss. Sharpie," she tells her. To me, she says, "You know, if you don't like it, just wash it off."

I steal another glance at myself in the mirror. I look so different. I don't look quite like the butt of Brynne Shawnson's jokes. In fact, if you didn't look below the neck or above the hairline, I could almost pass for one of *them*. I mean, my eyes—am I even allowed to think this?—are nearly as pretty as Brynne's. Nearly. I get a secret little thrill, just for a second. But reality sets in quickly. I must look as uncomfortable as I feel. I probably couldn't pull off "pretty" if you paid me.

So even though a huge part of me doesn't want to, I do wash it off.

By the time we get back to the Bored Game Club, Phoebe and

Joey are in opposite corners, playing separate games of solitaire. Monopoly sits high on a shelf behind Ms. Greenwood.

The bell rings and we leave the room together. Joey peels off as soon as we're out the door. "Bye, everyone except Phoebe," he says.

"What was up with him?" I ask, once he's gone.

"He *was* kind of a basket case today. Can boys get PMS?" Mandy jokes.

"Well, no, I don't think they can," Phoebe says, as if it were a real question. The rest of us hide our smirks. "But, yes, I agree. He was worse than usual."

"Oh well, he'll get over it, whatever it is," Delia says.

"Yeah, he's usually such a joy," Mandy adds. We all start heading in different directions, making our ways to our lockers and buses; and even though everything seems to be business as usual, I think about what I saw in that mirror, and I start to feel anything but usual inside.

When she's bored with everything going on around her, Brynne gets everyone on the bus to bark at me. So I guess today she's bored. The barking starts the minute I step on. You'd think I'd be used to it by now, but instead I feel my heart sink into my bowels and perhaps even embed itself in my small intestine. When the bus driver is good and sick of the noise, she hoists herself around, twists her face into a mask of anger, and screams, "Shut up, every-one!" It's like something you'd see on *Supernanny*—one of those bad moms whaling on her children—but it's like beautiful music to me.

The bus is full, so again I sit next to the booger kid, who, as usual, is too involved in his *Car and Driver* to acknowledge the world around him. I'm a little envious. I close my eyes and try to zone out, too.

And when I open them, I see Brynne Shawnson kiss fart-breath Danny Pritchard *on the lips*. As grossed out as I am, I'm still a little envious. Could I ever be the girl that someone wants to kiss?

If I really was that girl I saw in the mirror, maybe the answer would be yes.

New Tricks

AFTER SCHOOL, I'm lying on the couch, petting patterns into Oomlot's coat. I give him racing stripes by raking my fingers through his fur, then pet them out and go for a wave pattern. Bella waddles in, sniffs Oomlot's head, and lowers, sighing, to the floor next to him. Her coat is too short and smooth for patterns, so I just pet her with my bare foot.

I know it doesn't look like I'm doing much, but I'm also thinking. I'm thinking that being the girl in the mirror takes more than just a swipe or two of mascara. It takes guts. And I'm not just talking about your run-of-the-mill liver or garden-variety gland. I mean the kind of guts that make you feel the very opposite of hollow.

I guess I don't look busy enough, though, because Corny walks in and asks, "Wanna go for a ride?" Oomlot's ears perk up, and he brings himself to a hopeful sitting position. Queso, having heard one of the magic dog words, comes bolting into the room, skidding to a stop in front of Corny. Even lazy Bella lifts her head and gets out a couple of interested tail thumps.

I'm not nearly as excited.

"Unfortunately, she's talking to me," I tell the dogs.

She smiles. "I've got an appointment with Kisses and I could use your help."

"Can't I just stay here?" I ask.

"Oh, come on," she says. "We'll have sundaes after."

Although I'm disgusted with myself for being so easily lured, I lift my hand so she can pull me up off the couch. Oomlot follows, practically dancing. "You're staying here, pup," Corny tells him. He sighs loudly, his brown eyes dark with disappointment, and he flattens with a thud to the floor. Bella lays her head back down. Queso just stares at us with those big Chihuahua eyes, like she can't believe we're really not taking her with us. It's like she's saying, *You're really going to leave me here with the dogs? But I'm so portable!*

Corny must see it too, because she laughs and says, "Not this time, Queso. We can't give Kisses another reason to misbehave."

I give Queso a little scratch of apology behind the ears as Corny calls for Tess. Tess is sort of our babysitter. While we're away, the monstrous Ferrill stays in his favorite spot on the porch and keeps an eye on things outside, while Tess keeps watch inside. She makes sure that Oomlot stays away from food in the kitchen and Bella isn't tempted by a delicious-looking sofa leg.

I put on my shoes and get in the car with Corny, but I'm exhausted. Corny notices. As soon as we pull out onto the narrow road in front of our house, she asks, "What's the matter?"

"I don't really have the energy for Kisses," I tell her.

"Are you sure it's just that? You're not worrying about those elections, are you?"

I just shrug. I'm afraid of what will come out of my mouth at this point. I told her about the elections, of course, but she can't know about our plan. She'd either be delighted and tell everyone, thus ruining the plan, or she'd call it unethical and then triple my pooper-scooper duties and lecture me.

She pats me on the leg. "You know, I've got a lot of confidence in you. If you start to feel overwhelmed, just think about what you're capable of. And how far you've come." She gives me another closed-mouth smile. "I think you can pretty much do anything you want to do."

She's referring again to last year, when I first got here and had to get over my fear of the dogs. Corny likes to say I came way out of my "comfort zone" with everything. And I guess I did, but that doesn't make me a superhero or anything, no matter what Corny thinks.

"I'm just not sure I feel like a pack leader right now," I tell her.

"Well, you're out of practice," she says, as we continue down the road. "Everything takes practice, even once you're good at it. It's all up here, remember." She taps her temple.

I guess she's right. When you're training dogs—or people, as the case may be—you kind of have to change the way you think. It doesn't sound so hard—I mean, it's not like you have to solve some horrible word problem, or lift a thousand pounds, or learn Chinese, or something like that.

But your own head—and everything that's in there—can be harder to change than anything else in the world. And that's exactly what I need to do now. I think this has been the problem at school; I've been going through the motions without changing what's been going through my mind, and it's been obvious.

So now, instead of just adjusting my shoulders and my spine, I'm moving things around in my brain. I'm putting the words *pack leader* and *alpha dog* toward the front, and stuffing words like *mother* and *crazy* down into the butt-end of my brain, into that weird little round thing that helps you with balance. I don't remember what that part's called, but in my science class, we learned that thoughts don't really happen there, so those words should pretty much just stay there and leave the rest of my head alone.

By the time we get to Kisses's house, I'm starting to feel a little bit more like I'm in control. My body snaps into a confident position almost on its own.

"Ready?" Corny asks, as we pull in front of the row of tightly packed identical houses, surrounded by flat, treeless land. It's kind of like middle school—people crowding together even when there's room to branch out. I guess even in the grown-up world, people are a little afraid to be all on their own. *Pack mentality*, they call this kind of thing in the dog world.

"I think so," I say. Kisses sees us and busts through the screen door, howling and jumping as usual. Mr. Dewey comes running out after her, with her leash in hand. He appears to be trying to lasso her.

"Oh, no," Corny says. She steps out of the truck, and Kisses charges toward her. Corny doesn't flinch—just stands there, quiet, looking as calm as if she were waiting in line at the grocery store. The dog stops a few feet in front of Corny and lets out a howl. Corny ignores her still. Kisses lowers her head a little, her howls becoming more like whines, and starts to scoot away.

"What's she doing?" Mr. Dewey asks, looking worried. "Kisses, are you okay?"

Corny touches her fingers to her lips, signaling for him to be quiet. Then she turns to look at me. It's my turn.

I take a big breath, remind myself that this dog is scared to death of helpless, harmless blades of grass, of all things, and open my door. Kisses starts acting like a predator again, and lunges toward me, but there's one thing giving her away. Her little back legs are trembling. She's afraid.

She starts growling at me. Mr. Dewey opens his mouth, but Corny shakes her head no before he can call out to Kisses. A lot of people think that yelling at a dog or shouting its name will make the dog calm down, but all that noise and excitement can make things worse. Sometimes standing your ground and keeping quiet and calm—basically ignoring the dog—is the best thing to do. I guess it also doesn't hurt to know I can always jump over to the grass, where Kisses doesn't have the guts to go, if this ignoring thing doesn't work out.

Which, eventually, it does. Kisses's growls turn into whimpers and she runs toward the weak spot—Mr. Dewey. He starts to bend down to pet her, but Corny stops him right there. "You can't pet her now, not when she's fearful," she tells him. "That just reinforces her feelings."

He stands back up, but doesn't seem happy about it. "What am I supposed to do? Just ignore her?"

"Exactly," she says. "We'll show you how it's done. Right, Olivia?" Corny smiles at me.

Even though we're light-years away from our goal of getting this insane little dog out on the grass, it seems like we've already made a couple of big steps. The fear that I had is nicely tucked away. In fact, I feel like all the fears I have—like craziness and being terminally weird—are being nicely tucked away in that brain-trunk. I imagine them stored away in a vacuum-sealed Space Bag, out of the way of important and powerful new thoughts.

Such as the thought that, today, after sundaes, we're stopping by CVS. I'm *buying* that mascara. I've made a decision. I *do* have the guts to be the kind of person who looks like I did, earlier today, in the mirror.

"Right," I say, and smile back.

And besides, what's a layer or two of mascara anyway, if not good body language?

Teachable Moments

PHOEBE HAS BROUGHT a package of poster board to the Bored Game Club and is standing over us, distributing markers and insisting we come up with a slogan for Mandy's campaign.

"But I'm still working on standing up straight," Mandy whines.

"Don't write that down!" Delia yells at Joey, who has already started writing it out on the poster board with an orange marker.

Joey smirks.

"That's not funny, Joey," Phoebe tells him, and grabs the marker out of his hands. She starts to hand it to me, but stops and squints. "I still can't believe you're wearing makeup." She has been acting slightly betrayed since lunch.

"Oh," I say, and shrug like it's no big deal. "It's just a little mascara."

"Yeah. It looks good," Mandy says. "I've got some if you want to try it," she offers Phoebe.

"And risk *infection*? At a time like *this*? No, ma'am. We've got a campaign to run."

"You're just stressing everyone out, Martin," Joey says to her. His latest method of annoying Phoebe is calling her by her last name, like they're football buddies or something. "We're not ready for posters."

"Yeah, Pheeb," I tell her. "Remember? It's still top secret. You might have to tune out your inner working breed."

"Did Dennis Kucinich 'tune out his *inner working breed*'?" she asks, seething. In fourth grade, Phoebe took an online quiz that told her Dennis Kucinich, who ran for U.S. president in 2008, was her ideal candidate, and she's had a strange sort of loyalty to him since.

"Um, Martin," Joey starts.

"I DON'T CARE IF HE DROPPED OUT!" she yells at him. Ms. Greenwood looks up, eyes wide, mouth shut. "Sorry," Phoebe murmurs.

Joey stifles a laugh. "It's just so easy," he says. "I don't even have to say anything to you. You're just on auto-idiot."

Phoebe's right eye narrows and both nostrils start to flare. She takes a big breath as if she is about to seriously verbally assault Joey, but I flash back to our last session with Kisses, and I put my hand on hers. This is what they call a *teachable moment*.

I give her this really mature and patient smile, and say, "Ignore him, Phoebe."

"But—" Her face is tight with frustration.

"Sit down, Pheeb. Just stop. Relax. Don't even look at him." I glance at Ms. Greenwood, who appears, as always, to be engrossed in the papers on her desk. I whisper anyway. "Trust me."

Phoebe looks at me like she's offended, her mouth gaping. "Why should *I* stop?"

"We *all* have to ignore him. It's just like when you first meet

74

an aggressive dog. It may bark at you and try to scare you, but you have to completely ignore it until it calms down. It lets them know who's in charge," I explain. "So, for now, just keep doing what you're doing."

"Which was being a Marcie," Joey so helpfully reminds Phoebe.

I put my hand on Phoebe's elbow before she can launch into him. Then I say, "Boggle, anyone?" with a slightly forced, but still very wise, smile.

Phoebe exhales loudly and starts packing up her markers.

Delia reaches for the Boggle box, and Mandy starts handing out scrap paper—to everyone but Joey.

"Let me shake up the letters," Joey says. We ignore him. Delia gives me a look that says, *This is awkward.*

"C'mon, guys. *I'm sorry*, okay?" he continues.

Mandy stares up at the ceiling. Delia shifts in her seat uncomfortably. Phoebe has started laying out the game, her lips pressed primly together.

"I was being a butt, okay?" Joey says through gritted teeth, and sighs. "Now, can I *please* shake the letters?"

Sometimes you can see how twelve years old he really is. Mandy hands him the letters, and he suddenly looks completely, one hundred percent happy.

Lucky me. On the bus home, I get a chance to practice *that* teachable moment all on my own. I'm feeling a little like a scientist who just tested something in the lab (the Bored Game Club being our petri dish) and is now ready to try it in the field.

Today there's the usual barking, but it sounds more like a couple of restless poodles rather than a herd of pit bulls. I can feel Brynne staring into me, and I try to pretend she didn't just fake a cough and choke out "loser" as I walked by. I don't even blink when everyone laughs. I'm also pretty busy trying to keep my shoulders from creeping up to my ears, which is one of the all-telling signs of submission in the human world.

When I get to my seat, I pull out my Spanish textbook. With everything going on, I know I've gotten behind on my work, and to be honest, it's almost a relief to get my mind off of the training. I open my book and finally breathe—and almost relax. Until Brynne comes to the back of bus. "Hey," she says. "You."

I stare at the green vinyl of the seat in front of me and don't say anything. I'm too busy trying really hard to relax. You know how some people think about a beach or a park or something like that to make themselves calm down? Well, here's what I think about. Brushing my teeth. Washing my face. Those things you're supposed to do every day but sometimes don't because they're so incredibly boring. Flossing my teeth. I mean, if your world was really falling apart, the *last* thing you'd be doing is flossing your teeth.

"You think you can ignore me?"

And when flossing fails, sometimes hair washing works.

"*I said*, you think you can ignore me?"

Lather, rinse, repeat!

"Well, you can't," she says. She leans down close to my face. "No one ignores me."

LATHER, RINSE, REPEAT! I look back down at my book. My hands are gripping it so intensely that my thumbs are turning white. So much for relaxing.

But my nervousness actually works to my advantage. Because Brynne reaches her fist under my book and punches upward, but, as it turns out, I am holding on to it so tightly that nothing moves. And she looks kind of stupid trying to make it happen.

She stands up straight, nostrils flaring. "You *are* a loser." She holds her palms out and adds, "All's I wanted was a piece of gum," like she's a victim or something. Then she tries to storm back up to the front of the bus. Fortunately, we are making a turn and her balance is thrown. She plows into Kendall Kim, who, though pinned against the window, reminds her that his father is a lawyer. This time everyone in the back of the bus—the other losers like me—laughs. Not as loudly, not as surely. It might even be nervous laughter. But it still counts as laughter. And the best part about it is that no one is laughing at *me*.

It's a tiny victory, one barely visible to the naked eye, but still I feel a little rush of hope.

11.

Bites

WEDNESDAY AT LUNCH, Mandy walks in and slumps into her seat at the table. "Someone stop me before I strangle Corbin Moon. He is so aggravating."

She says this through lips that are especially black today, like she did a double dose of Sharpie. It also looks like she went outside the lines a little. "What did he do?" I ask.

"He commented on my lips. He kind of tricked me," she says, like she's a little embarrassed. "First, he goes, 'Wow, Mandy, there's something different about you today.' And the way he was saying it, I thought he was actually being cool for once. Then he tells me I look like I have a disease. This ignoring thing is really hard, Liv. I *so* wanted to tell him I'd give him a black *eye* disease if he didn't shut up," she says, balling up her fist as she talks.

"But you didn't," I say. Just to make sure, I ask, "Right?"

She sighs. "No, I *didn't*. But it's been such a sucky day."

"I know," Delia says, pulling strands of hair from her ponytail. Her skin may not be smoother, but since she and Mandy went shopping, it's a lot more even-toned. Not that it seems to matter at this moment. She's so upset, she hasn't taken a bite of her soyburger.

"Want to know what happened to me?" She glances around at all of us. "Tamberlin kept calling my name in third period. I tried to ignore her, but it got really annoying, and everyone else started poking me and calling me like they thought I couldn't hear her. So I finally turn around, and she gasps and makes this face like she's about to throw up, and tells me thanks, and says that looking at my face"—her voice cracks—"works a whole lot better than the appetite suppressants she's been taking."

I wince. Then I give her a shoulder-hug. "I'm sorry, Dee. It'll get better."

"Yeah, Delia," Phoebe adds.

"I just want to"—Mandy holds up her fist—"pummel her. Pummel them all."

"I'm sure your day wasn't worse than mine," Joey says, unwrapping a Ding Dong and stuffing it into his face. He talks through a full mouth. "I was copying the math equations from the board when Danny Pritchard just stole my pencil from me."

"And?" Phoebe asks, removing the crust from her turkey sandwich. "So what did you do?"

"Nothing," he says. "I just sat there looking like a total wuss, doing absolutely nothing. He laughed in my face." He picks up the wrapper and smells it. "This ignoring thing *blows*."

"You mean you just sat there without writing anything for the entire class?" I ask.

"Well, Erin Monroe ended up giving me a pen. Except it was stupid. It was one of those pens with the big flowery thing at the end."

In popularity rankings, Erin Monroe is no school celebrity,

but she's not a total Marcie either. "So someone bailed you out," I say. "That's a good sign."

"Whatever," he says with a shrug, fishing into his lunch bag for another treat. "I just think this is stupid." He pulls out a package of baby carrots and makes a face. "No idea what my mom was thinking here," he says, and then grabs my banana, which is weird, because the closest thing to a naturally occurring food item he's ever eaten in front of us was a packet of sugar. I decide not to fight for it.

Joey peels the banana and stuffs it into his mouth, almost violently. "Next time, Danny Pritchard's getting a *tameshi-wari* to the gut," he says, and while still chewing, demonstrates a karate punch.

Normally, this would be grounds to make some fun of our yellow-belt friend, but today I decide to leave it alone. If he's eating a banana, he's clearly upset.

"I know this is hard, you guys," I say, keeping my voice quiet. "But look, Joey, Danny's a terrier. He's determined—that's probably how he got Brynne to be his girlfriend in the first place. But now he's using this determination to try and bring you down. You just can't let him. Terriers aren't easy to control at first, but it's not impossible."

Phoebe lets out a sigh. "Brant's a sporter," she says, staring dreamily across the cafeteria at him.

Mandy scrunches up her face as if to say, *Where the heck did that come from?*

But Joey holds back a smile and says, "Yeah, I guess I can see that, Martin."

"Really?" Phoebe asks, surprised. For once Joey's not arguing with her.

"Well, yeah. 'Cause he's *definitely* playing some kind of game with you," he says.

"You know, Joey, you're just a—" Phoebe yells, and hurls a desperate last-resort insult, "a *dum-dum*." She pushes back from the table, bunches up her still-full lunch bag between her hands, and storms out of the cafeteria. She's about as graceful as an ox, so it does look a little funny, but it unfortunately looks even funnier when the über-beautiful Peyton Randall gets up and does an impersonation—with just a little more flailing.

The entire table of Brynne minions laugh. I wonder if being that mean feels pretty good, because it certainly looks like they're enjoying it.

Mandy grits her teeth like she wants to say something, or worse, do something. Delia shoots me a worried look. Joey, as usual, is directing his angst toward anything edible, practically turning his lunch bag inside out in search of a treat.

"Just ignore them," I say, keeping my voice low. "Remember. The. Plan."

But I glance back at Brynne's table, and I secretly wonder if we need to step it up somehow. Because you know that expression *Nice guys always finish last*? I'm starting to suspect that it's true.

Not-So-Well Bred

MONCHERIE'S WEARING a pink sweater that has thick shoulder pads in it. It looks like she's got boobs sprouting up near the sides of her neck. Even I know it's disastrously unfashionable—and keep in mind, I've been known to wear Velcro-strapped sneakers to school before. Not that I'm proud of it or anything. I'm just saying.

I follow her into her office. She takes her seat in the armchair, and I sit in the folding chair facing her. It's cold and hard, and I think I've learned where my coccyx is—we studied it on the skeleton in Science today. I move around in my seat and end up perching on the side of my thigh.

"Oh." Moncherie crinkles her nose. "Not comfy, huh?"

I shake my head no.

"Sorry to hear that. So how are you otherwise?" She squints. "Are you wearing *mascara*?"

"Do you like it?" I ask.

"I think—" she starts. "Never mind. It's not important what I think. What's important is how *you feel* about it. But I'd go with a brownish-black, if I were you. But I'm not." She smiles.

I nod, like it's an acceptable answer.

"So, how's school?"

"Okay."

"Good to hear." She checks off something on her notepad. "Now—" she says, and at the same time I say, "It still sucks," and we sit there staring at each other, like each of us is afraid to keep talking.

She takes a breath. "Okay, you're sending mixed messages, Olivia. Which is it?"

"Well, it still sucks, but you're not going to believe this," I say. After our last session, I think she might really want to hear this. "My friend Phoebe? Well, this totally popular guy asked her to the Fall Ball. It's got to be a joke but—"

She is nodding, but she has this pained look on her face, like I'm giving her the details on a frog dissection or something. I stop and ask her what the matter is.

"Well, Olivia, it's just that you're here for a reason. We're supposed to be talking about the issues regarding your mother." She taps the notepad with the tip of her pen, leaving a stipple of frustration on the page.

Just when I was actually beginning to like her.

Her eyes go a little soft. "I'm sorry. It's just that you always find other things to talk about."

I study my cuticle and find a spear of skin to pull off. My houndlike destructive behaviors always seem to kick in when I'm stressed.

"Olivia?"

I don't answer. I hit blood and reach for a tissue to blot it.

"How do you feel, Olivia, about your mother—and where she is now?"

I just shrug. I have no desire to unpack that Space Bag, to unload any of the baggage in my brain-trunk. Everything is fitting back there nicely enough, thank you.

She sighs and slumps a little, which makes me feel like I'm letting her down. So I decide to give her a little something for her notepad. I don't have to dig too deep in the trunk for this one. It's sort of like the souvenir you might pack in your carry-on luggage. Not like a snow globe or anything fun, but something with some shock value, like the paperweight with a dead scorpion in it that my dad brought back from a trip to Arizona. I remind myself that I'm breaking my bathroom-wall rule *yet again* for her. "I think she's got a boyfriend."

She sits up a little straighter and her eyebrows move into that concerned position. "And how do you feel about that?"

So I tell her. "It's just gross."

She's quiet, like she's waiting for me to add more, and I wonder, doesn't she know me by now? Good thing she's not holding her breath.

"Okay, Olivia, good," she says gently, showing me mercy. "Why don't you finish telling me about your friend?"

"Phoebe?"

"Sure."

So I start to tell her about Phoebe again, and she puts down the pen. It's always better when she puts down the pen. She's actually a lot easier to talk to when she stops trying so hard to make me speak.

Panting

IT'S SATURDAY, and it's been an exhausting week. I've had to do a lot of ignoring. On Monday, as I walked by her on the bus, Brynne sniffed the air and said, "German shepherd! No, Rottweiler! No, wait! I got it! Husky!" On Wednesday, in P.E., Brynne publicly declared that she didn't want me on her soccer team because I was "overheight." What was even worse was that Mr. Mack assigned me to her team anyway because he said "overheight" wasn't a real condition—like it would have been an acceptable reason if it was. And on Thursday, Carolyn harassed me because my jeans were a millimeter too short, and then Tamberlin took over and carried the joke even further, into my socks. "Is that a tube sock? Oh. *My.* God." And even though it *wasn't* a tube sock, I kept my mouth shut.

After such a grueling week, I'm glad to be in the company of Loomis, the neurotic bike-hating dog.

"Places, everyone," Corny says, like she's directing a play rather than running a dog-training drill. She stands on Mrs. Taylor's lawn, with her hands clasped together in front of her chest and a hopeful look on her face.

Mrs. Taylor steps to the sidewalk, holding Loomis's leash, and glances over her shoulder at me with a worried look on her face. I steady myself on the bike and turn around to smile at Delia, who is sitting safely on the hood of the pickup truck. She gives me a thumbs-up, fully playing up her role as my moral support.

"And, go," Corny directs.

Mrs. Taylor starts down the sidewalk with Loomis, who, at this point, is behaving like a show dog. He's a little chow and a little golden retriever, so of course he's too mixed-up to make it into one those snobby shows, but right now he's pretty convincing.

I wait for them to get about two houses away, and then I push off, bringing my standing leg to the pedal and lifting my butt off the seat to get some speed. As I get closer to them, I see Mrs. Taylor's shoulders stiffen, and I hear her voice getting higher in tone and pitch. "No, Loomis. *No*, Loomis. No, *no*, Loomis!" And then Loomis goes crazy and starts cussing me out with these big, loud, insulting dog barks, which startles me and makes me freeze up. I fall to the ground, my helmet thudding against the pavement.

Corny and Delia rush toward me, cooing concern. Mrs. Taylor apologizes and strains to hold back Loomis, who looks like he's grinning, but he's really just threatening me with his fangs.

I sigh, completely humbled. "I'm okay," I say. I start to brush off the pebbles and leaves sticking to my whole left side. Corny latches one of her bony hands around my forearm and pulls me to standing. She may be old, but she's strong. Delia slaps the debris off my jeans, so it looks like she's spanking me.

"You got a rip," she tells me, still absentmindedly beating the crap out of me.

"Um," I say, "you're sort of hurting me."

"Oh! Sorry!" She backs away. "I think those jeans are beyond repair."

Corny is standing on the sidewalk with Mrs. Taylor, counseling her. Loomis has gone back to playing Good Dog, and sits there panting and just looking around, relaxed and happy.

"What happened with Loomis?" Delia asks. "Hasn't your grandma been working with him for a while?"

"Yes," I tell her. I point out the way Mrs. Taylor tensed up when I approached on the bike, and the way she started yelling at Loomis. "She got really nervous because she thought he was going to go crazy when he saw the bike. But it wasn't really the bike that set him off—it was her reaction. She got scared, so he wanted to protect her."

"Wow," Delia says. "That was actually pretty sweet of him, then."

"Don't tell *her*," I say quietly to Delia, "but I think she's really the one we're training. Or *trying* to."

"We'll try again next week," I hear Corny tell Mrs. Taylor. "In the meantime, keep walking him and don't let yourself get nervous."

Mrs. Taylor looks a little embarrassed, but Corny gives her a little shoulder hug and says, "It's never really easy." Which I have the bruises to prove.

Corny feels so bad about my torn jeans and about, well, using me as bait that she drops me and Delia off at the mall and gives me money to buy some replacements.

"You know," Delia says gently, "they do make jeans in long sizes."

"Not where my dad shops," I say, trying to make it funny. It might be if it weren't true.

"Maybe it's time that your dad stops doing all the shopping." She says this so nicely, so sweetly, that I just nod and start to feel a little grateful. She's absolutely right.

I follow her into a store where everyone looks like a model— well, not like the six-foot-two *magazine* models, but like perfect little models of what people who make jeans expect people who buy them to look like. You know, no crazy, jutting hip bones, or warped butts, or tree-trunk thighs. "I'm not sure about this," I tell Delia. I can't help but stare at one salesgirl who's so pretty and willowy she almost looks like she's been drawn by some expert artist with a nice flowing charcoal pencil. Everything about her looks perfectly put into place.

I, on the other hand, look like I was drawn by that artist's third-grade student. I try to explain this to Delia, but she just hands me six pairs of jeans and leads me into an ant-sized dressing room. We cram in together, and when I slip out of my awful jeans, she takes them and looks at the tag. "These are guys' jeans."

"Yeah, well." I shrug. I don't tell her about the other pairs my dad bought me that have tags that say *irregular*. And yet seem to fit me.

The first pair mocks me by riding up in the crotch. The second pair plays a trick on me by making my butt magically disappear. The third pair serves me up a generous portion of muffin top. After the fourth pair just whines at me and sags so much in the crotch that I look like I've changed genders, my frustration

88

takes over. "This is why I just give up." I reach for my jeans. "Why even bother?"

She snatches them out of my hands. "Last time I shopped for jeans, I tried on fourteen pairs!" Which I know is only because she was seeking absolute perfection, not simply trying to be passable, like I am. She may have acne, but she's like a little mannequin. Clothes look as good on her body as they do on the displays.

Three stores, nineteen pairs, and one heated argument later (about which was worse, cystic acne or bad bone structure), I find them. Two pairs! On *sale*, even! They are magical. I can't help smiling when I see them in the mirror and find that I look incredibly normal. Somehow they've made my legs look less like odd appendages created strictly for the function of walking, and more like flowy things a dancer might have. Okay, that might be pushing it a little, but still, I *do* feel a little graceful in them. There's a shape to my butt, and it's not a rectangle. The crotch is perfectly gender-appropriate. It's just—normal. And acceptable. Both such beautiful, glorious words.

14.

Good Grooming

I AM MAKING my way to first period on Monday morning when I hear the word "Holy," right behind me. I turn around and see Mandy staring at my new jeans. "Cow," she finishes.

I disregard the Hubert C. Frost "Rules of the Road," which are posted every twenty feet in every hallway, and pull her across the hall to where a line of lockers ends, providing a small bunker. "Delia and I went shopping," I explain.

"You look so *different* in them," she says, but with a little shock.

"Thanks," I say. But she stands there kind of wide-eyed, looking me over. "What? Don't you like them?"

"Well, yeah," she says. I expect her to smile, but she doesn't. "I mean, they work."

My own smile starts to fade. "But?"

"But nothing," she says, and then adds, "Just don't change too much, okay?"

I give her a bewildered laugh. "The only thing that's changed is I have a couple of pairs of new jeans."

"And a shirt," she says. "Which, I have to say, is cute."

It is. It's a button-up with little pinstripes, and it goes in at the waist so I look a lot less pointy. "I borrowed it from Delia. Her aunt sent it, but it's like eighteen sizes too big for her."

"And mascara," she continues.

"Um, *hello*? Your idea."

"I know, but." She pauses. "I thought that was just mascara. But now the clothes, and I don't even know what else. You just look so different."

"Do I have to remind you? I *have* been working on my posture. Like you're supposed to be doing." I do a few shoulder slumps (before) and squarings (after) to demonstrate.

"I know and you're probably right," she says. "It's just, I don't know, every day you look less and less like my strange little buddy."

I snort out a laugh. "Oh, and by 'little,' you mean 'freakishly tall,' right?"

She shrugs. "So you've got a couple of inches on the rest of us. Big deal. In some cultures, that's a good thing."

"Yeah, well, so are bound feet," I say.

She laughs. I do too.

"Anyway." I bring my hands to my mess of hair. "Does the fact that my hair is still a big poof of frizz bring you any comfort?"

"Actually," she says, smiling, "yes. I think it does."

"Gee, thanks." I was kind of hoping she'd say that *it* looks different too, because I put some "all-day control" spray on it this morning—some stuff I found in the back of my grandma's bathroom cabinet. The label was yellowed and peeling, and it had a name like Georgie Girl, but I thought it was worth a shot. Apparently not.

I'm giving up. It's just going into a ponytail.

"Just so you know," Mandy says, "*I'm* not going mainstream."

"I'm not either," I argue. I mean, I doubt I'll ever be able to pull that off. Seriously. "I'm just trying to look halfway normal."

"Whatever you say," she answers. "Just don't become one of *them*." But then she gives me a soft punch in the upper arm, so I know she wants me to think that she's kidding. And I give her a soft arm-punch back, because I want her to think I am, too.

Puppy Steps

MR. DEWEY WAVES from his front stoop as we pull up after school. Kisses is next to him, on a leash. "Would you just look at that?" Corny beams.

But when we pull into the driveway, Kisses runs toward the car—as far as her leash will let her. She doesn't make the usual scene, but she looks like she's thinking about it. When she starts to lower her head and pull her lip back just a bit, Corny taps on the horn. Kisses startles, jumping away from the car. "Now, that's an easy distraction." She laughs.

We open our doors and I go around to the back of the truck. It was Corny's idea to bring sod today. It's like little squares of lawn. She thinks if Kisses can handle walking on a small strip of grass, it may be the stepping stone to bigger things, like backyards and parks.

"How's it been going?" Corny asks Mr. Dewey.

"Better," he says. Kisses starts to mash up her face. As her sharp teeth start to show, a low growl comes out of her. "Except she still acts like this whenever we have company."

"All that growling and teeth-baring is telling you that she feels anxious. When you see these cues, you've got to distract her immediately, before she can start acting on those feelings. Watch," Corny says, and claps her hands together just once. Kisses's lip drops a little and she tucks her head back.

"So when you tapped your horn . . . ?"

"Right. That was a distraction too. Sometimes you have to get creative."

We follow Mr. Dewey through the house and out to the back patio—a little stone surface surrounded by grass. I place the sod down on the stone. Then Corny hands Kisses's leash to me.

There's not much room out here, but I need to get her used to me handling the leash, so I walk her around in a loop until she seems comfortable. Then I walk her up to the square of sod. She growls and pulls back.

"That's a cue," Corny says. "So you need to distract her. Give a little tug on the leash. Gentle, but firm."

I pull upward on the leash, and her growling stops.

"Now, have her sit," Corny continues. "She needs to relax."

Luckily, Kisses listens to me. She sits down, still two feet from the sod.

"Good. Now try again," Corny says. This time Kisses takes two steps forward and one step back, pulling again. We do it all over again.

On the third try, Kisses gets close to the grass, even sets a tiny foot on it for a brief second, and then starts pulling and growling. Corny takes her leash. "Just a second too late on the distraction, Olivia," she tells me.

I'm ready to try again—I mean, her paw made contact with

grass!—but she tells me it's time to give it a break, that we'll be back soon to try again.

"Ah, well," Mr. Dewey says. "At least she's going on the paper now." He's talking about her potty habits. "I couldn't even get her to do that before."

"That's better," Corny says. "But we'll get her going back out here again. Just not today."

Later, on the way out to the pickup, she says, "Don't worry. It's okay. You did really well with her. In cases like these, it's always baby steps."

I'm already thinking. Cues and distractions. The next step in our plan.

16.

Natural Instincts

BETWEEN FIRST AND second periods the next morning, I see Phoebe engulfed in the herd making its way down the hall in front of me. "Hey, wait up!" I call to her.

She shoots a panicked look over her shoulder at me and slows down. The other kids move like liquid around her. "I'm stressed," she says as I catch up. "I've got a quiz this period."

"You always get A's," I remind her. "You're lucky."

"It's not luck," she says, eyeing me.

"*Hiii Phoeee-bee,*" we hear, in a booming, slow, and extra-syrupy boy-voice. It's coming from the gorgeous-toothed, sweepy-haired Brant, who happens to be traveling in the crowd moving toward us.

"Oh hi, Brant," she says, with a wave of her hand. "Can't talk!"

He gives her an exaggerated frown and floats away in the human river. For a second I am speechless. I'm wondering if maybe she's finally getting it—that maybe she knows, or at least suspects, that he's mocking her.

But I'm wrong again. "I *told* him I had a vocab quiz third

period," she says, shaking her head. "Who has time to talk when you've got a quiz?"

Over near the doorway of a classroom, the little kid from the bus, my silent seatmate, is trying to get across the hall. He eyes the traffic hesitantly, like a chicken trying to cross a busy road. He jerks his body forward, and then quickly back—a false start. I wonder if we should stop and help him or if that would make him feel worse, when we hear the chanting.

"S-P-I!" Pause. "R-I-T!" Suddenly the human waters part clumsily, and a blue spandexed line of about fifteen Spiritleaders starts snaking down the hall toward us. And—

Blam!

Little Kid has chosen the wrong moment to cross, and now both he and Head Spiritleader Brynne Shawnson are on the hallway floor. For a second they both flop around like fishes. Except for the flopping, the hall is pretty quiet—just a few sharp intakes of breath, a stray "Oh. My. God." Or two. But then the laughing begins.

Brynne makes it to her feet first, dusting off her unitard. "I'm okay," she says, neither sounding nor looking it. Her head starts to tilt back, and I quickly nudge Phoebe.

"Watch this," I whisper.

"What?" she whispers back.

"What she's doing! See?"

Brynne's lip starts to curl and her shoulders start to square as she eyes the kid. And then a stream of cruelty spews from her mouth. "You *idiot*! What were you thinking!? Are you blind or just *stupid*?!"

Little Kid gets up, blinking, and picks up his books. "Sorry," he murmurs, and shuffles quickly across the hall.

"God, Brynne, calm down. He was like, *eight*," Corinne d'Abo, one of the other Spiritleaders, says to her.

"So? I was just *kidding*," Brynne says back. "Let's go!"

The Spiritleaders shuffle back behind Brynne. "ARCTIC WIND!" she calls out. They organize themselves in a single-file line, facing sideways. "Let's get ready to *bloooowww*!" People start bumping into each other, scurrying for safety, as the Spiritleaders cartwheel down the hall like whirling blue death stars, the kind you see in ninja movies.

I turn back to Phoebe. "So did you see what she was doing?"

"Didn't *everybody*?"

"I'm not talking about the obvious stuff, Pheeb. I'm talking about the way she moved her head, the way she curled her lip—the stuff she did right before she started yelling at that kid?"

"Oh. I guess so. Why?"

"*Why*? Only because it's one of the most important parts of this plan."

"Liv, I've really got to go," Phoebe says. "That quiz—"

And then she's off. Thanks to the Spiritleaders, the crowd in the halls has thinned, but the floors are littered with wreckage—loose papers thrown about, full binders splayed open, even a random but seriously unfashionable clog. I'm sure somewhere in the school, a Teen Life teacher is walking lopsided, mourning its loss, but thanking her lucky stars that she escaped the hallway with all limbs intact.

I'm almost to my classroom when I slip on someone's algebra homework. My foot shoots forward, and I wind up on the ground in what a P.E. teacher would call a hurdle stretch. Luckily I scramble to my feet before I hear "You okay?"

I turn around and see Uncle Jesse. From *Full House*. Only

much younger and much more three-dimensional. This version also has a better haircut. I try to speak but can't. And then the Young Uncle Jesse smiles, and you can almost hear the roar of blood rushing to my face, prickling every nerve from my belly button to my sagging ponytail. I mean, the way he looks at me makes me feel like I'm some type of fancy show dog.

The bell rings, making us both officially late, but neither one of us moves. Me, because I'm physically paralyzed. Him, because—well, that part I can't figure out. Maybe my crazy gene has kicked in and I'm seeing things? Maybe I have a concussion from my fall? Maybe I'm actually dead and in heaven?

Finally, I get it out. "I'm fine." And then, before I can stop that stubborn inner dweeb, I hear myself say, "I'm Olivia."

"Oh. Well, I'm Caleb. I'm new."

New? So he doesn't know about my reputation as a Marcie? The misfit? The outcast? The smelly dog-girl? He's never seen me with too-short—and irregular—jeans? Or with anything *but* long, lush lashes and Caribbean green eyes?

I laugh. But nothing's funny, and now I've just made it even more awkward. But instead of getting all squirmy, he laughs a little too. And then I notice a little red patch on his chin—zits!—and I feel a flurry of hope. Because maybe wherever he came from everyone looked like the salespeople in the jeans store, and just having oily skin demoted you to Marciedom. Maybe he doesn't realize how out of my league he is here, where standards are so much lower!

And then, my heart quickening all over again, I start to wonder—could he actually, just maybe, perhaps, I mean, I know it's a crazy thought, but could he actually . . . ? Just a little . . . ? You know, be *liking* me?

But then he says, "This is probably a stupid question since I see you've got two on your feet, but any chance you lost a shoe back there?" And he dashes my dreams. He brings me back to cold, hard middle school life. Did I really think I could put on a new pair of jeans and suddenly stop being a Marcie? Because anyone who could possibly think I'm dorkish enough to own a clog can't possibly like me like *that*.

I realize I still haven't answered his question, and he's starting to look a little dismayed. He's probably wishing he could think of a polite way to end this conversation. So I help him out.

"No," I say, and turn away, starting toward my class.

"Well, nice to meet you," he calls to my back.

"You too," I mumble. But then I turn around just one more time. "Thanks," I say. I mean, sure, I'm mortified, but what does it hurt to get a second glance? And then I'll never think about him again.

Really.

Signs of Aggression

IT'S LATER THE same day and we're in Bored Game Club, but the games all remain in their boxes. Word has spread throughout the school about Brynne and Little Kid's hallway collision, but now it includes stuff like ambulances and comas, so Phoebe and I, as eyewitnesses, are trying to set the record straight.

"There wasn't even any blood," I explain to Mandy, Delia, and Joey.

"What does 'critical condition' mean?" Joey asks.

"He's not in the hospital, dummy!" Phoebe says to him. "He probably just got sent to the nurse's office and went home."

"Not if Mrs. Arafata's still in charge," I remind them.

"Those Spiritleaders," Phoebe says. "It's really only a matter of time before someone *is* hospitalized." Last year, Phoebe warped her braces when she fell down half a flight of stairs trying to escape their dreaded "Spirit Snowball" move, in which they somersault down the halls in rows of three across. Usually what happens is that half the snowballers get dizzy and disoriented, roll off course, and trap the slowest runners against lockers and walls. Phoebe says it set her orthodontic plan back about eight months, which is why she's still wearing braces today. "They're just so reckless," she adds.

"If I'm elected, you think I could get rid of them?" Mandy asks.

Delia perks up to say, "Oooooh. Good idea!" at the same time Phoebe says, "I doubt it," and before the two of them can start arguing about it, I say, "If we're going to get Mandy elected, then we've got to keep working on the plan."

"Okay, fine. So what's next?" Mandy asks.

"Cues and distractions," I tell them. They all look at me like living question marks, even know-it-all Phoebe.

"Oh! Cues! Like you were trying to show me today," Phoebe says suddenly.

"Exactly." I turn to the rest of them. "You know how when a dog starts to get upset, sometimes its hair stands up on its back, or it might start to growl? And if you're watching it closely, you can see it in its eyes. Their focus starts to change. We saw Brynne do that earlier today."

Phoebe jumps in. "Oh, yeah! Right before she started yelling at that boy, she tilted her head back a little. And did you notice that weird thing with her mouth?" She demonstrates, bearing her teeth. Well, braces.

"Exactly," I say. "There's always some type of cue before an attack, and we've got to start noticing these signs."

"And then what?" Mandy asks.

"A couple of things. First, stay calm. Don't get scared."

"Yeah. Just imagine she just cut one," Joey advises us. Then he makes a loud farty sound with his mouth. I guess we're still suckers for these jokes even though we are in eighth grade, because everyone except, of course, Phoebe, starts laughing so hard that Joey cuts one for real.

"Joey!" Phoebe yells, obviously upset. The rest of us are busy fanning our faces and trying not to laugh in the fumes. The tips of Phoebe's ears are red, and her hand shields her face.

Ms. Greenwood gets up quietly and, with her usual expression of mild but persistent disgust, opens a window.

"Okay, okay," Delia says, dabbing her eyes. "That was sick, Joey."

"What I mean is, even though she's a total hottie, she still goes to the bathroom." We all open our mouths to try and shut him up, but then he says something that actually sounds smart. And not math-genius smart, just real-life smart. Wise, even. "What I'm *trying* to say is that she's no better than anyone else."

We're all quiet for a minute. Delia looks surprised but nods in agreement. Phoebe leans back, thinking it over. Mandy and I exchange glances.

Joey looks around at us like he's making sure he's got our attention. Then his eyebrows lower and he starts to smirk. "In other words," he adds, "she's just as gross as the rest of you."

Okay, so that wise thing? It was just a fluke.

"Joey, you just did it," I say.

"That was like five minutes ago!" he argues.

"Not *that*, Einstein," I say. "You just gave a bunch of cues before you insulted us. Did you guys see that?"

"Oh, *yeah*!" Delia says, excited. "The eyebrow thing!"

"Yeah, and that evil little smile," Phoebe says. She stares at him angrily and waits for his reaction, but he just colors in the tread on the bottom of his shoe with his pen.

Mandy turns her head to the side, and her gaze floats toward the ceiling. "Now that I think of it, Corbin did this little quivery nostril thing that day he said something about my lips." She demonstrates. "I thought it was kind of weird at the time."

"See?" I say. "They all do *something*. It's pretty cool if you think about it."

"What's so cool about that?" Phoebe asks.

"Because once you see the cues, you can create a distraction. It's all part of the training."

"What kind of distraction?" Delia asks.

"Anything to get them off track," I say. I tell them about Kisses, and add, "You basically want to interrupt their train of thought and get them to focus on something completely different." Then I turn to Mandy. "Let's think about the other day. What could you have done to knock Corbin Moon off course?"

"Oh, I could have knocked him off course, all right," she says.

"If you had hit him, not only would you have been expelled, but you would have totally made him more interested in getting revenge," I explain. "But if you distract him, he's confused. He doesn't know how to react, or what to say, or really what happened at all. And best of all, he can't seek revenge because there's nothing to seek revenge *for*."

"So what do I do? Tell him his fly's open?"

"It's a little obvious, but I guess it could work," I say.

"Lame," Joey says, but he discreetly peeks down to check his own.

"How about a jumping jack?" Phoebe asks.

We all look at her like she's crazy.

She shrugs. "Stupid?" she asks.

We nod.

"Oh! How about a Fighting Serpent!" Joey says, and jumps

to his feet. He then crouches, lifts one leg, and holds his arms in front of him, hands curved down like a praying mantis.

"Absolutely. No. Karate. Moves," I tell him.

Joey gets back into his seat, grumbling.

"But see, none of you guys have acne," Delia says. "How can I distract someone from this?" She points to her face.

"It's not *all* luck," Phoebe says, but Mandy cuts her off before she can start describing her own face-washing rituals. Mandy also tells Delia her acne's not that noticeable. A lie, but sweet.

"If it's so *not that* noticeable," Delia says, "why does Carolyn Quim point it out every time I see her? And the way she does it—she's sneaky. She always starts by, like, asking me how I did on the math quiz or something. She pretends she's being nice. Then she says something like, 'So, do you eat a lot of chocolate?'"

"You don't, though, do you?" Phoebe starts. "'Cause I hear—"

I throw her a look, and thankfully she shuts her mouth.

"What are Carolyn's signals?" I ask Delia.

She twists up her face and thinks for a minute. "I guess she usually stares at me for a second or so, and then she kind of clears her throat a little. It sounds like a little grunt, I think."

"So while she's staring, you could ask her if she wants to borrow your Scope," Phoebe offers. We don't remind her that she's the only one in Hubert C. Frost Middle School who actually brings Scope with her wherever she goes.

"I don't know. Maybe I could just ask her what time it is or something," Delia says. Which sounds way too nice to me.

So I say, "Or tell her that you don't care what everyone else says, she is *not* getting fat. Be like, 'I have *no idea* what they're thinking.'"

Mandy, Delia, and Joey burst into laughter—even Phoebe

manages a smirk, which signals a huge accomplishment on my part.

"Oh, that's so evil," Mandy manages to say once she catches her breath, but she looks at me with something like admiration.

Joey smiles big. "Or just high-five her and say, 'You know, my friend Joey said you're an awesome kisser.'" Which leads to a chorus of disgusted moans, and I start to appreciate all over again how much fun my friends really are.

I get on the bus and walk, head down, through the narrow aisle. And then I hear her voice. "*Oh. Em. Gee,*" Brynne shrieks. The hairs on my arms start to stand up. My tongue feels heavy and my stomach churns, but I'm ready for this. For once.

She has this sickened look on her face. She looks at me and sniffs the air. "Do I smell—"

"Oh my God!" I find myself saying. My tongue is still heavy, but I sound only a little impaired. "What's that?" I am looking straight at her, pointing at the space between her eyebrows.

Her hand claps over her forehead and her eyes widen. She squeals. "What? *What?*"

I squint my eyes and lean forward. Her head tucks back. "*What!*" she yells again.

"Oh," I say. "Never mind. I think it's just a little zit." I even smile. Except for the tiny scar on her chin, her face is as clear as porcelain, but I'm sure I've touched a nerve. And then I walk on.

She turns to Carolyn, who has been watching, like everyone else, with her mouth hanging open. "You didn't tell me I had a zit!" Brynne says to her, angry.

"What? I didn't see a zit," Carolyn says apologetically.

"I can't trust you at *all!*" Brynne seethes. That's all I hear out of her until we get to her stop and she leaves the bus, walking down the street ten feet in front of the pleading Carolyn.

And I think, *Yay, me.*

When I get home, there's a letter from my mom waiting for me. I slide it under my mattress with the other ones I haven't opened. And then I turn on the TV and watch a rerun of *Full House*, where I can enjoy the *real* Uncle Jesse, and don't even have to think about what's inside the envelope, or what my mom might be doing right now at crazy camp. Not at all.

18.

Go Fetch

AFTER SCHOOL on Wednesday, Moncherie practically pulls me into her office. "I've got something to show you," she says, closing the door behind us with her foot. "Ta-dah!" she sings, and waves her hand in the direction of a big wooden rocking chair with a little cushion on the seat.

I smile. This is *so* much better than a folding chair. Maybe I'll actually be able to relax in here with her. Maybe she *can* actually fix me. Maybe one day I will once again be a normal person—someone without gaping, obvious problems like social awkwardness and damaged hair.

"Hey, wait a second. Wow," she says, stepping back to look me over. "First mascara. And now a new style. You look very—well, I don't know what to say."

You'd think someone who's twenty-six years old and went to college would be able to think of *something* nice to say.

"My friend Delia and I went shopping for some new jeans." And then I wait patiently for her to compliment me.

But instead she just says, "Shopping, huh?" then clasps her hands together and tells me to take a seat. Next she asks me how I felt about the "experience" in three different ways, with this little glint in her eye like she's a cat ready to pounce on a helpless baby rodent.

Now she's on her fourth version of the same question. "So, did the experience bring up any surprising feelings?"

I am only half joking when I say, "Well, I was pretty surprised to find some jeans that looked half decent on my weird body."

Normally when you say something like this around an adult, they start to argue and throw all sorts of compliments at you, which—even if they are complete lies—are still kind of nice to hear. So, of course, it sort of bothers me when she just sits there and says, "Hmm."

So I add, "It's kind of hard when you're as big as I am."

And instead of telling me how I'm *tall*, not big, and that one day I'll probably be happy about it, she just says, "And you feel"—tilting her head to the side and making a sweeping movement with her hands like she's conducting a symphony—"*blank* about that?"

"Well, not really *blank*," I explain, to my weird-and-getting-weirder therapist. "I mean, I feel like—*hello*, just stick me in a cornfield somewhere and you won't have to worry about crows."

The glint starts to fade. She sits back and sighs. She starts tapping her pen on her notepad. "I meant," she says, sounding exhausted, "fill in the blank. You're supposed to *fill it in*."

"Oh," I say quickly. "Sorry." Okay, so I'm not only *not* funny, but I'm also a moron.

"Let's try this another way," she says after a few moments of uncomfortable silence during which I completely but accidentally pick away the cuticle from my right thumb. "So you have some new jeans."

"Right."

"And they're different from the jeans you normally wear."

"Yes."

"How are they different?"

"Because they look okay—I mean, pretty good. I guess."

She starts to sit up straight again, gaining strength. "And why don't the jeans you normally wear look good?"

Okay, so much for *any* sort of compliment. I sigh.

"Because my dad buys them."

Her eyes start to shine again. "And *why* does your dad buy them?"

Oh. Right. And here we are. Her right hand, holding her pen, hovers hopefully over her notepad.

But I don't feel like dealing with anything that will bring her a check mark, not today. I'm actually feeling a little okay with myself, so why ruin it? I mean, looking decent in jeans, that's a pretty huge thing for someone like me. So I just say, "Because that's what he's supposed to do?"

She deflates. I mean, literally. Her breath leaks out and she begins to slump, like a helium balloon three days after a party. Her hand falls to her side, the pen dangling between her index and middle fingers. Her eyes are closed and she has this tight little smile on her face—not really a smile, I guess, just these tensed-up face muscles that make it look like she's living through some kind of pain, perhaps even torture.

It's time to throw her a bone. A little one. A Milk-Bone,

maybe, not like one of those meaty, gristly bones from the butcher shop. "My mom?" I say/ask.

Her eyes snap open. Wide open.

"Fashion was never really her thing either. It kind of runs in the family." Like other things, I think, but don't say—like, oh, *insanity*. Or like a total inability to lead a normal, acceptable life—you know, that sort of thing. And then I give her this smile that's supposed to tell her I'm kind of sad, and she starts to nod and give me this little sad smile back. And just before the timer dings, setting me free, her hand creeps up to make another check mark in my file.

Right before I go, she yells out one word: "Fetching!"

I guess my confusion shows on my face, because she says, "Sorry—that's the word I was looking for. You look very *fetching*."

"Uh, fetching is what dogs do," I remind her.

She is smiling. "No, no. That's not what I meant. It means something else in the human world. It's a good thing—it means attractive."

Attractive. Which is like acceptable, but even better. In fact, it's sort of like the opposite of misfit.

I smile back. As ridiculous as her human-world compliment sounds, it almost makes her interrogation worth it.

19.

Gentle Leader

ON THURSDAY at lunch we compare notes. I've been talking about the bus incident for the last two days, and now Mandy and Delia are reliving something that happened in the hall yesterday, between lunch and fourth period.

Delia is giddy. "He didn't even know what to think," she says, referring to their encounter with frequent Mandy-taunter Garrett "Glass Eye" Pearson, who, when he sees Mandy approaching, sometimes shouts, "Outbreak!" and asks everyone around him if they've been vaccinated against bubonic plague.

But yesterday, just as a twinkle of excitement was forming in his good eye, Delia and Mandy planned and carried out their distraction. It involved Delia "going long" and Mandy launching a pudding cup, sailing it just inches in front of Garrett's nose— which caused him to duck and cover, and most importantly, scream like a nine-year-old girl.

"He was *so* embarrassed," Mandy laughs. "He had no *clue* what happened."

"Well, that's nothing like my technique," Joey gloats. We

all roll our eyes, but start laughing all over again. Corbin, whose favorite name for Joey is simply "Nancy," had bumped into Joey at the trash can during lunch, and opened his mouth to rail into him. But while Corbin was busy cueing—his eyes narrowing to slits, his nostrils starting to flutter—Joey, very clearly and very calmly, said something else very simple: "Balls." That was it.

Corbin's mouth had trembled; he grasped for something to say. But by that time, Joey had perfected his smile and walked away, slowly and straightly and just *oozing* confidence. It was practically beautiful.

Phoebe's nibbling on a date bar, looking happily lost in thought.

"What about you, Phoebe? Anything to report?" I ask.

"Well, there's Brant, of course," she says, shrugging shyly.

"Oh, God, Martin. Let's please not hear about Brant," Joey groans.

Phoebe puts down her date bar and glares at him.

"Well, Pheeb, you know," I say. "The thing with Brant, well, it happened way too early to be a result of the training—"

"And we're still wondering why," Joey interrupts.

"He *likes* me!" Phoebe yells at Joey.

"Don't get your panties in a wad," Mandy says. "Just stop focusing so much on Brant and start working on the other people, who aren't so . . ." She pauses and adds, even though it clearly pains her, "Nice."

Phoebe's face softens. She sighs and goes back to her nibbling.

Just then, Delia's head goes low and her eyes widen. "Isn't that the new kid? What do you think he's *doing*?" she asks, her suspicious herder gene on red alert.

I follow her gaze. And there he is—Caleb, a.k.a. Young Uncle

Jesse. He's going from table to table. He's talking to people and actually shaking hands. Doesn't he realize this is *middle school*? He stops at Peyton Randall's table, sweeping a hand through his dark hair, nodding, talking. Peyton grins. One of the other girls scoots over like she's offering him a place to sit. But thankfully, he just sticks out his hand again, and the girl shakes it, and he moves on to the next table.

Delia pokes me. "So what do you think he's up to?" And that's when I realize I haven't taken a breath in the last three minutes.

"Well, he's definitely introducing himself," I say. "But why? I'm not sure."

"Maybe that's what people do wherever he comes from," Phoebe suggests.

"And where's that? *Uranus?*" Joey adds, but it doesn't matter, because just then Mandy whispers, "*Shhh*. He's coming!"

He approaches our table with not so much a smile but a look of contentment. "Hi there, sorry to interrupt, I just wanted to—" He cocks his head to the side, looking directly at me. "I know you, don't I?"

I look down at the table and find a nice grape-juice stain to study, just as Phoebe says, very quickly, "It's not true, whatever you heard."

My jaw clenches, but I keep my gaze on the stain. I am starting to think I should maybe look for the face of Jesus or his mother or something else that proves that miracles just might exist, but all I see is an ordinary splat. I finally take a quick breath and look up. "We met in the hallway the other day."

"Oh. right." And then he *doesn't* laugh, which not only makes him polite but so very thoughtful. "It's Olivia, isn't it?"

My name. He remembers my name! My eyes jump up from

114

the juice stain and practically leap into his. And then. He smiles. My heart is doing so many ridiculous little dances in my chest that I feel like it could short-circuit.

While I'm busy accepting the fact that I am probably having a heart attack, and actually happy enough at this very moment to be okay with that, he introduces himself to the rest of my friends. "Well, for those of you who I haven't already met, I'm Caleb Austin." He pauses, so Phoebe jumps in and starts rattling off everyone's names.

"Where are you from, anyway?" Joey asks—or actually, accuses.

"Saudi Arabia," he tells us.

Joey gives us a very smug smile, like, *What did I tell you?*

"Then why don't you have some kind of accent?" It's Delia and her wary herder gene again.

So he tells us about his dad being some kind of diplomat, and how they were in Saudi Arabia for two years, and how he went to American schools, and how before that, they lived in California. By the time he gets to that, Delia's paranoia has disappeared, and she, too, is practically scooting over to make him room and offering him some of her (unsweetened green) tea, courtesy of her granola mother. That is, until he tells us *why* he's introducing himself—which we've forgotten even mattered.

"Well, it's been really nice to meet you all," he says. "And I hope you'll think of me on October seventeenth."

And this is how off track we've gotten. How utterly, completely, ridiculously off track. Mandy picks at her eyebrow scab between sips of her smoothie. Phoebe is barely there, her gaze focused across the cafeteria on Brant. Joey is making strange shapes with cheese that he's stolen from the distracted Phoebe.

And Delia's guard is down by her ankles, which is proven when she asks, through a mouth full of sunflower seeds, "Oh, why? Is it your birthday?"

"Oh, no." He laughs. "It's election day." And as my dumb little overactive heart slams into a rib, he adds, "And I'm running for president."

In Dog We Trust

IT'S FRIDAY after school. I step onto the bus and make my way to the back, passing by Brynne and her sidekick Carolyn, who barely glance up at me. Brynne sits slumped in the seat, her knees raised to rest against the seat in front of her, where Danny sits. Tamberlin is nearby—though she chews her gum with a wide and open mouth, she is silent. I brush by their clump, surprised and relieved by their unusual quiet.

I sit down in a seat by myself and pull out *A Wrinkle in Time*. I'm only halfway down the page when I hear my name being called. I look up. The entire population of the bus looks back at me.

"Does your grandmother drive a pickup truck?" Tamberlin asks.

I have that sinking feeling again in my stomach. I'm sure they're setting me up for some sort of joke, like they used to do with the granny panties. Just when I thought we were really getting somewhere! I push my gaze back into my book. It's too late for a distraction, so I will *try* to read. I will *try* to ignore it.

"Olivia!" I hear my name again. It's Carolyn this time, and she sounds exasperated. "Isn't that your grandma?"

A horn sounds. I look out the window. It *is* my grandmother. She's pulled the pickup truck up next to the bus, and is waving wildly. Although I'm majorly embarrassed, I'm even more relieved. For once I'm not the butt of some sort of joke. "Thanks," I say to Carolyn as I squeeze past her.

She gives me a puzzled look back. "Okay. Whatever," I hear her say just before I step off the bus.

"What are you doing here?" I ask Corny as I climb into the passenger's side. But as soon as I sniff the meaty, yeasty smell of homemade dog biscuits, I know. "We're going to see Kisses?"

She nods. "You're doing such a good job with her."

I sigh. I'm tired and hungry, and I'd rather be home watching *Full House*. But I manage to give her a smile.

She smiles back. "She's one of the toughest cases we've had, and I think you deserve this." She hands me a root beer Slurpee. It's sweet and cool, and even though I know it's just mostly sugar and ice, it makes her words feel almost true.

So. Yeah.

Turns out I'm supposed to use the bone-shaped dog biscuits to "reward" Kisses the same way Corny used the Slurpee to "reward" me. Not that she's put it that way, but it's pretty obvious. Nice.

"It's not like I'm a dog, Grandma," I remind her.

"I know. But I don't care—I love you anyway."

This time, not only does Kisses *not* attack the car, but she seems almost happy to see me and my good posture. She wags her little stalk of a tail, and I start to notice how cute she actually is when she's not acting like an assassin.

We go back around to the patio, and Corny sets out the sod again—this time four pieces together to make a larger square. I walk Kisses in circles around the little lawn squares for several minutes, and then I start to walk her right up to them. When her head lowers, I tug gently up on the leash. She raises her head and takes another two steps forward before stopping just in front of the sod.

"Sit," I say, and she does. I'm tempted to give her a piece of the biscuit, but Corny tells me not yet. So I just say "Good girl" and take a step backward. I'm standing on the sod.

We do it again. She takes a step forward, and then hesitates. And then another. Her front paw is standing on top of a grass square. "Good girl!" I practically squeal. Corny gives me permission to give her a small piece of the biscuit. But I have to place it in the center of the sod, surrounded by the grass blades.

You can tell she's torn. She wants to pull back and go forward at the same time. Her teeny neck stretches ahead, she takes a couple of steps and sniffs the biscuit. Then, lightning-bolt fast, she dips her head into the grass to grab the treat, and runs away from the sod as far as her leash will allow.

Corny clasps her hands together and smiles. Mr. Dewey brings his palms together like a prayer. And then Kisses comes back toward me. "Another step farther," Corny coaches me. I plant a piece of biscuit in the far end of the grass. Kisses slowly steps onto the sod, her little twig legs shaking as she advances. She dips into the grass, grabs the biscuit, and tries to run away again. This time I hang on to her leash so she has to chew while standing on the sod.

Now I've got to get her to sit down. I give her the sit command and she moves around on the sod in a semi-squatting motion, her rear end grazing the grass and then popping back up again. I tug upward on her leash and push gently down on her back, and then finally, believe it or not, she officially sits down on the sod. I feel the thrilling rush of success as I give her the full biscuit. She lowers onto her belly, holding the bone-shaped treat up between her two front paws to better gnaw on it. We all cheer.

I'm finding this reward thing pretty rewarding all by itself.

When I get home, I have a letter from my dad. It's a card with a black-and-white picture of a sleeping cat on it. It looks just like a skinnier version of Grey, my old cat. My dad kind of spoils her. Sometimes I think my mom replaced me with her new life, and my dad replaced me with Grey. I give him a little more slack—he was both father and mother to me for a while, so he's got to do something with those parental instincts now that I've moved away.

I open the card and a check falls out. It's forty dollars I wasn't expecting, which should make me pretty happy since it means another pair of delightfully normal jeans, or maybe a decent shirt. But his note leaves me feeling a little sad.

> Liv—
> We might as well enjoy the unfortunate success!
> Miss you and love you—
> oxoxoxox Dad oxoxoxox

I guess this shows how powerful a reward can be. In this case, money. It's the whole reason my dad is staying in Valleyhead, where he has no life outside of work.

It's just another example of how people aren't that different from dogs at all.

Kibble

IT'S MONDAY AFTERNOON. Phoebe and Joey have wasted the first five minutes of Bored Game Club arguing over whether to play Yahtzee or Boggle, when Delia walks into the room, practically glowing.

"Oh, good," Mandy says. "Now we outnumber them. Who's up for Upwords?" She raises her own hand and looks expectantly at Delia and me.

"Yeah, sure, that's fine," Delia says, still smiling.

"You hate Upwords," Joey says, eyeing her suspiciously.

"Yeah, and why are you smiling like that, anyway?" Phoebe adds.

"Okay, I know this shouldn't be a big deal," Delia says, as she sits down between Mandy and me. "But just now, Carolyn came up and started talking to me about the math test. And I was totally ready with my distraction—"

"Which was?" I ask. Delia's "distractions" have been, to be honest, pretty bizarre. Her most famous one at this point was when Tamberlin came up to her in the hall, totally cueing with the beady-eyed fake smile that we've come to expect. So Delia asked her how many teeth humans are supposed to have. And Tamberlin actually stood there, stuck her fingers into her mouth, and counted them.

"Oh. I was going to ask her for a pad. With wings."

"Ew," Phoebe says.

"Gross," Joey says. *"Wings,"* he repeats under his breath.

I look at Delia. "Really?"

"I thought it would definitely get her off the subject of my face, and who knows? Maybe she'd even feel a little sisterly bond."

"Wait. What are wings?" Joey asks, more quietly than usual, but no one seems to be paying much attention to him. We're all caught up in Delia's moment.

"That's so *brave,*" Mandy says.

"Thanks. But the good news is I didn't even have to ask her. She actually just wanted to talk about the math test—she was worried she got half the answers wrong! Not one single mention of my zits. I mean, she didn't even look at me strange!" She smiles. "It seems like it's working."

I feel myself grinning along with Delia.

"I know, Dee, it's awesome," Mandy says.

"Sounds promising," Phoebe adds.

"Your *mom* has wings." That's all Joey.

"You know what?" Usually I like to let the room air out a little after his comments, but today I jump right in. I can't help myself. I'm excited. "I think we're ready for the next step. Rewarding good behavior."

"Yeah, but," Mandy says, "at this point I'm lucky if Glass Eye just ignores me when I see him in the hall, or if Corbin walks by with just a weird stare. It's not like either one of them is like,

122

asking to carry my backpack, or like, helping me to get to class when I lose a clog or something."

I swallow. I always hoped the fact that we were considered dorks was really just a case of bad packaging. Now I'm starting to wonder if this dorkiness thing we've got going on really *is* more than skin-deep. Am I the only one making an effort here? "That was *yours*?" I ask.

"Well, technically it was my mom's, who, by the way, almost killed me when I came home without it." She eyes me. "Don't you remember me having to wear my ugly gym shoes that day?"

Well, no, I didn't, because one, I was too busy not thinking about Young Uncle Jesse, and two, Mandy wears her ugly gym shoes four out of five days of the week. But a clog—that's just bad judgment. I make a mental note to talk to her about this later.

"Okay, well, here's the thing," I say. "Garrett or Corbin just walking by without saying something mean is good behavior."

"I'm not really understanding how this will work, Olivia," Phoebe says.

"Once you start to see good behavior—and this could be your tormentor just treating you like any other person, or it could be something more—then you can reward it. Candy, gum, all that stuff works," I say. "For example, next time Carolyn wants to talk to you, Delia, about anything other than your complexion, you give her a piece of gum."

"Isn't that going to seem weird?" Delia asks quietly.

"Seriously, guys, who *doesn't* want gum? Or candy?" I ask. "I mean, has anyone ever stopped and asked why you're offering them a piece of gum? No! They just grab it and stick it in their mouth like it's going to explode if they don't."

"I guess you're right," Delia says.

"But gum? Candy?" Phoebe, whose diet-obsessed mother doesn't allow any sort of refined sugar in the house, acts inconvenienced. "What am I supposed to give for a reward? Molasses chews?"

"That's so Amish," Joey tells her.

"See?" Phoebe turns to me, actually agreeing with Joey.

"It doesn't have to be something you eat. Just bring in something tomorrow, Pheeb. I'm sure you have *something* people would be happy to get," I say, although I'm secretly wondering what that might be.

Treats for Good Dogs

THE NEXT MORNING I raid Corny's purse and find a nearly full pack of spearmint Freedent. It may not be Bubble Yum, but it's about all you have on hand when you live with a sixty-year-old.

When I get to school, Phoebe's waiting for me at my locker, looking impatient but excited.

"You found something, Pheeb?" I ask.

She nods. "It's not a traditional reward, but I think it might work. Instead of handing out sugar for positive behavior, I'm going to hand out office supplies." She says this like she's proud, so even though it sounds a little ridiculous, I hold back my laugh.

"Like *what*?"

She looks at me like *I'm* the weirdo.

"Like refillable lead pencils. Tiny staplers. That sort of thing. Stuff from my mom's shop." As funny as it sounds, I know she's got a point. Those lead pencils are probably more popular than candy. Now my Freedent really seems stupid.

I try to stuff it into my pocket and turn away. But she sees it and coos. "Oooh, Freedent! Perfect for orthodontia! Can I have a piece?"

"Sure. Only a couple more weeks, right?" I ask. Phoebe's finally getting her braces removed.

"Right. Just in time for the dance." But before it gets awkward, she asks, "Want a pencil?"

"Oh, God, yes," I say, very quickly. I laugh, and she gives me one of her strained little smiles that shows that somewhere, maybe buried under the layers of her very big brain, she does have some hint of a sense of humor.

"You think—" she starts, then stops.

"What?"

"Nothing," she says, and shakes her head.

"Phoebe, *what*?"

She looks at me, blushing. "You think—I mean, since my braces will be off, you think Brant might try to, you know"—her eyebrows raise—"kiss me?"

"*Uhhhh,*" is all I can say.

Then there's a little squeak of a sound coming from her. It stops just as soon as it starts. She's red, but her eyes are wide with excitement. And then she says, "J.K."

But my mouth still hangs open.

"J.K.," she says again. "Just. *Kidding?*"

Okay, so it's a totally wack sense of humor, but yes, it does exist. It might just need a little tweaking. But then, really, what doesn't?

"So," Delia asks at lunch, "anyone have anything interesting to report?" She's gloating over the cranberry-applesauce oatmeal-butter cookies that her mother made and she's brought in for rewards. Carolyn called them "The Best Cookies On The Face Of The Planet," and now everyone seems to want one.

"I'm working on it," I say, and sigh.

Mandy sniffs the air with a slightly puzzled look on her face. "You smell like my great-grandfather. Is that Dentyne?"

"No," Phoebe says, shaming me with her look. "That's Freedent. And she's *supposed* to be saving it for her rewards."

"It's not what you think," I tell them. The truth is that I've been jamming the gum into my mouth between every single class since I ran into Caleb on my way to first period. Yes, I like, literally *ran* into him. I was walking and reading, trying to review my periodic table, and the crown of my head slammed right into his very firm chest. He said, "Ouch?" like it was a question. I stepped away and knew I should have been feeling pain, but all I felt was a lingering warmth in my scalp. I think I apologized, but he just gave me that adorably lazy smile and said, "Be careful with that head of yours. It's practically a weapon." And even though he's new at school, everyone within earshot laughed good-naturedly because he's the kind of person that doesn't have to train people to like him—they just naturally do. So the gum, well, it's just in case this happens again. The last thing I want to be accused of is having fart-breath like Danny Pritchard.

"Well, I'm sure it'll get better," Phoebe says. Then she empties her stash onto the lunch table; there are only three pencils left and a foldable ruler.

"Cool," Mandy says. "So who got the goods?"

"Let's see. Peyton Randall, for one. I had some toilet paper stuck on my shoe, and she offered to step on it so it would come off. Earned herself some number seven lead refills." She takes a bite of her tuna sandwich. "Who else? Oh! I gave a packet of colored paper clips to Morgan Askren because she said hi to me."

Morgan Askren is practically untouchable. She's popular even though she doesn't go to parties or talk to anyone in school. It's like she floats above it somewhere. She's supposed to be related to Angelina Jolie. I don't know if it's true or not, but the rumor alone has made her a legend.

"Oh, and Brant, of course," Phoebe adds. "I dropped my math book in the hall and he came over and picked it up. He's just so nice."

Joey says, "Get a clue, Martin."

"Stop it, Joey. He was really sweet. I gave him a mini-stapler."

"Your *mom* gave him a mini-stapler."

Phoebe looks at Joey like she's ready to throttle him. He's being annoying enough right now that I'm not so sure we wouldn't pin him down for her if asked. "For your information," she says through tight lips, "he smiled. Like he meant it."

"He was just smiling at how stupid you are," Joey mumbles.

Delia jumps in. "Joey, just let her—" She sucks in her breath; it's obvious that her words aren't about to comfort Phoebe. "I mean, we all know—" she tries again. Finally, she says, "Just shut up, Joey."

Phoebe looks at us all and gets up, throwing the rest of her lunch into the gaping trash can with a strong jerk of her arm. Delia runs after her.

"Wow, Joey," I say. "That was brutal. What is up with you?"

"Well, we all know what's going on. How can you guys just

keep humoring her? She's gonna get wrecked when it finally sinks in!" He's practically yelling at us.

"I know, I know," I say, hoping to quiet him. It's strange to see Joey all worked up like this, especially about Phoebe's *feelings*. Weird. "We just have to be nice about it, okay? She seriously likes him."

He puts his head down on the stretch of table in front of him and thumps his forehead against it three times.

"Yeah, just calm down, Joey. You're being a major smear," Mandy tells him. He doesn't raise his head.

No one says anything for a minute. Mandy pulls the pepperoni off my slice of pizza and eats it. I roll up the rest and eat it like a burrito.

"Now I need something sweet," Mandy says, after she's through with her scavenged lunch. "Joey, you got any Ho Hos left?"

This morning, Joey brought in a big box of them to use as rewards.

"No," he says from his face-plant.

"Well, why not?" I ask.

He doesn't answer. Mandy looks at me knowingly.

"Did you eat them all, Joey?" she asks.

He doesn't answer. He doesn't even lift up his head, not even a little.

"I hope they were worth it," I say, trying not to get too mad. Joey's such a *liability* sometimes.

"I'm sugar-crashing now," Joey finally says, his nose still pressing into the table.

"God, Joey," Mandy says, and shakes her head. "From now on, nothing edible for you. You've got to bring in something that you can't stuff into your mouth."

He raises his head, finally. "Like what?" He appears to be completely stumped.

"What do you have a lot of?" I ask.

"Uh, Yu-Gi-Oh! cards?"

Mandy shakes her head. "Look, alpha dogs don't play Yu-Gi-Oh!, okay? Let's just get that straight. What else you got?"

He shrugs.

"What about office supplies? Can you buy some of those?"

He cocks his head as if it's the stupidest thing he's ever heard. "*A*, I haven't gotten allowance in two years, and *B*, Phoebe already cornered that market."

Mandy looks at me. "We need something free. What costs nothing?"

"*Nothing* costs nothing," I say.

Joey puts on a sickeningly sweet face, full of sarcasm. "A smile is free," he says, reciting the line from yet another "inspirational" poster tacked up by the soda machine. We all gag out loud. And then I get an idea.

"Compliments!"

Mandy stares at me dully. Joey says, "What about them?"

"They're free!"

"So's your advice! No offense, but sometimes you're such a tool," he tells me, his face contorted with disgust and disbelief. "You've got to be kidding."

"Seriously, Liv," Mandy says. "You think a person like Brynne is going to care at all if she gets a compliment from someone like Joey?"

"Hey!" Joey says.

"I see your point and all, Mandy, and I don't think anyone would admit it," I say. "But think about it—at first they might be like, 'Who's that stupid kid and why should I care if he thinks I'm pretty?' But then they'll go home and look in the mirror and think, well, if it doesn't get any better at least I'll have Joey Spagnoli."

She glances over at Joey, who looks like he's injured, and pats his arm like it helps somehow.

"Well, it's got to be true," I say. "If it wasn't, would there be all this self-esteem stuff splattered all over the walls?" I gesture toward a poster of a warthog. Above the warthog are the words I'M FINE . . . in a large bold font. Across the animal's feet, in dreamy italics, are the words JUST THE WAY I AM.

"I guess you're right," Mandy says, and turns to Joey. "It could work."

"I don't do compliments," he says, his voice a monotone. "They're just stupid."

"Only sometimes," Mandy says.

"*All* the time," he argues.

We both look at him. If only he was willing.

"What?" he says, raising his palms up. "It's just that they're so embarrassing."

"Joey, do you want to be a Marcie all your life?" Mandy asks.

"I'm not a . . ." he mumbles, trailing off. Giving up.

The three of us are quiet. Joey shuffles a little in his seat and avoids looking at either one of us. He takes a deep breath. "Okay, okay, whatever. Will you guys just, I don't know, give me a list or something?"

Mandy and I smile at each other.

"All right, Joey," I say. "We'll give you a few starters. Then you're on your own, okay?"

He shuffles his feet under the table and gives us an I-surrender-but-this-is-ridiculous face.

"Look, they're coming back," he says. We turn around and see Delia and Phoebe heading back to our table. Delia's arm is wrapped over Phoebe's shoulder.

"Quick," I say to Joey, "you've got to give Phoebe a compliment!"

"But why? She hasn't done anything to earn a reward!"

"Just for the practice," I tell him.

Mandy slaps her hands on the table excitedly. "Tell her she's hot. *Smokin'* hot."

He looks at us like he'd rather eat a plateful of raw broccoli, which, for Joey, is worse than eating, say, live parasitic worms.

"Okay, *fine*," Mandy says, as she and I laugh. "Then just tell her you like her hair like that."

"Like *what*?!"

"Just say it," Mandy tells him, practically gritting her teeth.

"You all right, Pheeb?" Mandy asks, as Phoebe and Delia sit back down at the table.

"Fine," she says, though she doesn't seem it.

"What did you do to your hair?" Joey asks.

"What? What's wrong with it?" Her hands fly to her head and shake out her hair as if trying to forcibly remove a trapped spider.

"Nothing. It looks—fine," he says. I tap my knee against his under the table. "I mean, nice. Kind of good, actually." He is red, as if in pain from the stress of giving the compliment.

She eyes him distrustfully.

Joey sighs. "I like your hair, Martin." And then he looks down and away, fidgeting with his hands. It's a little uncomfortable to watch. I have to look away for a second, too.

Phoebe is trying to grasp what's just happened. "My hair?" she's saying, touching it, this time lightly, and looking bewildered. "Really?" She stops and gives us a questioning look. "Thanks, I guess, Joey."

And then I see that, despite being the color of a stop sign, Joey is smiling. Just a little bit.

And then Phoebe does, kind of, too.

Scents and Sensibilities

ON WEDNESDAY, I run into Mandy between first and second period. She's so excited she is practically violating the Emo Code of Ethics. If you get past the scabbed-over eyebrow piercing and black lips, her face looks like a kid in a Disney World commercial. Her eyes are like little green Christmas lights, and she is smiling. Beaming, actually. And bouncing toward me.

"What's going on?" I ask. I try to smile, but she's acting so different from her normal self that I'm sure I just look constipated or something.

It doesn't seem to bother her. "It works!" she says, nearly glowing.

"What happened?"

"Okay, so I was in the bathroom putting on my lips, and I hear this flush, and Tamberlin Ziff comes out of the stall. I thought for sure she was going to start with that 'Bubo' thing, you know like she used to? Like *bubonic*?" Her head is bobbing with excitement and she is talking very fast. "So I go, 'Cool necklace,' you know. To distract her. And she was like, 'Thanks.' And then she was like, 'Is that really a Sharpie?'" Mandy's eyes are wide. Practically innocent.

I smile. But there's a little part of me that holds back—the part that's full of doubt and stuff. "Okay?"

"She said she'd never really thought of using a marker."

I'm still smiling, but I say, "Most people"—I fight the urge to add *outside of the asylum*—"don't." I remind myself that I still haven't talked to her about the clog.

"I know it's not exactly normal," she says, "but, personally, and I told her this, I like the fact that it stays on and doesn't feel greasy. She said she was going to try it, but that her mom would probably make her use the nontoxic washable kind. And that she'd probably go red. And so I gave her a treat!"

When I don't say anything, she says, "You know, a reward. Like we talked about? *Hello?* What's wrong?"

I sigh. "Are you sure it's not just something for one of their Spiritleader Dress-Up Days? Like a Wacky-Tacky theme or something?"

"What?" Mandy looks injured. "No! I don't—I don't think so. You know, I'm not like Phoebe, Olivia. I can usually tell when someone's trying to make fun of me."

Which is why I'm surprised right now. I just say, "I know. I guess it's just kind of hard to imagine that Tamberlin's going to start putting marker on her lips because some Marcie—in *her* eyes, I mean—gave her a piece of gum in the bathroom."

"Life Saver," she corrects me, her mood crumbling a little. "Pep-O-Mint. Olivia, she listened to me. It worked," she says again, and walks away.

135

I feel like a real dolt when I see Tamberlin at lunch later. Not only does she have bright red lips—quite possibly a primary-colored Crayola washable marker "borrowed" from the arts alcove—but when she sees me, our eyes meet, and then she just looks away. Like we were just two normal strangers who, for just a second, were accidentally caught in each other's eye-lock. That would never have happened a week ago.

Mandy was right.

Then I think about what Mandy said when she saw me in my new clothes, how she told me she wasn't going "mainstream." Well, maybe she won't have to. Maybe she is changing the definition of cool. Could we all be wearing clogs by the time this year is over?

And it gets weirder.

Because I'm almost to my fourth period classroom when I hear *"ICICLE STORM!"* And then the Spiritleaders are whirling through the scampering crowd, coming right smack toward me. They are jumping, twisting, kicking, and flailing, in their interpretation of a natural disaster of which I, being immobile with terror, am about to become the first victim.

But just then I become aware of a hand on my upper arm pulling me through a doorway. And then I am standing in front of a urinal, facing cute Jell-O fan and English classmate Max Marshall, who is trying to catch his breath. "You okay?" he asks, panting.

"I think so," I say. "Are you?"

He nods. "Sorry about pulling you in here—it was the safest place."

"No, that's okay," I tell him. I mean, I'm safe. I'm alive. And I'm in forbidden territory—the boy's bathroom. I just always expected something a little more interesting than this. It's disappointing—you can practically map out the social hierarchy of Hubert C. Frost Middle School by reading the girls' bathroom graffiti. But in here, the most fascinating thing is the urinal. There's a puck-looking thing sitting in the bottom of it. "What *is* that?"

"That's a little something they call a urinal cake. *Not* edible, though." He smiles. "Just in case you were tempted. Come on, let's get to English before we get detention."

We walk to our classroom together. Max takes his seat in front of me, and I look at the back of his honey-brown head and wonder if he would've just let me fend for myself two weeks ago, or even just two days ago.

But then he passes a little slip of paper back to me. I open it up. He's drawn me a cartoon—a urinal cake with candles in it. Next to it he's written, "Make a wish!"

It makes me laugh. What's weird is that this whole thing feels like one big fat wish. And what's even weirder is that I feel a glimmer of hope that it could actually come true.

And before I forget, I pass a stick of Freedent up to him.

There's no more barking on the bus these days. In fact, lately, when I get on board, Brynne just turns and looks away. She doesn't even try to insult me anymore, at least not to my face.

But today, as I pass through the aisle by her seat, I hear her quietly mumble, "Granny panties." To which Carolyn just sighs and says, "God, Brynne, move *on* already."

Yes, this wish. It could possibly be coming true.

Underdog Railroad

IT'S FRIDAY after school, and we're setting up for Monopoly. Joey has gone to, quote-unquote, "puke his lungs out" because he complimented Corinne d'Abo on her small nostrils. "It was either that or her bra size, and I panicked and didn't want to get expelled," he'd told us, before suffering an attack of dry heaves. Ms. Greenwood had taken the opportunity to make it perfectly clear that there would be no vomiting permitted in her room.

Phoebe unfolds the board and eyes the game pieces. "I think I deserve the shoe today," she announces. "Especially after what I had to endure."

"Yeah, maybe you do," Joey says, coming back into the room. And then he smirks and adds, "To the back of your pants!"

"Shut up, Joey," she says.

"Your *mom* shuts up!"

The rest of us look at each other and sigh.

"So, Phoebe," I say. "I vote you get the shoe if you tell us what happened."

She looks down at the table. "Okay, so I was standing in

line at the vision screenings, and Brynne and Danny Pritchard were behind me. And Brynne said, 'I'm getting an attack of the Phoebe-Jeebies.'" She gives me a slightly tortured glance. "The *Phoebe-Jeebies*! I thought that was behind us. Especially after all the mini-staplers I've gone through."

My heart drops. "I'm sorry, Pheeb. Maybe it's just a minor setback."

"And don't forget—it's Brynne we're talking about. She's the worst, so she's going to be the hardest," Delia adds.

It's true. I wish there was some special supplemental training just for her.

Mandy adds, "And Danny. Jeez. What a butt-crack he is."

"Actually, Danny wasn't *awful*. In a way, he stuck up for me," Phoebe says.

"Oh, first Brant's in love with you, now *Danny*," Joey says in a mocking tone.

"I didn't say that—not about Danny!" Phoebe says, her pale skin turning pink.

"Pheeb," I say, trying to get her to refocus. "Explain. How did he stick up for you?"

"Well, first he groaned, and then he rolled his eyes. And then"—she looks at me—"he *shushed* her!"

"Big deal," Joey says.

"Actually, Joey, it *is* a big deal," I say. "For him to be shushing her is *huge*."

"Yeah," Mandy adds. "Danny's like her slave boy."

Then an idea hits me. "Okay, listen, you guys," I tell them. "Next time something like that happens—next time one of Brynne's minions stands up to her or says or does something mean to her—you're giving them some sort of reward."

They all sort of stare at me. "I don't get it," Phoebe said. "I thought we were rewarding *good* behavior."

Delia looks uneasy. "Yeah, so now we're supposed to reward mean things?"

"It's more like we reward anti-Brynne behavior. Look, Delia already said that Brynne's the hardest to train. And Mandy—you just called Danny her slave boy, right?"

They both nod slowly.

"So we're just going to help a little with the revolt. Think of yourselves as abolitionists," I say. "Freedom fighters."

Delia looks at me sideways.

"Like Sojourner Truth," I add.

"Sojourner Truth was a hero," Delia says. "I don't know, Liv. That might be a stretch."

"Or like, what was that lady's name? The one who wrote that book about Uncle Somebody's cabin?" Mandy says.

"Harriet Beecher Stowe," Phoebe says. "But as far as abolitionists go, I much prefer Francis Ellen Watkins Harper."

"And I much prefer *your mom*," Joey says. Then his smug face morphs into a blotchy panicked one, and he starts apologizing. *Apologizing!* I mean, this is Joey we're talking about! "Uh, sorry, guys, but—" he stammers. It's awkward—and not the funny kind of awkward, just the squirmy, uncomfortable kind.

Mandy tries to put him out of his misery. "That's okay, Joey. You say stupid things all the time."

"Oh," he says. "I'm not sorry for that. I'm sorry because I'm about to cut one."

Ms. Greenwood yells out in disgust. Mandy quickly jumps up and pulls Joey out of his seat. She pushes him out into the hall and closes the door. A minute later we hear a gaggle of laughs and a guy's voice saying, "Nice one, Spagnoli."

Joey opens the door and comes back in, wide-eyed with excitement. "Holy crap! Corbin Moon just high-fived me," he says. "Man, this plan *rocks!*"

I hear a squeak come out of Phoebe—it's the same squeak I heard the day of the office supplies. But now it's followed by a strange howl-cackle. Phoebe sounds like she's in great pain. It takes a moment for me to realize it's a laugh. She's *actually* laughing. We all look at her, surprised. "What?" she asks, when she realizes we're staring at her. "It was *funny.*"

Joey looks stunned—seriously, I've never seen him look this way. Nothing shocks this kid. Mandy's blackened mouth is hanging open.

Phoebe turns a deeper shade of pink. *"What?"* she asks again.

So, even though part of me wants to bury my head in shame for Joey, I laugh. We all laugh. Loud. Ms. Greenwood yells at us, but we are laughing too hard to hear her. Even Phoebe is laughing. Especially Phoebe.

While we were so busy being amused by Joey's bodily functions, Brynne was busy getting an illegally early start on her campaign, plastering the school with her face. It's only been an hour and seven minutes, but her campaign flyers have been jammed up the vent of every locker, and the halls and stairwells are now lined with "Win With Brynne!" posters, featuring her larger-than-life-size headshot, which looks like it was taken at Glamorland. In the photo, she has this sort of dreamy look. Her hair is wavy like a mermaid's, and the scar on her chin is nonexistent. If I didn't know better, her picture might convince me that she's some sort of superhuman creature, maybe even an angel.

Two things become clear. One, it's time for us to go public with our campaign. And two, anyone who says pictures don't lie is most likely a moron.

25.

A Leg Up

WE'VE SPENT ALL weekend coming up with a slogan and making posters, and on Monday, the public part of our campaign officially begins.

"What the crap is this?" I hear Carolyn Quim say, as she stands facing one of our campaign posters. I walk carefully behind her, undetected.

We've ended up using an idea of Delia's—"Have Some Candy, Vote for Mandy"—for two reasons. One, it really drove home the reward concept, and two, Joey made good on a claim that he had access to an "event-sized" bag of Jolly Ranchers, which, we all agreed, were colorful, indestructible, and tastewise put most other hard candies to shame.

"I don't know," Tamberlin says, not sounding too concerned. She grabs a green-apple-flavored piece off the poster, unwraps it, and sticks it into her mouth.

I continue down the hall to science. Before I go into the room, I turn and look back. The two of them are still standing there, looking utterly confused.

And then someone says, "Oh, yum. Is that one water-melon?"

We're at lunch and Phoebe is telling us about her first act of abolitionism.

"I gave away my last Neo-Gel pen today, but it was worth it. Carolyn Quim rolled her eyes when Brynne called me an Albanian!"

"I think she meant albino," Mandy says.

Phoebe gives her this confused look and asks, "Why would she call me an albino?"

Mandy shrugs, smirking.

Delia smiles. "Well, guess what happened to Olivia and me? We were walking down the hall and Brynne handed Corbin Moon a stack of flyers, and he was like, 'Oh my God. You know what I just realized? Your initials are B.S.!' And then he started laughing so I slipped him one of my mom's cookies." She looks over at me. "Crazy, isn't it?"

But I can't answer. I've overstuffed my mouth with Chikkin M'Eaties and am now having to chew three times my normal speed, as Caleb Austin approaches our lunch table, flanked by preppy-boy Carson Winger and Sudoku Club president Ryan Stoles. I'm also banging the table with an open palm to get every-one to shut up about the plan. But they stare at me like I'm weird until I can finally swallow and tell them, "Caleb Austin is coming."

They look up just in time. Caleb reaches out his hand for Mandy's, which she extends slowly and suspiciously. I wish he'd hold out his hand to *me*. "Congratulations," he says to her. "I see you've started your campaign."

"Uh, yeah. Thanks."

"Always glad to have another candidate on the books."

Mandy laughs a little and says, "Really?"

"Sure. This is a democracy, isn't it?" Then he looks at me and shoots me one of his award-winning, heart-melting smiles, and I totally soak it in. When he rips his gaze away, it almost smarts.

"Do you all know Carson and Ryan?" he asks.

We nod. Phoebe hums an acknowledgment that sounds kind of like a low growl. Phoebe's never really gotten over the Sudoku Club Incident from last year—where they stole our Bored Game Club membership drive idea and doubled their roster.

"Well, they're going to be helping me out on my campaign," Caleb continues.

"I'm campaign manager," Ryan says.

"Hang on, dude," Carson argues. "I've done this before—"

"Yeah, in fourth *grade*," Joey whispers, as Caleb calmly quiets his campaign staff. "And he *lost*."

"Well, we just wanted to stop by and wish you and your staff good luck," says Caleb, turning back to us.

"You too," Mandy says. As he walks away and I try not to look at him too longingly, Mandy winces. "That was so totally awkward," she says.

"Why? He's not *that* hot," I say. Okay, I lie.

"Good *lord*, Olivia," Mandy says, her nostrils flaring. "I didn't say he was *hot*. I just mean that was awkward. He's only been here a couple of weeks and already people are fighting over him."

"Yeah, I know," I say, and shrug. I try to look casual.

145

"Anyway, I think he's totally weird-looking."

"I think I know what's going on and I'm getting really grossed out," Joey says. "Olivia's in love or something."

"I am *not*!" I yell. "He looks like a—" I realize I have no idea what to say, because the words that are coming to mind are things like *Spanish prince*, or *incredibly successful underwear model*. "Chocolate Lab," I finally manage. I mean, his hair is brown and thick and smooth. His eyes are that deep, thoughtful brown. And he kind of has that Labrador personality—easygoing and attentive, and he might even save your life.

They all give me these grins that I don't like, but luckily Phoebe starts coughing from swallowing her chocolate milk down the wrong pipe, and everyone gets too involved in walloping her on the back to continue that conversation.

"Is she okay?"

The ridiculous walloping stops, and we all glance up. Max Marshall is standing there, looking both amused and concerned.

"She's fine," I say, embarrassed.

But he smiles at me and makes it better. "Okay, just making sure."

And then, over Mandy's shoulder, I see Brynne, who's been watching Max and me from her table. She's decked out, like all the Spiritleaders, in bright orange sweats (Spirit Dress-Up Day. Theme: Jailbreak). She has a broccoli floret up to her mouth but hasn't taken a bite. When she catches me looking, her eyes flit to the side as if to pretend she hadn't been watching at all. Averting her eyes. A sign of submission? *Good girl*, I find myself thinking.

146

On the way to the buses, Delia and I stop by her locker to get her science textbook for homework. She's telling me that she passed Joey in the hall on the way to sixth period and, for the first time, she didn't hear him before she saw him. And Erin Monroe was walking next to him, appearing to be actually listening to whatever nonsense was coming out of his mouth.

"No way," I say.

"It's true. It was like it was an after-school special, and someone else—a normal person—was acting the role of Joey," she tells me.

Then Phoebe strolls by and waves to us. "See you tomorrow," she calls from the crowd passing through the hallway.

We hear a voice call to her. "Hey, Phoebe. Wait up!"

It's Brant Farad pushing through the crowd to catch up to her. And then they get to the exit. He does the nice-man thing where he lets her through first and then follows, like they're on a date or something. Sort of like a grown-up, human version of the command *heel*.

I actually get goose bumps.

26.

Destructive Behaviors

BESIDES BEING FORCED to undress in public, there's another form of twisted abuse going on in the Hubert C. Frost Middle School gym, and it's called Sleeterball. Sleeterball was created by Colonel Sleeter, who taught P.E. at the school for like a million years and, lucky for me, retired the year before I got here. When dodgeball was outlawed in the county in 1998, Colonel Sleeter dreamed up this supposedly more humane version, so it's basically the same game with a somewhat lighter ball, fewer ball-launchers, more inner-circle victims, and specific (but completely ignored) rules about hitting only between the shoulders and belt.

When you "play" Sleeterball, it becomes pretty clear that the school board overlooked the fact that Colonel Sleeter had extensive military expertise in "ballistics and trajectory weapons," which really means missiles and bombs.

So it's Tuesday, and I am in the middle of the Sleeterball circle, scared out of my wits. There are five of us left inside, and only one of them has a larger body mass index than me. His name is Charles Wooten, and he moves faster than you'd think—certainly too fast to hide behind. And yes, I've tried.

One of the other potential casualties is none other than Brynne Shawnson.

Amber Menendez, who seems to be looking for extra credit, shoots the ball across the circle at us, and we all scamper successfully and breathe a collective sigh of relief.

But it gets worse, of course. Tamberlin catches the ball. She narrows her eyes and looks at me. I hop around, having abandoned any sense of dignity for the more important goal of survival. I run to the back of the huddle, which opens up and exposes me. We are all running around like roaches under the nozzle of a can of Raid. It is every roach for himself.

Finally, having nothing to protect me from Tamberlin's angry glare, I crouch and cover my face. I bring my arms close in to my body. I don't have much, chestwise, but what I do have, I would like to protect. My body squeezes up and prepares for the pain. And then I hear the slap of rubber meeting flesh. And then a wail.

I look up. Brynne Shawnson is doubled over, rubbing the red welt on her thigh. Her face is crunched up like she's about to cry. "You're out," Tamberlin says, and cracks her illegal gum.

Brynne stumbles toward the bleachers, and I blink and look at Tamberlin. She gazes back at me vacantly. I look for her eyebrows to lower, her lip to curl at me in disgust, for some sign that she still hates me. And then—

Thwack.

The ball has hit me in the back of my knee—Amber's doing—and my legs buckle. The sting of the rubber is almost unbearable.

149

"Whoops, sorry, Olivia," Amber says, and appears to mean it.

"Why weren't you looking?" Charles asks, and gives me a look that tells me how stupid I am, just in case I had any doubts about it.

I scoot out of the circle just as Tamberlin fires the ball back in. It hits Charles with a rich splat, square in the belly. "Awwww," he moans, and bends forward, his hands on his stomach.

I am back on the bleachers by the time he throws up. Everyone acts like it's the most exciting thing that's happened in weeks.

But I am busy mulling it over, marveling at the fact that Tamberlin chose to assault Brynne instead of me. Marveling at the fact that Brynne is sitting thirty feet away from me, alone on the bleachers, nursing not only her injury but also her ego.

Because I can't exactly hop across the court and stick a piece of lame Freedent into Tamberlin's hand, I stare at her until she glances in my direction. And then I "reward" her with a smile.

Of course she doesn't smile back. But what she *does* do is look away very quickly, and then back at me, and away quickly again. And it's the weird nervousness in her glances that makes me really, truly believe that yes, Mandy could be right. And yes, Delia could be right. And yes, maybe even Phoebe's right.

It feels too good to be true. Could the plan really be working?

That afternoon, Corny and I go to Kisses's. By now she's mastered the sod, although she still won't step out onto the lawn. But today I get this wild idea all on my own. I take a few extra patio stones and make a short path on the grass. You can tell she's not happy about it, but I get her to walk three stones out. She's surrounded by all this enemy territory, but she manages to stay sitting on the third stone for close to five pretty calm minutes.

She's almost there. And maybe we are too.

Like I said. Maybe it really is working.

Off-Leash Training

THAT EVENING, Delia calls me at home. Corny answers and comes to get me. "I think it's the one who used to have all those pimples," she says. She doesn't mean to be rude, it's just that in the dog world, people use words like roach-backed or dish-faced to describe a characteristic, and it's a perfectly acceptable practice.

"Guess what I just got?" Delia says, her voice full of exclamation points. "An Evite to Erin Monroe's party!"

"Really?" I say. *Oh.* "Wow. Congrats."

"You *too*, you goof. We all got invited—you, me, Mandy, and Phoebe. Obviously not Joey, since it's a sleepover."

"Wow," I say again, feeling a little shocked. It's the first non–Bored Game Club sleepover I've been invited to in the year I've lived here, and I'm having visions of my eyebrows being shaved off while I sleep.

"It's the night before the Fall Ball, so everyone's probably going to practice makeup and show off their dresses and stuff," she tells me.

"Well, then, what the heck are *we* going to do?" I ask.

"What do you mean?"

"I mean, none of us is going to that dance. Well, Phoebe thinks she is, but by then—"

"Don't say that," Delia says. "You don't know what's going to happen between now and then. I mean, a month ago you would never have believed we'd be invited to this."

"True," I sigh. Okay, I'll give her that. But it makes me nervous because I don't want to get my hopes up that much. Caleb Austin's face pops into my head, and I close my eyes and forcefully bury it in the thought-free trunk of my brain. That part is getting so filled with things that if I ever have a problem with balance—or is it vision?—I'll know why.

"So you want to go to Erin's sleepover?" I say.

"Of course I want to go! Are you *crazy*?"

"Mandy and Phoebe do too?"

"I'm sure they do," she says. "Come on, Liv. Aren't you excited?"

"Well, yeah, sure," I say. Because I am. And I'm also terrified. It's amazing—we're getting what we wanted, and it's great, but all of a sudden there's a lot to lose. "Just don't freak out with your response and act like we're lucky to be invited."

"I *know* that. I'm not going to even respond for a little while."

Right away, I go check my e-mail. Sure enough, there's the Evite in my inbox. Brynne, of course, is on the list. She's already RSVP'd, which isn't something I'd have expected from someone like her, who should be WAY too busy for a stupid Evite. But the strangest thing is her response—OMG I'M SO THERE, ILY BFF!!!!!!!!!! There's like twenty zillion exclamation points—so many that it takes up an additional five lines.

I feel weird, because her response sounds more than a little desperate. And also because that gives me a little thrill.

Digging for Bones

"DO YOU REMEMBER your class elections?" I ask Moncherie during my Wednesday afternoon psycho session, after I've given her an update on how the campaign's gearing up.

"Hey, don't worry, okay?" she says, giving me one of those wincing smiles. "I know it's rough, but it'll be over before you know it. One day, middle school will just be a distant memory." I guess she thinks she's comforting me.

"But I actually think we might have a shot," I tell her, feeling frustrated. "I mean, things are going pretty well in general."

"Well, good," she says, but in a way that makes me think she doesn't believe me. Not really. "But remember, you don't want to set yourself up for disappointment."

"I'm not," I say, a little hurt. I don't bother telling her how much we've already done so far. She just doesn't need to know that—or anything about the plan.

She taps her pencil against her palm and looks down at her notebook. "So, how are you feeling today?"

"Like I said. Things are actually going okay for once."

"That's not a feeling," she says. "That's just a . . . statement. A speculation. I need to write down—I mean, I need you to tell me how you're *feeling*."

"I'm feeling *good*," I say quietly.

She exhales loudly. "*Good* is not an emotion." She leans forward and starts making little round cartoon faces on the back of the manila file for my case. "This is happy," she says, drawing a smiley face. She draws another, almost identical, but the smile is upside down. "This is sad." Then she draws upside-down arches over the eyes on the next. "This is disappointed. Now, do you see 'good' anywhere on here? Good is—I don't know—a three-bedroom ranch house with a fenced yard, or a, uh, spacious city condo. Or maybe a small cottage on the beach where you can hear the waves lapping the shore—no, actually, that would be *great*. But good is not an *emotion*!"

I'm sure I give her a strange look, because she says, "Sorry, got carried away, but you know what I mean." She opens a bottle of water and takes a sip. "Look, Olivia, I'm sorry. I don't mean to force you—" She stops talking and shakes her head. "It's just—well, if you don't want to talk about the issues with your mother, can you just think about *why* you don't want to talk about it?"

My throat starts to feel tight. I clear it as quietly as I can, and say, "But I thought you were interested in what happens at school."

"I am!" she says loudly. "Look, if it were up to me, we'd sit back and drink sodas and eat popcorn and talk about all those terrible—*girls* at school. But the fact of the matter is that I care about helping you. I'm your therapist. And you're my head case."

I'm sure she means this as, like, "lead case," or maybe "most difficult/challenging/troubling case," but because she's totally not aware that she's just called me a *head case*, it strikes me as funny.

155

Very funny. And I start to laugh like a seriously sick-in-the-head, put-me-in-a-straitjacket-and-haul-me-away kind of crazy person. And the more I laugh, the more I feel like I might start to cry— and I start to worry that my brain-trunk might just fly right open.

Uh-oh. I think my gene is showing.

"Olivia, I know you've got some emotions going on there." Moncherie says this with lots of pity and stuff, but also with a little enthusiasm. I guess when therapists smell tears forming, they get excited.

I've got to distract her. I blink back the wetness in my eyes and say, "I should probably tell you something."

"Yes, please," she says, looking like she might have just struck gold. She sits up straight and positions her pen above her notepad.

"Now, you can't tell a soul," I say.

"Olivia, I'm a therapist. I'm *sworn* to secrecy," she says, holding her hand up to emphasize the swearing-in part. Her foot bounces around with impatience.

"My friends and I . . ."

"Yes?"

It's my last opportunity to bail on telling her. But I don't. I ignore my bathroom wall fears and take a breath. "We're dog-training the entire school so that Mandy can win the election."

There, I think. That'll keep her busy. Too busy to make me talk about my mother.

She squints her eyes and cocks her head. "You're doing *what*?"

I say it again. Her face tightens, and I'm starting to get nervous she might bail on the secrecy thing, so I add, "I thought you'd be proud of me. It's like dog psychology, but we're using it on people. So we're kind of like junior therapists."

Moncherie still looks worried. She walks over to her desk, rummages through the top drawer, and pulls out a laminated rectangular piece of paper. "Is this," she asks, then reads from the paper, "'a danger or risk of danger to yourself or others'?"

"No, no, nothing like that, not at all," I say, wishing now that I had kept my mouth shut. What if she decides to shut down the whole project? I add, "It's totally legal. And mostly just for fun."

She still stands there stiffly. "Does your grandmother know about this?"

"No," I say. "And you can't tell her. You already swore on it. And I'm telling you things, aren't I? Secret things. I would never have told you a secret like that a month ago."

She starts rubbing her temples. "No." She exhales loudly and sits down. "No, I guess you're right."

"This is supposed to be a *safe environment*," I say, using the words on her that she's used many times before on me.

"Yes, yes, Olivia. You're right. Of *course* you should feel free to talk to me about anything," she says, and gives me a weary smile. "I'm proud of you for opening up."

I smile back. I wonder what I'll end up confessing next time she starts up with the mother issues again. I'm going to run out of material soon. Watch me pour my heart out about Caleb Austin and the freakish effect he's been having on me lately. Ugh.

The dollar-store timer dings, and Moncherie stands up, still with that droopy smile. "Well, it's been a productive session, wouldn't you say?" She looks down at the notepad in her hands and makes a large check mark across something on the page, which seems to make her happy. Very happy.

I'm glad to see this therapy thing is working for *one* of us.

Pedigree

ON THURSDAY, right before lunch, I pass Caleb in the hall and he says my name. "Hey, Olivia."

I like the way he says it. He slows down and smiles at me.

I slow down and smile too. And then I say, "Hi, Caleb." Except I don't just say it. I *spray* it, and I'm pretty sure I douse his nice sky-blue shirt.

That blasted hard C! Why couldn't his name be Neal? I think it's virtually impossible to spit when saying *Neal*. Or John. Or Rob, even.

But he doesn't seem to notice. "Wanted to ask you something," he says.

I dare to raise my eyes. My heart starts to float a little, like a helium balloon. "You did?"

"Yeah." He does this little embarrassed laugh that's adorable. "This is a little awkward—"

"Hey." The back of Ryan Stoles's big fat head pops in between us. "No fraternizing with the enemy," he says. He lets out an obnoxious wail of a laugh. "Dude, what are you doing?"

Caleb smiles. "Hang on, Ryan."

Just then Phoebe appears at my side. "Coming to lunch?"

Caleb and I exchange glances. "I'll just talk to you soon, all right?"

"Yeah, okay," I say.

"What was that about?" Phoebe asks.

"No idea," I say. "But I spit on him."

"Oh. Why?"

"Is that really a question? I didn't mean to!"

"Oh."

We're the last ones to get to our lunch table. When we sit down, Delia's explaining something to Mandy and Joey. "I swear it's true," she is saying.

"Danny, as in Daniel Pritchard?" Mandy says, eyes growing wide. "Isn't he Brynne's?"

"Maybe not so much anymore," Delia says. Delia's locker is three doors down from Danny's, and two days ago, he was there with Brynne. He went to kiss Brynne good-bye, but she said, "*Oh. Em. Gee.* Did you just eat a turd or something?" And Danny slammed his locker shut and said, "I think I'd rather eat a turd than kiss *you!*" And when Brynne stormed off, Delia—in true freedom fighter fashion—handed him a cookie. Apparently, he's been following her around like a puppy dog ever since.

"What's going on?" I ask.

"Danny asked me to the dance," Delia says, with something between a smile and a look of concern on her face.

"Danny Pritchard asked you to the Fall Ball?" Phoebe can hardly contain her excitement. "Let's double-date!" she adds, eyes wide and hopeful.

My mouth drops open. "Because of that cookie?"

159

"No, it was later. We were just talking and he said he never thought Brynne was all *that* anyway. So I told him he looked like he was going to be tall one day. You know, a compliment, sort of. I just needed some type of reward. I guess he thought I was hitting on him, and he asked me to go."

"Too bad he's such used goods," Mandy says.

"I know—but I kind of *do* want to go." She glances down at her Tofurky sandwich, which Delia's mom credits for her smoothing skin. "I've never been to one of these things. Plus, I mean, he was Brynne Shawnson's boyfriend. It's like, what if Zac Efron asked you out?"

"I don't like Zac Efron," Mandy reminds her.

"I *know* that," she says. "But still—on one level, it would be like, wow! You know how there are different pedigrees of dogs? Like different classes of dogs? Well, it's like he's in a higher class than us. I mean, you can't help but be flattered in a strange sort of way."

I don't want to admit it, but I know exactly what she's talking about. I mean, look at Brynne. I would never say this out loud, but I do sort of want her to like me. To admire me in some way, at least. I mean, until recently—like a-couple-of-weeks-ago kind of recently—it always seemed like people would run in the opposite direction from me. My own mother ran away, didn't she? So the thought that someone like Brynne could like me—someone who likes practically *no one*—well, in some twisted way, it could mean that maybe I'm not such a freak after all.

I still can't believe the plan is actually working—it's working! But just for a second I start to wonder if this growing power we have is good or evil.

Because I look over at Brynne's table. She's quiet, contemplating her veggie pack. The people at her table are all laughing at something. She's the last one to join in—it's like she pushes out a few giggles and then, completely unnoticed, she's back to staring at her baby carrots. She bites into one, chews, and swallows. Just like anyone else. Chewing and swallowing, the simple act of eating, just trying to stay alive in this insane world.

For a second, it makes me feel kind of sad and melty inside.

Which is *ridiculous*. So ridiculous that when Phoebe says she thinks she saw Brynne standing alone at her locker today, wiping her eyes with a clump of toilet paper—which would make sense if puny little Danny dumped her—I make myself laugh out loud, as loud as everyone else.

Okay, maybe even louder.

Every Dog Has Her Day

I THINK I hear someone whisper my name.

It's later on Thursday and we're in English, serving out the mandatory forty-five-minute monthly reading session, "Rock-n-Read!" The only thing "rock-ish" about "Rock-n-Read!" is that you get the feeling that if you don't do what's required, you just may be stoned to death. It's basically when teachers pace the aisles like prison guards, making sure each one of us is reading something of our "choice." It can be anything, as long as it meets the requirements (*No comic books*; *no bottles or other packaging*; *no magazines with faces on the cover*—which was later changed to include *or other body parts*). It's also when kids try everything to drive the teachers crazy by finding loopholes. Last year, it got so bad the list of requirements were just about narrowed down to *Must have both "Catcher" and "Rye" in title*.

Anyway, "Rock-n-Read!" is just another thing, like Sleeterball, which starts out as someone's idea of fun and ends up as a feeder program for detention.

I hear my name whispered again, I'm almost sure of it. I look up from the *Composting: The Delight of Decay* book I have been sentenced to read since I left my copy of *A Wrinkle in Time* at home, but no one seems to be looking at me—let alone whispering my name. I once heard something on the radio where someone was talking about how in cases of extreme boredom, like being isolated in prison or marooned on a desert island, the brain starts making up things for the bored person to hear. They interviewed someone who heard a whole opera! I thought that was pretty nice of the brain to do that. So I figure that what's happening here.

But then I hear it again, only a little louder. "Hey, Olivia!"

And I look up again. Max Marshall is in his seat in front of me. He's got his hand cupped over his mouth, directing his whisper in my direction.

He passes a piece of paper back to me. On it, he's written, *What's superficial mean?*

I'm glad I know this. *Not deep*, I write back. I glance at his desk when I pass it back to him. He's reading *The Andromeda Strain*.

And then he scribbles something and passes it to me: *Awesome. Thanks.* And he's drawn this little squiggly-lined happy face next to his words. And when I look back up, he's glancing over his shoulder, giving me a crooked little smile. It's a nice smile.

I try to find something interesting-like in my book, but even the pictures are outrageously mind-numbing—charts that show the different but equally disgusting phases of decay; photos of soil in varying shades of dark brown; an artist's rendition of compost machines of the future. I pray that the class will be out of its misery soon, but I do so with open eyes to avoid being jabbed with a yardstick by Mr. Renaldi. I add a few other things into that prayer too. Like about a certain someone. An astonishingly hot someone named Caleb. I decide to let the bell be my *amen*.

When I get up, Max gives me another smile, but rushes off. Janie Lindy smirks and shuffles up next to me. "You know what I heard?" she whispers. "I heard he's going to ask you to Fall Ball."

I'm speechless. She just smiles at me, adjusts her hidden back brace, and moves on.

And you know why I'm starting to believe that I'm close to becoming an alpha dog? Because even though Max is a nice guy, and even a cute guy, I only consider it for a couple of minutes. Because you know that prayer I said? For the first time ever, it feels like it could come true.

But.

When I pass Caleb in the hall on my way to sixth period, he just smiles at me and gives me a little wave. He doesn't stop to ask me anything, like he tried to this morning. I tell myself that it's okay. First of all, he's not alone—he's hardly ever alone anymore. And second of all, I'm still hopeful that it's only a matter of *just yet*. We still have a little time before the Fall Ball, right?

Strays

JUST YET isn't happening quickly enough.

"So, I hear the campaign's going well," Caleb says to me on Friday morning. I am at my locker, and despite the fact that I've been waiting for this moment, he's caught me off guard.

"Oh, thanks," I say, and smile. I stand up straight like an alpha dog, but I'm feeling a lot more like a puppy. Then my eyes meet his and I'm stuck. I can't look away—they're too deep, with the pull of heavy-duty magnets. "How's . . . How's it . . ." My mind goes blank. "How's it . . ." I allow my eyes to blink shut. "Going for you?" I finally continue.

He looks a little confused. Adorably confused. "Great," he says. I nod dumbly while my eyes refocus on his. I didn't know I liked brown eyes so much, but something about my heartbeat is telling me that yes, I do. In fact, my pulse seems to believe that I *love* them.

"So—"

"So—" I repeat after him, and try to add a dazzling smile.

Just then, Carson and Ryan—now co-campaign managers—interrupt our moment and make me want to scream. Three Sudoku clubbers stand shyly at a distance behind them. "Dude," Carson says to Caleb, "want these guys to stick up some posters or something? They said they want to help."

"Sure," Caleb answers. He turns back to me. "Hey, I'll just catch you later, okay? Well, good luck."

He turns to leave, and I can almost hear my eyes thwack back into their sockets, like when I pull Corny's suction-cup soap dish off the tile above the sink. I blink several times and feel my entire head burn. My ears start to feel incredibly exposed.

And then I realize, he didn't ask me a single thing—not the whole three minutes we were alone together. Like, say, about the dance, for example.

"You okay?" Maria Trujillo, whose locker is next to mine, asks.

I turn back to my locker and pretend I *am* okay. "Yeah. Thanks."

"Don't let him get you all rattled," she says, looking sympathetic. "You guys have my vote."

I'm thankful for her misdiagnosis. Despite the knot in my stomach, I feel a slow smile spread across my face. "Really?"

"Well, yeah. I mean I'm not going to vote for a snob like Brynne, and who needs Mr. Rich Kid Show-Off?" She shrugs. I fight the urge to say something stupid, like *me*. "At least Mandy's like one of us," she says. "Kind of weird, but in a good way, right?" She slams her locker shut. "Well, see ya."

I take a deep breath. I should feel relieved. And I will, I'm sure, just as soon as my body returns to its regular boring state of being.

"Guess what?" Phoebe says at lunch. "We've got even more competition."

"Who?" Mandy says, more with curiosity than surprise.

"Dawn Lane's running," Phoebe tells us.

"The girl with the braid?" Delia asks. What she's referring to is the unstylish four-foot-long braided ponytail Dawn's been growing out since kindergarten. No one's really sure if she thinks it looks good or if someone, most likely a parent, has guilted her into it, but it's sort of kept her in the lower ranks of popularity. The difference between where she is in the ranks and where we used to be is this—she seems utterly unaware of her status.

Dawn Lane is the kind of girl to sign up to play "I Believe I Can Fly" on the recorder for the Spring Talent Show; the one who manages to wear flower-patterned dresses with watermelon-sized puffed sleeves and enormous lace collars, and clunky white canvas sneakers with every-color-of-the-rainbow racing stripes, all without the expected sense of shame. She's the kind of person who takes notes during school assemblies. Like I said, totally oblivious.

"Oh, her," Mandy says. "That's okay."

The teachers in our school always say the election isn't a popularity contest, but that's just another big fat lie that grown-ups tell you. And seeing as the training's worked and people really do seem to like us now, I'm actually starting to feel a little relieved that it is.

It's on the bus home that I realize Brynne and I have something in common.

She's standing next to Audrey Sharif, who has reluctantly agreed to share her Bazooka gum. Brynne actually looks excited about it. "Oh, this is the kind with the cartoon!" she says.

Audrey asks, "Why don't you ever seem to have your own gum? I mean, *ever?*"

"Yeah, it's getting kind of annoying," Carolyn chimes in.

Normally this would have brought out the Wrath of Brynne. But now, she just says, "Well, *sor-ry.*"

Carolyn and Audrey exchange glances and roll their eyes, turning away from Brynne, who continues to talk, this time to the back of their heads. I may be the only one listening. "It's because of my stupid little brother," she says, and then corrects herself. "*Half* brother. He keeps stealing my gum from me. And my mother keeps letting him get away with it."

A half brother.

Maybe Brynne's mother practiced—and failed—on her, and then decided to try for a new-and-improved version. Just like my mom practiced and failed on me, and could one day do the same thing with that guy Darren or maybe someone else. The thought of it makes me want to curl into a ball like those little gray roly-poly bugs. I wonder how Brynne deals with it. I'm not sure I could.

I must be staring at her, because she turns in my direction and her eyes meet mine. The normal gemstone blue of her eyes looks more like a rainy-day gray, and she surprises me with something like a smile, but very heavy and sad. I know that smile. It's the kind of smile you put on your face when your world has fallen apart and all you really want to do is go home and cry about it like a big baby.

Like I said, I *know* that smile.

I blink, and breathe, and quickly turn my gaze to the window. A billboard on the side of the road advertises Floyd County. There's a picture of the courthouse and the old church, and the high school we'll all be going to next year if we don't screw up too much. Despite the fact that the sun has faded the sign and the colors are worn, Floyd County looks a whole lot prettier on that one-dimensional poster than it does in the three dimensions of reality.

Too bad life's not that simple. Or people, for that matter. It would make them a lot easier to love—and a lot less complicated to hate.

The Collar

IT'S SATURDAY, and I'm supposed to be doing my homework. Instead, I'm watching another *Full House* rerun. I'm curled up with Oomlot, and we are both ignoring Queso's attempts to play, when the phone rings. My grandmother picks it up and calls for me. I tear myself away from the TV, accidentally exciting Queso, who does a little play-bow and hops around. I'm expecting to rush Mandy or Delia off the phone so I can get back to Uncle Jesse, but it is neither of them.

"Olivia?" the voice says, as my brain scrambles to identify it.

"Yes?" I say. Queso looks up at me expectantly. I reach into my backpack and pull out an eraser. She wags her whole tiny little body. I throw it and watch her scurry and skid across the floor, and finally go in for the attack. That'll keep her busy for a few minutes.

"It's Brynne," the voice says. When I am in too much shock to say anything, she adds, "Brynne Shawnson? From school? *Hellooo?*"

"Oh." *My. God.* "Hi."

"So, you have Mr. Renaldi for English, don't you?"

"Uh, yeah. Fourth period," I say.

"Oh, thank God. I have him for sixth, but no one in my class will answer their stupid phones."

I am quiet. I wonder if this is why she's calling me. If somehow she's figured out I'm basically the reason why.

But then she says, "So do you know what we're supposed to do for homework?"

"Oh. Yeah, hang on." I pull my notebook out of my backpack, still reeling, and tell her the assignment. We're supposed to write a scene of fiction based on the western pioneers' experience.

She is quiet for a second, then asks, "What did you write?"

I'm afraid she's going to ask me to read it out loud—which is terrifying—and then copy it—which is maddening—so I just say, "I haven't written it yet."

"Well, me either, obviously." She laughs. "They died a lot in those days, didn't they?"

"I think so," I say.

"YOU FRIGGIN' WASTE OF FLESH!"

My heart jolts. So *this* is what it's about. It's another joke on me. I'm about to hang up when she says, "*Oh. Em. Gee.* I'm so sorry about that." And then she screams, "GET OUT!!"

I'm frozen. Queso has laid the eraser by my toe and is patiently waiting for me to throw it again, but I'm too stunned to move.

"Olivia? Sorry, sorry! Just hang on."

Then I hear her slam a door. "My brother. He's only nine, but he's already a tool," she explains to me. "Sorry to bug you with this, but like I said, I just don't know what's going on. Everyone acts like they don't want to talk to me."

This is awkward.

"It's okay. I don't mind." I catch myself wincing in the mirror as I say it.

"Thanks," she says. "I probably shouldn't care anyway. Honestly, you're probably smarter and nicer than all of them put together."

I laugh nervously, unsure of what to say. A million stupid little things come to mind, but thankfully, none of them make it to my mouth.

Now I hear a woman's voice rising in the background. "*Okay, Mom*," Brynne whines. "I gotta go. I'll talk to you later."

She hangs up and I sit there for a second before picking the phone back up to call Delia and tell her what just happened. I still feel slightly stunned, and my words come out kind of flat and baffled, but Delia's full of excitement.

"This is incredible! You're a genius, Liv. I can't believe the plan is working so well!"

"Me either. I'm just—shocked. I mean, Brynne Shawnson calling me for help? Saying I'm smarter and nicer than any of her friends? It just feels bizarre."

"I know. Have you seen the new batch of Brynne's campaign posters? The ones Carolyn and Tamberlin did? They just took markers and wrote 'Vote for Brynne' on regular lined paper and stuck them up in the science hall with Scotch tape. And I heard Corbin Moon was supposed to do a bunch of posters, but just showed up with a pad of Post-its instead. He was going to write her name on them and stick them on the bathroom stalls, but Mrs. Vander-Pecker wouldn't let him go into the girls' room."

"Ugh. You think that's true?" I say, throwing the eraser again for Queso.

"That's what I heard," she says. "I mean, Corbin was calling it 'grassroots campaigning,' but who does he think he's fooling? It's like none of them really care if she's elected anymore. I'm telling you, Liv, it's all because of the plan."

I curl back up with Oomlot and remind myself of all the things Brynne's done to deserve this.

Survival Instincts

THERE ARE NOW *three* popular girls who have picked up on the lip-marker trend. And Joey and I actually witnessed Brant smiling at Phoebe—a real smile, not a smirk—in the hallway when we were all walking to the bus. And Delia's cheeks are looking clearer—not just her hairline. And when Joey spilled his Yoo-hoo in the ice-cream line in the cafeteria, small-nostriled Corinne d'Abo, who was in the line in front of him, ran and got some paper towels to help him clean it up. And I saw Corbin Moon glance at Mandy and look away, like she was just a normal person—maybe even a *pretty* person. But the real turning point for me comes at lunch on Monday, when Brynne walks over to our table. In front of everyone, she slips four stapled sheets of paper in front of me. "Will you read it?"

I pick it up and study it. Despite what she said on the phone, I'm still half expecting this to be some type of cruel joke—a petition voting us out of the campaign, for example. But all I see, centered in the middle of the page, is the word "Reclaimed." Under that is, "By Brynne L. Shawnson."

"It's my pioneer story," she says, her fingers clasping each other, fidgety. "Do you have time? Would you . . . read it over before I turn it in?"

"Okay." I swallow. "Sure."

Delia glances at the paper. "Nice title."

"Thanks." Brynne smiles kind of sadly. "Just let me know how suckish it is. I'll come by your locker after lunch."

She walks away, and everyone's eyes pop open. "Let me see," Phoebe says, trying to snatch the paper. I pull it away, like a reflex.

Delia asks me what I'll say to her if it does suck. I tell her I don't know.

"Wow, she's like totally over herself," Mandy says. For a second, she looks concerned. Then she bursts out with a laugh. She and Joey butt fists, and then, with his hands, Joey mimes a plane flying, falling out of the sky, crashing and bursting into flames, complete with all the expected sound effects.

"This is *awesome*," Joey says.

"She looked kind of, I don't know, *worn out* or something, didn't she?" Delia asks.

"Yeah, amazing what happens when you strip someone of their confidence," Mandy says, grinning. "Hey, am I getting any better looking?"

"Well, your scab's healed up pretty nicely," Phoebe tells her.

While they continue their self-congratulations, I grab a pen and start reading Brynne's story. With each sentence, I'm surprised. I mean it's a little far-fetched, but it's pretty good. It's about a prairie girl named Elizabeth, whose parents have died on the trip out west, and she has to find a family to adopt her.

"So *does* it suck?" Delia says, trying to look at the little notes I've written in the margin.

"It's actually not bad," I say.

"What's yours about?" Mandy asks. She hasn't written hers yet because she doesn't have to go to her fifth period class; her mother is picking her up for a dentist appointment.

"It's about this family that lives on a prairie, and they have a bunch of kids, and one of them gets really sick and almost dies."

"Oh," Mandy says. "Isn't that basically *Little House on the Prairie*?"

"It's similar," I admit. Suddenly I am disappointed with myself. The truth is I just wanted to get the story out of the way so I could catch the rerun of the very first episode of *Full House*, where the mother just died and Joey and Uncle Jesse move in with the girls and their father. It's my favorite episode. Sometimes I wish my dad had had a brother and best friend to move in with us when my mom left, but then I'd probably still be afraid of dogs, and I'd have never gotten to the point where a former celebrity like Brynne would be asking for my help.

"Well, I'm sure your story is much better than Brynne's," Delia says.

"I wish," I say. "But to be honest, hers is just a better story all around. She's actually a good writer."

"Careful, there," Mandy says, smirking. "Sounds like you're sympathizing with the enemy. Some abolitionist you are."

"Yeah, more like Benedict Arnold," Joey says.

"Wow, would you listen to yourselves?" Delia jumps in. "Olivia was just trying to say she liked her story. She didn't say she liked *her*."

"Yeah, I mean—okay, I guess it doesn't hurt that she's also being nice," I say. And before I really *do* start to feel like a traitor,

I add, "I'm just saying, we got her where we want her. We don't have to stick the knife in and twist it."

Joey starts acting out my words. He stabs and twists his milk straw into Phoebe's upper arm, and Phoebe yells at him about the difference between literal and figurative. And I'm actually relieved because I don't feel like I have to defend myself anymore.

And anyway, it doesn't matter how nice or smart or, okay, vulnerable, I think Brynne is. I'm not a traitor.

Agility

ON WEDNESDAY, I'm on my way to third period when I hear a squeal, then two bare arms wrap around my shoulders so tight it hurts.

It's Brynne. She's almost knocked down several seventh graders on her way to me. "*Oh. Em. Gee!*" she pants. "I got an A! Thank you! Thank you!"

I feel this weird little happy rush—her hug, her gushing appreciation, her acceptance of me. And then I have a panicky realization. I've been waiting for this moment. It's the stamp of approval I was hoping for. It's like I've finally been accepted into that country club, even if it *is* a little more like a rec center now.

"Which way are you going?" she asks.

"Oh," I say. "History. Knapp's class."

"Cool. I'm going that way." She walks next to me like she weighs twenty pounds, practically floating, while I thud away next to her trying really, really hard to think of something funny or enlightening to say. I get nothing.

"Mr. Renaldi even said that I've got talent," she practically squeals.

"Oh," I say again. Marvelous vocab I have. "Yay." Despite that secret inner thrill, my words come out flat and unimpressed. I wish I'd been prepared for this!

"I know, right?" She laughs. "Oh my God, I sound like such a spaz!"

"No," I manage to spit out. It seems one-syllable words are all I can handle.

"Well, see you at lunch," she says, and peels off to her next class.

"Bye," I say. I kind of want to smile, but then I remind myself not to let it go to my head. I tell myself whatever I'm feeling is just a little pang of success. It's not personal. I can't *really* like her and she can't *really* like me. She's just responding to the training like any dog would. It's that simple. Like any dog.

I don't get it. When I walk into the cafeteria, Brynne waves and slaps the seat beside her. I look over at my table. It's early—Phoebe sits alone, quietly disassembling a bag lunch. She spots someone and waves a bit ridiculously—I follow her gaze and see Brant waving back. Yes, that's still going on.

Then Brynne calls my name. I find myself being drawn in her direction.

And then I hear the sound of Delia laughing as she and Joey sit down at the table with Phoebe—it's something Joey's said—and I feel the tug of belonging in the opposite direction.

I throw a sheepish smile at Brynne and set my backpack down next to Delia, who—thankfully—isn't even slightly aware of my weak moral character. The fact that, for even a second, I could be lured away by someone else, let alone Brynne . . . I'm ashamed.

Peyton Randall appears. "You're sitting there? I asked Delia to save me a seat next to her."

Delia hears her. "Oh, sorry, Peyton. You can sit here tomorrow." She smiles up at me, but I don't smile back. Wait. Was she *really* going to let someone else have my seat?

Peyton sighs and heads to the other end of our table. Janie Lindy says hi to everyone and sits down across from Peyton. I'm starting to feel like the hound that I am. Territorially aggressive. This is my table, and this is my pack.

Delia is smiling at everyone like this is the greatest thing, these new people at our table. Her herd's growing, with people she's personally approved, so she's happy.

Stupid herders.

I mark my spot, leaving my backpack on the seat next to Delia, and get in the back of the lunch line. Mandy spots me and forgoes her better space in line to stand with me. I try to smile.

"You're quiet today," Mandy says.

"Sorry if I'm not a laugh a minute."

She looks at me like she's not really sure she gets me, and I know for a fact that, at this single moment in time, she doesn't. I'm not even sure *I* get me.

Mandy's black marker has worn away on all but the outer rims of her lips. For some reason, it annoys me.

"Your Sharpie's wearing off," I tell her.

"Oh," she says, and rubs at her mouth a little carelessly. "I'll fix it after lunch."

But it looks stupid *now*, I fight the urge to say. Don't you care that you look like a total Marcie?

We sit down in silence, and Tamberlin Ziff and Carolyn Quim approach our table, lips fruity red and clipboards in hand.

"We need some ideas for our Spirit Dress-Up Days, so we're taking down suggestions," Tamberlin explains.

"Um, Circus Day?" Janie offers.

Panic flashes across Carolyn's face.

"That's a little insensitive," Tamberlin chides Janie. "Lots of people are scared of clowns. It's an actual *syndrome*."

"Backward Day? You wear everything backward?" Delia says.

"That *sounds* good," Tamberlin says, "but it's just so *uncomfortable*. I mean, bras really don't work when they're put on backward. What else?"

"How about Favorite Scientist Day?" Phoebe starts. "That would not only be fun but edu—"

"Sorry, Phoebe, but *ehhhhh*!" Carolyn says, imitating a rejection buzzer, and giggling. "Olivia, don't you have any ideas?"

"Uh . . ." The problem is that I really want to have a great idea. I really want to impress them, but my brain is doing what it usually does when it's under pressure, which is to malfunction. My eyes dart around the cafeteria looking for something—anything— to offer. And here's what it comes up with. "Trash bags."

"Huh?" they both say.

I wish I could grab one of Mandy's Sharpies and scribble through my suggestion. But I can't. The only thing I seem to be able to do is stutter. "Um, I, I mean, um—"

Mandy rescues me. "She means Trash Bag Day. You can wear anything you want, as long as it's a trash bag. Great idea, Liv."

I glance at her. She's sitting up tall, delivering this with perfect spinal alignment and a confident tone—artfully, and perhaps quite magically, spinning my brain-doo into a somewhat reasonable-sounding idea.

"Oh my"—Tamberlin looks excitedly at Carolyn and squeals —"*gosh*! That's excellent!"

"This. Is going. To be. Great!" Carolyn says. "Thanks, Olivia!"

And I think, *Really?*

"Hey, anyone want a cookie?" Delia says, quick with the reward. Each of the girls grabs one and crams it into her mouth.

"Nice, uh, necks, both of you," Joey adds. "Very, uh, gooselike."

"Swan!" Delia corrects him. "He means swanlike."

They both laugh and say, "Oh, Joey. You are so funny!" before they scurry back to their usual table.

"Trash Bag Day," Peyton says, with a little admiration and wonder in her voice. "Huh. I would have never thought of that. You guys are so *interesting*!"

"*You're* interesting!" Joey says. It's the lazy boy's version of a compliment—a recycled one. Still, Peyton seems pleased.

"Peyton, would you care for some Wite-Out?" Phoebe adds.

While Peyton is being awkwardly flattered and begifted at the opposite end of the table, I say quietly to Mandy, "I should probably thank you."

"Yeah, you should. You know, you've been acting kind of weird, Olivia. This whole plan was your idea. You can't just start coasting now."

I look over at Brynne's table. I can't help but wonder—could Brynne and I really be friends? Could she really like me? The spot next to her is now filled by the willowy but incredibly whiny Izzy Van Norton, who is eating her daily half-pretzel and, no doubt, complaining about how full she is. For just a second, I feel a rush of regret at giving up my window of opportunity.

And then I sigh and tell Mandy that I'm sorry, because I know that despite the fact that I have Caribbean-green eyes and dancerlike legs and hair nicely controlled in a ponytail, *I'm* still the Marcie for even having my incredibly stupid regrets.

But I guess my eyes and legs and training abilities are worth something, because when I open my locker, a teeny tiny card falls out. It's shaped like a tiny oak leaf, and it's the color of a pumpkin. I know people think fall leaves are pretty, but they've always made me a little sad. I mean, these leaves are *dying*. I open the card, and there it is, written in Max's sweet, sloppy handwriting. *Will you go to FB with me?*

So Janie Lindy was right. I'm fluttery inside. I dread telling him no. But I can't say yes, because it's got to happen. I've seen Caleb's cues and I still think he's going to ask me. He keeps trying to, doesn't he?

Later, I pass Caleb in the hall. I make sure I'm standing up straight when I do. I look him in the eyes and think, *Ask me! Ask me!* I mean, time is seriously running out. But he just waves and smiles and stays with his crowd, which is moving in the opposite direction.

Basic Training

MONCHERIE'S OFFICE smells like chemicals when I walk in that afternoon, and she's blowing her beige-pink fingernails dry. "Lotus Blossom," she tells me, twinkling her fingers. "What do you think?"

It occurs to me that because I now wear makeup and look more like, say, a normal girl, I'm probably expected to have an opinion on things like nail polish. So I try to come up with one. It's brilliant. "Nice," I say.

Okay, I see *that* part of me hasn't changed.

"Went to this house that's for sale, and the bedroom walls were about this color. Well, come on in and sit down. We'll need to small-talk until this dries." She blows out a long gust of breath, letting her fingers dance around in the stream of air. She looks like she's playing an imaginary pan flute.

"How's school?"

"Pretty good, actually," I sigh. Do I tell her about the Fall Ball prospects? Am I really the type of girl now to be having this problem?

"Oh? Not 'fine'?" she teases. "How's that girl—the you-know-what?"

So I start to tell her about Brynne—the surprising things, like the fact that she called me, that I read her story. That she seems to actually like me. That she seems to be a little different now. Less full of herself.

Moncherie is waving her fingers furiously in the air. "Slow down, slow down," she says, and blows quickly on her fingers. "Hang on. My polish isn't dry." Then she stops and looks at me. "Okay, I'm probably going to regret this." I hear the creak of her top desk drawer opening, and she reaches in with both hands, trying to grab her pad and pen with open palms to save her not-yet-dry fingernails. I wonder if the fumes have gotten to her.

When I hear her start to make little gasps of frustration, I get up and help her.

She gives me a relieved smile. "Thank you." She takes the pen awkwardly between her fingers. "Now, I thought you didn't especially like this Brynne."

"I don't. I mean, I *didn't*," I explain. "She's just kind of interesting in a way. And probably a lot more complicated than I thought. You know she's got a half brother?"

"Oh," Moncherie says, leaning in. "A half brother." She might as well be rubbing her palms together with anticipation. "So her parents—are they apart too?"

I realize where she's trying to take us. I almost handed her the key. I catch myself before she starts unloading all my trunk baggage.

"I don't really know." I shrug. "Anyway, she's being sort of nice to me. It's because of the training."

She lets out a one-gust laugh. "Oh, yes. The training. Sure

would be nice if it worked on men. Now." She examines her polish by touching a tiny corner of her left thumb. It must be dry, because she adjusts her grip on the pen, smiles, and asks, "So, have you heard anything from your mother?"

I pounce on her last comment. "I bet it does work on men," I tell her. I mean, if my instincts and those rumors are correct, I could possibly have *two* invitations to the Fall Ball.

"You are *so* young," she sighs. She gives me a lopsided smile and shakes her head slowly, but it's clear that I've successfully distracted her. Standard training trick, right?

"I can tell how you it works," I offer.

"*Olivia*." She narrows her eyes in a teasing-scolding way. "Okay, okay. Just because I like dogs. How exactly does the training work?"

We spend the rest of my session going over "dog training" basics. She's put the pen back down, but she definitely seems to be taking notes.

36.

Pick of the Litter

I DON'T SEE Brynne on the bus Friday morning. In fact, I don't see Brynne until Delia and I are walking toward our second period classes. Only I don't recognize her—not at first—because she looks like a well-packaged pile of litter. Her hair is covered by a black trash bag, secured at the side of her head with a twist-tie. She is wearing another trash bag like a knee-length dress, upside-down with holes cut out for her neck and arms. A white trash bag with a drawstring makes a sort of belt, cinching the waist. She is wearing little else, unless you count flip-flops and a big, big smile. "Hi, guys," she says when she sees Delia and me.

"Hi," we repeat, our voices weak. We're a bit dumbfounded. It takes me a minute to get it. It must be Trash Bag Day. My brain droppings at work.

The crowd hushes and parts as she crackles and swooshes down the hall. You can't help but turn and stare. It's rare that you see so much plastic—especially worn with such aplomb.

Mandy finds her way to us. "Trash Bag Day! I'm so excited!"

she whispers, grinning. "I can't wait to see how stupid all the Spiritleaders look!"

Brynne's smile wavers a little as she spots Tamberlin and Carolyn, who are both in their regular uniform of tight jeans and overpriced T-shirts. "Hey," Brynne says. "Why aren't you—well, where are your bags?"

"At home." Tamberlin says, putting her hands on her hips. "Under the kitchen sink."

"But—why?" Then her smile drops completely and she slaps her forehead. "*Oh. Em. Gee.* I got the day wrong, didn't I? Is Trash Bag Day *next* Friday?"

Carolyn squeals with laughter and the crowd builds as Brynne looks increasingly confused. Corbin Moon sweeps down the stairs, chanting, "Hefty, hefty, hefty!" A few kids chant back with a high-pitched "Wimpy, wimpy, wimpy!" Soon at least half the crowd joins in.

Brynne looks around desperately. Then she starts to run. One of the guys grabs a wheeled trash can and starts pretending to chase her with it, but Brynne, thankfully, disappears into the bathroom.

So, they took my, well, "idea," and made it into a prank on Brynne. I wilt a little inside. It must show because Mandy looks at me and says, "Look, Olivia, don't get all racked with guilt. This is the *exact* same stunt she would have pulled if she still had her power."

"I know." I remind myself about a certain incident involving ketchup, which still makes me burn with embarrassment, And, of course, countless other indignities. I also try—really hard—not to think about the sad smile Brynne had on the bus the other day. And the nice things she said to me on the phone. And the way she looked just a few minutes ago, dressed in plastic, unaware that it was just a prank. Unaware that she was the target.

"Can you believe this?" I say. I feel dizzy. Almost sick.

"No," Delia says. "What should we do?"

"What do you mean, 'What should we do?'" Mandy says, laughing. "You got any cookies in that bag?"

"No," I say. "Bad idea. We can't reward this behavior."

"That's right. Plus, I only have two cookies anyway," Delia says, with slight relief.

"Oh, no problem." Mandy grins. She opens her own bag. "I was just going to resupply all the campaign posters anyway."

I take a breath. "Look, Mandy, okay, so we probably shouldn't feel bad for her. She's had it coming. But I don't think—"

"Um, hello?" Mandy leans in close to me. "Your idea, if I remember correctly. Freedom fighters? Ring any bells? Unless . . ." She steps away. "Unless you *are* Benedict Arnold."

"I'M NOT A TRAITOR!" I say too loudly.

"And you—" She points to Delia. "What about Sojourner Truth? Would she be proud of you for backing down from the enemy?"

Delia exhales, surrendering.

I shrug, throwing my palms up. "All right. Let's just get this over with." And then I feel the heft of the not-so-fun-sized bag of Jolly Ranchers in my left hand.

"Oh my God! Jolly Ranchers!" someone yells. And we are swarmed. It's like vultures picking apart roadkill, just a faster, more frenzied version. It's probably less than a minute until we are all rewarded out, which means that later, after fourth period, when Brynne resurfaces wearing *The Sassie Lasses(!)* I'll have nothing to give Corbin Moon when he murmurs, "Ugly girls say *what*?" and

Brynne seethes, "*What?!* What did you say?!"

Okay, okay. Not being able to reward that fool—actually, it's a little bit of a relief. Just not quite enough.

All weekend long, I keep trying hard not to think about that beatific, proud, trash-bag-wearing version of Brynne. On Sunday night I even work ahead in my algebra book in an attempt NOT to think about it. At least with solving equations there's a definite right and wrong. Unlike life.

The phone rings. I pick it up. It's Brynne. I almost drop it again.

She sounds nervous. "I have something to ask you," she says.

My heartbeat comes fast and erratic, but I try to sound cool. "Okay."

"Trash Bag Day." Her voice cracks. "I heard that was your idea?"

"No," I say, quickly. Then I correct myself. "Well, yes, sort of. But not like you might think."

And I tell her about Tamberlin and Carolyn coming over to the table, looking for ideas, and how I blurted it out. "I didn't know they were going to make it into a prank, though."

She's quiet for a second, and then she mutters, "*Trash Bag Day.* I can't believe I fell for it. I'm so done with them."

"Well, they'll probably get in a lot of trouble," I say.

"No they won't," she tells me. "I just told Vander-Pecker I got the day wrong. All she's going to do is make Dress-Up Day illegal."

I'm shocked. "But why'd you tell her that?"

She sighs. "I don't know. I was stupid enough to fall for it, for one. I mean, why drag it out? They're not worth it to me anymore. They're just not worth the trouble."

I turn the page in my math book, and for the first time ever, am relieved to see about fifty extra problems. That's another good thing about math. Math is fair. Life is not.

37.

Lost Dogs

I AM ON my way to the Bored Game Club on Monday afternoon when I hear my name called. I know it's Brynne before I even turn around. "I want to show you something," she says. "Come here."

I open my mouth, although I'm not sure what to say. "I can't," comes out.

"Yeah, you can," she says. "It's easy. Just turn around and start walking this way."

I give her a halfhearted smile. She smirks.

So I start walking toward her, totally going against all the proper training techniques. Like she said, it's easy.

She smiles a little, grabs my wrist, and starts running down the hall with me attached. I feel like a dog on a leash. Then she stops in the middle of the hallway, looks around, and pulls me into Mr. Renaldi's dark classroom.

My body becomes stiff. I have somehow got sucked into trouble. "What are we doing in here?"

"Just hanging out." She looks at me and laughs. "Don't tell anyone, but sometimes I come in here and just chill. He forgets to lock his door half the time."

"You hang out in here? Alone?"

"Pretty much. Especially lately," she says. "Sometimes I just read."

"Books?"

"Sometimes. But he doesn't have a lot of good ones," she says. She goes to the "Rock-n-Read" basket and picks up the composting book I was stuck with the other day. She looks at the cover, puts it back in the stack, and digs deeper.

"This is fun and all, but we should leave," I tell her. Everyone knows sneaking around dark, empty classrooms is considered trespassing, and I'm terrified of getting caught. Corny can be really sweet, but you don't want to cross her. She can bring a pit bull to its knees—well, you know, not knees, since dogs don't have those, but she can make it roll over and act like a major suck-up.

Brynne walks behind Mr. Renaldi's desk, pulls *Catcher in the Rye* off his bookshelf, and fans herself with it. "I like it in here."

"What if Mr. Renaldi comes back?"

"He won't. His backpack is gone. Plus, he always turns out the light when he leaves." She sounds like an expert.

Phoebe and Joey are probably fighting over who gets to be the little shoe piece in Monopoly, I think. But Delia and Mandy are probably wondering where the heck I am.

"Aren't you supposed to be somewhere, though?"

She lowers her eyebrows and stares up at me. "Like?"

"I don't know. Yearbook committee?"

"*Pfft.*" She sweeps my words away with a backhand gesture. "I've already taken a bazillion pictures. And before you say anything about Spiritleading, I'm glad to be done with it. That spandex was giving me a rash anyway. So it's either hang out here, or go home and fight with my butthead brother and my maniac mom."

"Oh," I say. "Sorry." And it's the truth—that's exactly how I feel for her right now.

She studies me for a few seconds. "You know, speaking of moms, you're lucky yours doesn't live with you. I sure wish my mine would like, go away or something, like yours."

My chest starts to feel tight, but I say nothing.

"You don't have to feel bad, you know. I know exactly what it's like. My mom's crazy too."

I swallow. How on earth could she know about that, when Delia's the only one who does?

"It's okay," Brynne says. "I know about your mom."

So many things start to creep up from the little round balance part at the back of my brain, and clog up my thinking. I mean, Delia would never—*ever*—

I somehow manage to ask, "What about her?" and I try to act like my throat isn't starting to close in on itself. "That—that she travels a lot?" The words sound ridiculous now. They probably always have. I've just been too stupid and too scared to admit it.

"That she went a little crazy and just left you. It's okay, though, you know. My mom's—"

"Who told you that?" I ask, but something tells me I don't want to know the answer.

She just shrugs and says, "Delia."

"What? *Nuh-uh*!" I know I sound like I'm four years old, but I guess that's what happens when you sense a crisis. Fetal position and thumb-sucking are also starting to seem like appealing activities.

This can't be happening.

"Yeah," she says. "Well, she's the one who called me, but your friends were all there. They had me on speaker."

All my friends. Were there. Which makes it all so much worse.

"Mandy too?"

"Yeah, the goth one, right?" She looks at me. "Yep. And Pheebie-Jeebie too. Even that fat kid."

I don't know which I feel more of—anger or hurt. "When was this?" I finally ask.

"Like a few weeks ago. Delia wanted me to leave you alone, so she pretty much gave me your whole sob story. But don't worry. Like I said, I can totally relate."

I sink down into a beanbag chair in the corner of the room. I force a few breaths down my tight throat. My entire head is stinging and throbbing, and if I were alone or in the company of dogs, just dogs, I'd be crying my eyes out.

But I'm not alone. Or am I, really? Maybe not physically alone in this room, but all alone in my crashing-down little world. The one person I trusted—Delia—has told my biggest secret. She and all my friends must have discussed me behind my back; they've probably made secret pacts never to mention it in front of me; they've probably told their parents. They probably all know that I go to therapy, where a weird lady with bad fashion sense tries really hard to get me to admit that my mom didn't want me. All because of Delia, and because of my own stupidity in trusting her.

Brynne pulls another book off the shelf and leafs through it. "You know, everyone used to think your mom was dead."

"Well"—I make myself exhale a little laugh, which sounds more like I'm choking—"she's not." Although that would be a lot easier to explain, I find myself thinking.

I keep my head down, but out of the corner of my eye I see Brynne look up from the book. "Well, duh, I know that *now*. My dad died, you know," she says, even though I didn't. "From an accident. I was with him but I was like, four. This is what I have to remember him by," she says, touching the scar on her chin. She might as well be talking about what she had for lunch—she sounds completely over it.

"Well, sorry about your mom," she continues. "But once you meet mine, you'll see how lucky you really are. Total nutter."

Yeah, right, I think. I'm so sure. Most people think their moms are crazy if they sing out loud in the car, or eat plain yogurt, or wear high-waisted jeans. She has no idea. Zero. *Zilch*.

"I'm talking one word here," Brynne says, as if reading my thoughts. "Prozac."

Okay, then. Maybe she *does*.

At this moment I feel so betrayed by Delia—by all of *them*—that it's almost a relief to think Brynne and I have this thing in common.

Suddenly, through the window in the door, we see the top of a graying head. "Hide!" Brynne yells in a whisper, and drops to a crouching position beside Mr. Renaldi's desk. I roll to the floor and move the beanbag chair on top of me. Over the loud beating of my heart, I hear the door open and then footsteps. I slowly open my eyes, which ache from squeezing shut, and watch a pair of wide sneakers walk by. For a second the trash can disappears, then it clangs back to the floor, and the sneakers walk off, shutting and locking the door behind them.

Brynne's voice rings out. "Mrs. Vittle, the janitor," she cries out, laughing. "*Oh. Em. Gee.* That was great."

I exhale with a laugh, relieved not to be in trouble.

"We really should go," I say.

"Good thing she didn't lock the door," Brynne says.

"But—I heard her key in the lock."

"You did?" She shoots me a look of panic that I'm sure I return.

"Oh, *no way*," she says, and scurries to her feet. She grabs the handle and turns back to me, eyes panicked. "No freakin' way."

I get to my own feet. "What?"

"We're locked in!"

"*What?*" I ask, even though I heard her perfectly. We are going to be in *so much* trouble. My voice feels shaky, and I dash toward the door.

But she grabs me before I can reach it, and a volcano of laughter erupts from her. "I'm kidding," she says, between gasps.

I grab the knob and turn. The door opens, so I shut it again quickly. She holds back her laugh with her hand. "The doors don't lock on the inside. You can always get out. Otherwise, we'd all burn to death if there was a fire."

"Oh. Right," I say.

"You should have seen your face." She stops laughing just enough to mimic my expression—a combination of terror and surprise. She looks like a caricature, her pretty face wrestling itself into something so ridiculous. Despite the fact that I'm upset, a laugh leaks out of me like a whine.

Then the bell rings, which causes us both to scream, which makes it even funnier.

"We . . . better . . . go," she tries to say through her laugh. We both take deep breaths, then she peeks down the hall in each direction. "Quick!" she yells. We scamper into the hallway and I trip and actually make a noise like *splat* on the floor, and by now

I'm doubled over with laughter and we're both finding it hard to walk. It takes us extra time to get outside, and when we do, we hear the buses start up. We begin to run—fast—and make it to our bus just before the door shuts for the last time, and she pulls me down to a seat with her and begins her interrogation for gum, like it's any other day.

I feel an empty churning inside my stomach. I break out a pack of Goldfish crackers from my backpack and offer a few to Brynne. But it's something other than hunger, because after downing all but about three of the crackers, the feeling is still there.

38.

The Pound

CORNY IS WAITING for me on the porch, her arms crossed over her chest, her lips pressed together in a thin line. She looks nothing like the normally sweet but very odd old lady that I've grown to love. *Nothing.* My already-troubled stomach sinks.

Even the good-natured Ferrill, who is sitting next to her, seems to be giving me the stink eye. This can't be good.

"Where were you this afternoon?" she asks, as I step off the bus. The bus moans its way down the narrow road behind me. Part of me wants to run down the road after it.

Queso pushes through the screen door. When she sees me, she starts acting like Corny Junior and launches into a yapping session. Her bark is high-pitched and nerve-racking. Finally Corny slaps her hands together and Queso snaps out of it.

"I was at school," I say. I look down at my fingers. I've been picking at my cuticles so much, they look like a hungry rat had at them.

"Why weren't you at that game club? Delilah called from the front office, asked if you'd come home sick or something." I don't even bother correcting Delia's name. Corny's words come too fast. Thankfully mine do too, although I'm not sure where they come from.

"I went to the library instead," I lie.

I feel her staring at me, so I add, "I had a lot of homework." I meet her stare, but she doesn't look satisfied.

"Is that so?"

I nod and roll my eyes. "Yes, that's so."

"Funny. 'Cause I called the library."

I hear the sound of a record scratch in my head. How could I be so stupid? Why didn't I think that my grandmother would call the school looking for me, especially if Delia called, worried. For a minute my mouth seems like it's moving without words, then something seems to take over. "*Oh.* You must have called the school library." I shoot her a look that says *silly old lady*. "I went to the regular library. The *public* one."

Her face goes blank. I start to feel like I'm winning. I walk up the steps to the porch and lean down to scratch Ferrill under the chin. He lets out a big sigh and drops his head to the floor.

"Well, it's just down the street from school. I made it back in time for the late bus, didn't I?" I feel lighter again. This is working. I open the screen door and walk inside, holding it open for Oomlot to follow. Queso runs in front of him and enters first.

Corny starts inside too, not ready to drop it. "I never gave you permission to leave school grounds," she says, practically through her teeth.

"I know, and I'm sorry." I stick my bottom lip out for effect. "I just didn't figure anyone would really miss me—"

"Why didn't you tell your friends? Your best friend?"

"Well, I mean, we just—I just needed my space." A little part

200

of me wonders why I didn't start with this. This is something Corny would probably understand. And it's pretty true—well, almost. But it's too late to undo all the other lies.

"Well, you're grounded," she says. "You won't be going to that girl's sleepover." She's talking about Erin Monroe's party, which is at the end of next week.

I suck in a breath. I feel slapped. My chest gets tight and the back of my eyes start to ache. "What about the dance?"

She looks at me and softens just a little. "I said the sleepover, didn't I?" I am slightly relieved. But only slightly. "Now," she continues, "call Delilah right away. Just let her know you're safe."

Talking to The Great Betrayer is the last thing I want to do. I start to argue, but Corny cuts me off and says, "I told her you'd call." So I know now I have to.

"It's me."

"Hey! What happened? Why didn't you come to the club?" Delia sounds genuinely happy to hear from me.

I say nothing. It's one of those moments where's there too many words to say, and any one of those words might mess up the nicely packed vacuum-sealed Space Bags in my brain.

"Olivia? Hey, are you mad at me or something?"

I take a breath and blurt out, "You told Brynne about my mom, didn't you?" It barely sounds like a question, and I barely want to know the answer. There's one little shred of hope that this is just a lie that Brynne made up, or maybe some stupid misunderstanding—the kind that happens in sitcoms on TV. "In fact, you told all our friends, didn't you?"

"Olivia, our friends know you don't live with your mom— that's not a secret."

"But the fact that she went crazy and just took off is!"

"Olivia, all I did is stop rumors! And it's not like I broadcast it to the whole school, Liv. I just told our friends. They were hearing all sorts of weird things. People were saying that you were a juvenile delinquent and you were arrested in a Greyhound station! Some people were trying to say you were taken from your mom because she kept you locked in a room!"

"So then once you told them—once you all became experts about my life—you decided you'd get on speakerphone and tell Brynne all my business!"

Now she's saying nothing. Not a good sign.

"I can't believe this," I say. "All of my friends—you, Mandy, Phoebe, even *Joey*—have been hiding the truth from me for how long? Like, more than a month! What did you have, a secret pact not to tell me what was going on?"

"I'm really sorry! I thought it would help. It was right after the ketchup thing and I was just trying to get Brynne to lay off! Remember? I was trying to help you and I didn't want to do it alone, that's all."

"Trying to *help* me?" I yell, and let out a low, sarcastic laugh. "How?"

"I was kind of hoping she could relate. Remember, I used to be friends with her. I know how craz—I mean, unstable—*her* mom is. I thought if she knew what you were going through, she'd be decent enough to stop torturing you and the rest of us. But obviously, she's not!"

"So you wanted her to feel sorry for me? Of all people, Delia, I thought I could trust *you*! You know who's stupid? *Me!*"

"Olivia," she pleads. "Honestly? You're not being fair."

I start to hang up, then yank the phone back to my ear. "And you know what? You're right about something. Brynne *can* relate."

And then I slam down the old phone, thankful for the satisfying clang that rings out for mercy when I do. And a second later, when it rings, I pick the phone right back up and get to make that clang again.

And then I call Brynne.

I tell her about how Delia nearly caused my grandmother to have a heart attack. I tell her about how I called Delia—I even make my voice all high-pitched and nasally when I imitate Delia asking me if I'm mad at her, and Brynne laughs like I knew she would, and says, "*Oh. Em. Gee.*"

And then I tell her I'm grounded this weekend, and that I can't go to Erin's party next weekend.

And she says something that changes everything. She says, "Well, then, I won't go either."

All night, I think about the Fall Ball. I think I should probably give Max his answer soon. I'm thinking maybe it should be a yes. Maybe I was wrong about Caleb after all. I mean, he's got a bunch of prettier, more naturally likable girls helping him out on his campaign—and maybe they all feel the way I do around him. You know, special.

And—news flash!—prayers aren't always answered. You think I'd know that by now.

On Tuesday, Brynne and I sit alone at our own lunch table, and I make myself look like I'm having a grand old time. Even if Peyton Randall is sitting in my old seat next to Delia. And even if Joey is acting like Gallant, instead of Goofus, from *Highlights* magazine, and is doing polite little Gallant things like *eating chicken salad*! With his lips *closed*! And even if Erin Monroe is laughing about something Joey said, and Phoebe is joining in like she's been doing *this laughing thing* her entire life! And even if CALEB AUSTIN is stopping at the table and saying something to Mandy, who nods and smiles like she's some regular, ordinary person who always does things like smiling and nodding and not just being the HUBERT C. FROST MIDDLE SCHOOL *SHARPIE QUEEN*!!!

I take a deep breath. That's all right. It doesn't matter. I just picture myself washing my hair, and when that doesn't work, I move on to flossing. When that doesn't work, I give up. Alpha dogs don't floss anyway.

39.

The Other End of the Leash

WE HAVE A sub in English on Wednesday, so it's basically every man for himself. The sub has turned on his iPod and tuned the class—and its spirited desk-hopping contest—out. But Max is unusually quiet.

I tap him on the shoulder. "Max?"

He turns his head around slowly.

"Hi," I say.

"Hi?"

"How you doing?" I ask, buying time. I still feel nervous about saying yes. Caleb will just miss out. Like I've said before, stupid Caleb.

Max ignores the question and turns his head away from me.

"Um, hey," I say. "About the dance—"

"Oh. It's okay," he says.

Huh?

"It's okay. Don't worry about it. You don't have to go with me." He seems a little annoyed.

"But—I—"

"I'm not stupid, you know," he says. "If someone doesn't say yes, then I can figure out it's a no."

"But that's not what—"

"I'm going with Izzy Van Norton," he says—meaning the half-pretzel girl—and turns around, leaving me feeling completely like a lost puppy.

It's Friday, and I've successfully avoided Delia, Mandy, Phoebe, and Joey all week. I am getting my backpack out of my locker when something hits the back of my head. People around me giggle, and I turn and see Peyton Randall walking away. "Delia wanted me to give you this," she says, in a disgusted voice. There's a small triangle-shaped note on the floor. One kid accidentally steps on it, oblivious. I reel it in with my foot before it gets crushed again.

My name, which Delia wrote in a triangular pattern to match the shape of the note, now bears a gray sneaker mark. I dust it off and hear, "What's that?"

It's Brynne. She's got her backpack over her shoulder and a slight sneer on her face, like she's hungry for something to make fun of. I'm glad it's not me, and I stuff the note into my pocket and say, "Just trash."

On the bus, after Brynne gets off at her stop, I read the note.

Dear Olivia:
Will you please CALL ME? I'm sorry!
Delia

Then I crumple it up noisily in case anyone's watching. When I'm sure no one is, I stuff it into the side pocket of my backpack. I feel only slightly bad about the fact that I'm not going to call Delia—not just now. She needs to learn a little lesson about betrayal.

Later that night, my dad calls. It's obvious Corny called him earlier, and I can just imagine how *that* went.

Corny: She's acting so weird! I think it's happening! She's starting to crack!

Dad: But it's so early. She's barely through puberty!

Corny: I know, it's a shame. A darn shame.

My dad asks if everything is okay, but in that careful way—with tight words that sound like they could easily fall to the ground and shatter.

I try to act casual. "Everything's fine, Dad." But I just prove that it's possible to *talk* out of tune, which sounds the opposite of casual.

"Are you sure? I can come up for a quick visit if you need me."

I make myself breathe. "I'm really busy with school and stuff."

"Oh."

He sounds a little hurt, so I add, "It's just been stressful with the campaign."

"No, I understand," he tells me. "I'd vote for Mandy if I could."

"Oh, great. Thanks," I say. It makes me sad to hear him say it, especially because I'm not so sure I would say the same.

Common Traits

"CAN I ASK you a question?" I bring myself to say to Brynne. It's Monday, after school, and we are at my house, sitting at the kitchen table, being stalked by Oomlot and Queso since we are making peanut butter and sugar sandwiches. I'm only slightly ashamed that I don't have real Nutter Butters to offer.

"You just did," she says. But then she flashes a smile. "What's your question?"

I hesitate. I almost don't want to go down this route with the M-word. I think about chickening out and asking her about her shampoo or her favorite character on *Full House*, now that she's seen a marathon with me over the past weekend and seemed to really like it.

"Um, Ryan Stoles," she says.

"Huh?"

"My secret crush." She laughs. "Isn't that what you were going to ask?"

I laugh. "Well, no, but *really*?" I think about Ryan, Caleb's co–campaign manager. He's sort of wiry and boyish. If you put a thick pair of glasses of him he would be a Classic Geek. But then I think about Danny and I realize Brynne has a definite type.

"A little, I guess," she says. "Your turn. Let me guess. Caleb Austin."

An electric bolt of panic shoots through me. I stammer, "I don't . . . I mean . . . he's . . . I mean—"

She laughs loudly. "It's okay, Olivia. Seriously. He's a flirt. Everyone kind of likes him."

I smile with embarrassment.

"Anyway, sorry." She laughs. "What did you really want to ask me?"

Even though it's a lot more fun to talk about Caleb, I take a breath and ask the question that's been on my mind a lot lately. "When you found out about—about, you know, my *mom*"—I swallow—"did you tell anyone?"

Her smile fades. "Sometimes I wanted to. But, no."

"Thank you," I finally breathe.

"I mean, I wouldn't want anyone knowing too much about *my* mom. Plus," she says, "what could I say about your mom that people couldn't say about mine?"

"Yours doesn't sound too bad, though. At least she still—" I start. I can't believe I'm having this discussion with anyone, let alone Brynne. Moncherie would be *so* jealous. "She still lives with you."

She laughs. "Oh, lucky, lucky me. She totally babies my brother and treats me like a felon."

"Is it really that bad?" I ask, beginning to feel a little sorry for her.

"When she takes her medicine, no. I mean, it's not horrible. But then after she takes it for a while, she starts feeling normal, so she goes off the pills and then everything sucks all over again." Her eyes soften. "So, is your mom like, in like—sorry, I don't know what to call them—one of those loony bin places?"

"Yeah," I admit.

"Oh. That's got to be weird. But now do you believe me that my mom is crazy?" She starts to smile.

"Okay, I do."

I wonder how she feels about carrying around her own little personal crazy gene. If she worries about it rising up and taking over too—if it's not starting to already. I imagine us old and graying together, in some white-walled institution somewhere, weaving brightly colored pot holders even though neither one of us is allowed near kitchen knives or a hot stove.

"You know what?" she says. "You're a way better BFF than Carolyn ever was."

BFF. The letters swell in my head, both thrilling me and making me want to run at the same time. All I can choke out is, "Really?"

"Yeah. I can't really talk to her about this stuff. You know, the deepest conversation I ever had with her was about hair products." Then she stops abruptly. I notice she is staring at my hair. "I mean, sure, sometimes there's a *need* to talk about hair products—" She sees me watching her, gives me an apologetic smile, and continues. "But not like every single second, you know what I mean?"

"Yeah," I say, embarrassed. Ugh. My hair. I can change my posture, my walk, my clothes, even intensify the color of my eyes, but I seem to be stuck with this clownlike hair. I could use all the Georgie Girl in the world, and *still*. I decide to change the subject. I look over at her flattened PB&S sandwich. "Sorry I don't have anything better to eat. Unless you like lentils."

"Oh, that's okay," she says. She takes another bite and smiles. "I think my EpiPen's in my backpack, so it's fine."

"EpiPen?" I ask.

"Oh, that's just a shot I have to give myself. Peanut allergies."

Peanut allergies. I've heard all about peanut allergies. In fourth grade, I watched as Kipper Moore's face swelled to the size of a watermelon after he picked up an empty dry-roasted peanut wrapper during lunch duty.

I look at her. She's waiting for a reaction. So I say, "You're joking, right?"

"See?" She laughs. "I'm *so* not funny anymore! People used to think I was funny, and now they don't. They act like they don't even like me!"

That's because they've been trained not to. I feel a little jolt of guilt, but I brush it off and make myself laugh instead. "You're still funny," I say.

"No, I'm not." She pinches off another piece of her sandwich and flattens it between her fingers. She lifts her gaze to me for a second, before lowering it again. Her voice gets kind of wobbly— just a little—and she asks, "Will you still be my friend even if no one else thinks I'm funny anymore?"

For a second, I forget to breathe. "Sure," I finally say.

She looks up and smirks. "See what I mean? I was totally *kidding!*"

"Oh," I say, reddening again. She laughs, and then I do too. And she seems relieved. And I wonder, is this what you find when you socially dissect a popular girl? When you get to the center, are they really this insecure?

211

New Pets

ALL WEEK LONG, Brynne and I have been pretty inseparable. We eat lunch together, we walk to our classes together, we hang out together at my house after school. She's all I talked about this week with Moncherie—and guess what? I got to talk about Brynne's mother instead of finding excuses not to talk about mine. *Score.*

It's Friday night, the night of Erin Monroe's party, and Brynne has stayed for dinner. Corny makes stewed beef, which she unfortunately declares "the perfect dog/man meal," but Brynne doesn't seem as revolted as I would have expected.

"What time will your mother be picking you up?" Corny asks.

Brynne dismisses herself to call her mom as I help Corny fill the dog bowls. When Brynne comes back, she says, "My mom says I can spend the night if it's okay with you."

Brynne Shawnson. Spending the night. Here. My anxiety level starts to rise. What if she sees that I have a whole drawer *full* of granny panties? What *then*? Or what if I talk in my sleep and reveal *all*? Assuming I can even sleep!

"Oh, well, then," Corny says, and looks over at me, eyebrows raised. "Liv? How's your room? Clean?"

"It's—" I start to answer but find myself grasping for words. "It's fine. We were up there earlier."

"Yeah, and it's much cleaner than my room," Brynne says. She starts to smile, but it falls away as she looks between Corny and me. "I'm—I'm sorry. You know what? You probably have plans. I should probably just have my mom pick me up. We haven't really—" She looks at me, slightly panicked. "We haven't really been friends long enough for me to just invite myself to spend the night. I'm sorry."

Corny and I stand there. My body is frozen but my mind is racing. My heart feels like it's gotten trapped in one of my lungs or something. Then Brynne gives a humble smile and turns back down the hall toward the phone.

"No!" I shout. She turns around, eyes wide. "No, don't," I continue. "You can spend the night here, can't she, Grandma?"

Corny blinks and relaxes. "Well, of course. You're welcome to stay, um, B— Brah—"

While Brynne's head is turned toward Corny, I stand where Corny can see me and begin to silently shape Brynne's name with my mouth in an exaggerated, slow-motion movement. It's like doing the breaststroke with lips.

"—Brynne!" Corny says. Then she smiles in that way that makes me want to hug her, despite her grayish teeth.

"You sure?" Brynne asks.

"Positive," I say. "We insist."

She looks at me with a little doubt.

So I finally say it.

"Come on, we're BFFs now, aren't we?"

And then she breaks into a big smile and says, "That we are."

213

Obedience

IT'S SATURDAY NIGHT. Nine p.m. Brynne is still here.

And there are four reasons why.

The first is that I have glossy hair.

Turns out Brynne has a big secret—that she actually looks a little like a pretty-faced version of that comedian Carrot Top when she's not using *product*. That's what she calls it. Not *a* product. Not *the* product. Just *product*. And I guess it really doesn't matter, because *I* call it sweet, sweet magic. Last night, after dinner, she handed me this tube of stuff and told me her hair would look exactly like mine if she didn't use it. And when I smeared some over my frizz poof, my hair practically became silk. It's a pretty big deal—I mean, it's like my hair was a disease and *product* was the cure. Brynne even told me I looked a little like Jessica Alba, so I've been sneaking peeks in the mirror to see if she is right.

The second reason is that last night, when we went up to bed, she said, "I guess I need to borrow something to sleep in," which nearly sent me into a panic, because what on earth do I have that she would actually wear? I apologetically handed her some sweatpants (my favorites) and a "Vote for Pedro" T-shirt. She went to change in the bathroom, and came back, hair in a lumpy ponytail, face scrubbed of all its makeup, swimming in my sweats. And at that point she looked like she could be a *real* friend of mine, not just an artificially induced one.

The third reason is, after she sat down on the foam pad that's served as Delia's bed many times before, she said, "I've got a surprise for you." Then she reached into her bag and pulled out a little black case, which she unzipped to reveal Travel Scrabble. *Travel Scrabble!*

"So you really *do* like board games?" I asked.

She looked up at me and smirked and said, "Yeah, actually. I really do." Then she broke into a smile. A really nice one. "I'm a geek. Scrabble's one of my favorites. I've just been in the closet for like, the last three years."

And she won with the word *toxic.*

And the fourth reason she's here, is that today, when we went with Corny to the Food Lion, my grandmother let us hang out at the coffee shop in the strip mall near the store. And when we were sitting there sucking down our vanilla cream caffe lattes, Carolyn and Tamberlin walked in. For a few minutes we went unnoticed—just two sloppy thirteen-year-olds in flip-flops and rolled-up sweatpants. (Okay, *one* with glossy hair!) But then it happened—the second glance. "Oh. My. God. Is that Brynne?" Tamberlin asked. And then Carolyn said, "It's either her or her homeless cousin." Then they both laughed. Brynne looked down into her shake and stirred her straw around. They got their mochas, and as they walked toward the door, one of them said, just loud enough for us to hear, "God, she's really let herself go."

"Bet Danny's glad he's not going to the dance with *that*," the other one said.

I looked over at Brynne—with her head low, and her naked face glowing red, and her gem-blue eyes starting to turn muddy— and cringed to think how I would have rewarded their behavior just a couple of weeks ago.

And then I heard myself say, "You know, I think you should stay over again tonight."

So now, at nine o'clock on Saturday night, while everyone else is at the Fall Ball, Brynne and I are here. She contemplates the dance from a reclined position on the floor, and snaps photos of Oomlot with her cell phone. I eat plain M&M's one at a time, eyes shut, trying to guess which color is in my mouth. Oomlot is sitting at attention, hoping I'll be a truly awful owner and give him an M&M, which I won't because they're poison for dogs.

"I don't even care about it anymore. I'm glad I'm not there tonight. Is that weird?"

"I don't know. Maybe," I say. I crunch. *Green?*

"Well, Olivia, if you wanted to go, why didn't you go with Max Marshall? He's not bad."

"I know. I waited too long, I guess."

She looks over at me. "I mean he's a lot hotter than Danny even." I don't tell her that most of the school is, except for maybe Joey. It's at this moment that I truly start to believe the old saying that love can be pretty blind. She crunches into an M&M without even trying to close her eyes and guess the color.

"Want the truth?" I ask.

She looks up at me, her eyes wide.

I take a small handful of M&M's. "I was kind of holding out for Caleb."

"I thought so!" She laughs.

"Well, he kept trying to ask me something," I say in my defense.

"Oh, he does that with everyone. He just wanted to ask if you could change one thing about the school, what it would be. It's part of his campaign strategy. You know, people feel like they're being listened to."

Oh. Crap. I'm such. A sucker.

She continues. "You know he's there tonight with Audrey Sharif?"

Audrey Sharif. Tall, pretty. A former friend of Brynne's, but more recently, a Caleb Austin campaigner. It figures.

"Don't worry; it was a total last minute thing. I kind of *do* think he likes you, though."

"Yeah, that's *likely*." I close my eyes and bite an M&M in half. I chew and guess red. I open my eyes. Wrong again. Brown.

Brynne gets up on her elbow. "Honestly, Olivia. Haven't you seen yourself lately? But you know what? Even if he was madly in love with you or something, he would have had to be stupid to ask you to Fall Ball."

"What do you mean?"

"Um, *hello*? Elections, maybe? He's Mandy's main competition. You were Mandy's campaign manager. Remember? Don't you think that would have been really weird? Haven't you ever heard of 'conflict of interest'?"

Oh. Right. All that waiting and hoping, and there it was, plain as day. So maybe she's right. Maybe he *does* like me! I feel a twinge of appreciation for my new friend for pointing that out.

She lies back down with a huge sigh. "Oh, God. Why'd I bring up elections?" she whines. "No one's going to vote for me." She takes a picture of herself and then frowns at the image.

"Sure they will," I say. I want to be nice back. I close my eyes and take another M&M.

"*Seriously*, Olivia," she says.

"I *am* serious," I lie. I crunch a couple of times and then stick out my tongue. "What color? Blue?"

"Gross," she says, and twists up her face. "No. Yellow." Then she snaps a picture of me.

"No more pictures," I say. "You've been doing that all day."

"Just one more of us."

"Last one," I say. I stick my face next to hers, and we mug for the camera and laugh like we've always been best friends. Oomlot gives up on begging for the candy, sighs, and lowers himself to the floor. Bella—a.k.a. the Dog Formerly Obsessed With Wood—rolls over onto her back and puts her paws in the air. I pat her belly.

Then Brynne yawns and stretches out on the floor, accidentally exposing her belly button. Like Bella, she's gotten so trusting. Here I am, in a room with two of my training success stories. What does it matter if one of them is human? Even if it didn't turn out exactly as planned, it was for a good cause, wasn't it?

Despite the fact that I'm starting to feel a little sick to my stomach, I cram a handful of M&M's into my mouth. I've given up—all the colors taste exactly the same, just like they always have.

"Maybe I should drop out," she says.

"Nah, don't do that," I say, through my full mouth, although I start to wonder if maybe it is a good idea. I like her better this way. A little dorky. A little Marcie-like. Kind of like my old friends. I think of them, and for a second I feel their absence before I remind myself of Delia's betrayal, and push it all away. "Anyway, you can't. You need that social studies credit."

"You'll vote for me, won't you?"

"Of course," I say, swallowing. It's just one vote. One vote Mandy doesn't even need.

The Loyal Companion

ON MONDAY MORNING, as I pass through the halls on my way to first period, I notice former Mandy-harasser Garrett "Glass Eye" Pearson taping up posters for Mandy's campaign. Peyton Randall, a.k.a. My Replacement, walks behind him, holding a massive bag of Jolly Ranchers.

Then Corbin Moon's voice booms behind me. "Hey, G.E., you need some more tape?" He rolls a gigantic spool of tape down the hall toward Garrett, and I almost trip trying to stay out of its way.

I head down the hall, avoiding the traffic jam of people near Mandy's locker. The mostly blank wall is decorated with a few Dawn Lane posters (she's made them as long green strips, like street signs; "Dawn Ln" is shown intersecting with "Presidential Blvd"). I notice something sticking to my shoe—it's an old yellow "Vote for B.S." Post-it. I peel it off and throw it away so Brynne won't see it.

I go early to first period just to try and escape the halls— to escape any sign of the election. Ms. Flamsteed is writing the definition of mechanical energy on the whiteboard, which is already making me sleepy. She puts the marker down and turns around to the classroom—vacant, except for me, in my front row seat.

"Oh! Olivia," she says, surprised. "You're early."

And then Brynne walks into the room. She's dressed in the same sweats she was in all weekend, and her hair is wet and pulled into a ponytail. It looks just plain brown, like a bag when it's wet, nothing like its usual radiant auburn. I start to wonder if she gave me her only tube of *product*. It also doesn't seem like she's bothered with makeup since she washed it off at my house Friday night. Without it she's still pretty, just a little less colorful.

"Hi!" I say, surprised.

"Hey!" She smiles a little, then looks around and slips into the seat next to me.

"Oh, Brynne, dear—not there. Your seat will be in the back row, third desk over."

She looks pained. "It's just that—Ms. Flamsteed? I don't know if Mrs. Vander-Pecker told you, but I can't sit back there. I'm nearsighted."

Ms. Flamsteed exhales loudly. "Well, no, she didn't, but I guess you can stay there if you need to. As long as Maria doesn't mind moving."

My mouth drops. "Are you in this class now?"

"Yep," she whispers, smiling sneakily.

"But *how*?"

"Never underestimate the power of the parent," Brynne says quietly. "I told my mom I was going through something and felt like I needed to change classes to get away from the usual people. It's *kind of* true."

"So they just switched you? Just like that?"

She stifles a laugh with her hand. "Trial basis, but yep."

"Wow," I say. And I am kind of excited. Because it'll be fun to have someone to laugh with whenever we have to watch a stupid science video, like last week's *Let's Get Electric!* And it'll be nice to have an actual lab partner again, and not have to pair up with Ms. Flamsteed, which happened last week when we had to swab our filthy, bacteria-laden mouths and watch the germs swim around, confused and out of place, under the microscope. I mean, I don't need science to tell me how gross I am—I'm starting to feel that way again every time I set foot in this building. It's like when I gave up my friends, I gave up the chance to be socially acceptable altogether. And this, despite the fact that I now have socially acceptable—even brilliant and glossy—hair.

Which is further proven when Maria comes in and acts sincerely thrilled to move four seats back from me and next to Dawn Lane.

I'm on my way to Spanish. In the hallway, Erin Monroe acts very inconvenienced but does her civic duty and tells me my shoe's untied.

I make a "traffic violation"—as it's called at Hubert C. Frost—and stop to tie it. Someone runs right into me, like they were following too closely. I tumble forward onto the dirty gray tile. Even though I'm supremely mortified, I kind of hope to look up and see Caleb's face, just for a taste of the old thrill, as pathetic as that sounds. Instead I see Brynne's.

"Sorry, Liv," she says, helping me up.

"I thought you were going to fifth period."

"I am." She smiles. "Mr. Chang for Spanish."

"But that's my class," I say, stupidly.

"Like I said, never underestimate the power of a parent."

On our way to class, we pass by her "Win With Brynne" posters, which are worn and torn in places. She now looks completely unrecognizable from the angelic picture of her former preplan self, but it doesn't seem to bother her.

"Don't you want to put up some new posters?" I ask, because the whole thing seems so sad. It's like when I was little and someone was building a house on the land next to us, and I guess they ran out of money or lost interest, because it never got finished. It just kept standing there untouched, like a skeleton of a dream, and eventually became what my dad called "dry rot."

"Nah," she says. "I don't really care about the election anymore, but it's the only thing keeping me from failing Social Studies and spending another year in this hellhole."

"I know," I say. "But still. We could make some new ones after school." To be honest, I don't want her to give up. Maybe because that would confirm to me that I've pretty much ruined her life. And am probably an evil person.

"No, seriously, Olivia," she says, sounding a little upset. "Despite what everyone thinks, I'm not some ditz. Look around. I don't have a prayer. Dawn Lane will get more votes than I will."

She doesn't get to sit next to me in Mr. Chang's class, but she does manage to pass a note up to me. The kid behind me kicks me in the anklebone to make me turn around, and then shoves the square of paper into my palm so hard it hurts.

I try to unfold it quietly, but I'm not quiet enough, because the girl next to me shoots me an annoyed look. The note says,

Don't forget to wait for me after class!!!!!

I slowly turn around and give Brynne a smile that says I think she's crazy—*good* crazy, not seriously mentally ill. *Although.* She smiles back and her face softens, like she's a little relieved.

But *I'm* not, I realize after I turn back around and it hits me. I think about Bella, and how when some dogs start to feel insecure, they begin to fixate on something. In Bella's case it was wood; in Brynne's case, well, I'm starting to think that it's me.

It's not just any Monday. It's Worm Day.

I know that sounds gross, but I love Worm Day. It's the one day of the month that the dogs get their heartworm medicine, which comes in meaty little chews. The dogs are crazy about these chews—I'm talking *nuts.* Worm Day is when the dogs pull out their best tricks—rolling over on command, turning in a circle, shaking hands, that kind of thing. I'm trying to teach Queso to high-five me (with no luck) when the phone rings. It's Moncherie.

"I can't do our session this week," she tells me. It's good timing because I've just received another Spokane-postmarked letter, and I know how much she loves to interrogate me about them. I file it away, under my mattress, unopened, with the others. "Something came up, but I'll call as soon as I can to reschedule."

She sounds a little excited.

I wonder if she's got a date or something. And I wonder if maybe she used the training I told her about to get that date. And then I wonder if she knows what she's getting into.

44.

Separation Anxiety

I WALK INTO the school lobby Tuesday morning and try to squeeze past a crowd. I slide sideways, sucking in my gut, tolerating elbows and shoulders digging into my ribs, and knees bumping into my shins. I stand on my tiptoes to see what's in the center of the crowd.

It's a table, full of campaign buttons that just say, really big, MANDY! Behind the table are the four of them—Mandy, beaming and looking almost glamorous with her black lips, like some oddly attractive work of art; Delia, with her caramel complexion practically glowing; Phoebe, looking polished and professional, with naked, perfect teeth that you can see really well because she is *actually smiling*; and Joey, all dressed up, with a belt and even a hint of a waistline. Hands are reaching over other hands to grab the buttons. I feel pressure at my back and I'm swooped forward. I try to turn around and swim out of the crowd, like you're supposed to do when you get sucked into a riptide, but the crowd doesn't yield. Someone behind me says, "I'm just trying to get to English. Are you trying to make life difficult?" I crane my neck.

It's Caleb. He's smiling at me. I'm so flustered that I say something dazzling like "No!" I'm just *that* smart.

But the moment is gone because the crowd pushes forward again and forces me closer to the table. My arms and legs are struggling against the force. And then I hear Delia's voice.

"Olivia?" For a second, our eyes lock, and I can't remember why I'm mad. All I feel is panic and sorrow and the hollowness of missing someone pretty badly. Even if that someone betrayed you. The crowd squeezes forward again, spitting me out sideways, where I beach and catch my breath.

But my head is still swimming.

Is it possible to forgive someone who betrayed you even when it still hurts? And if it is, *how?*

In the hallway I trip over my own ankle. In Algebra I pick at my cuticles and bleed so much that I start to wonder if there's an artery in my thumb. In History I find myself glancing over at the back of Joey's head so often that I get a crick in my neck. For the first time ever, I'm dying to know what's going on in that round little head of his.

I still don't know exactly how you forgive someone, but I think I'm ready to try. Maybe I can start with Joey. I decide that I'll kick him in the butt on our way out of class. That's how guys make up after fights—some type of casual violence. I've seen it myself. Last week, Blake Edward and Nissen Gambrill got in some fight about a basketball foul. A couple of days later, Blake sneaked up on Nissen and put him in a headlock. They've been inseparable since. And wedgies. Those also work. But I decide a nice swift, but gentle, kick to the left cheek should do it this time.

But I never get the chance. I try to follow him, but the minute we get out the door, I run smack into her. Brynne.

"Hi," she says. She's waiting for me. "Do you need to go to your locker first or you want to go straight to lunch?"

It's a little weird how things have changed. Okay, a *lot* weird.

I sit beside her on the bus, like I always do now. The popular kids that she used to hang out with in the front of the bus are still there—and still popular—but we've managed to secure our own little spot in the backseat. It's like we've been banished. Being her friend is not at all like I imagined.

I think about all the training we'd done, and I so wish I could rewind everything. I miss Delia with an almost physical pain. I want to cry—in a good way!—when I see Phoebe, for Pete's sake! I almost stopped in the hall and hugged Mandy today, and would have French-kissed Joey if I could just have him back as my friend. I miss them all so much. As mad as I've been, I *know* them. Delia did something stupid, but it's only because she was trying to protect me from something worse. They all were.

Brynne starts. "Did you see what your ex-best-friend did with her hair?" She's referring to Delia's new updo, her hair swirled up and away from her face. Knowing Delia, it probably took hours to put it up and days trying to overcome her insecurities to do it in the first place. Just thinking about her little familiar quirks makes it hard to breathe. "I think I liked her hair better down, like when she had pizza-face."

"You're being kind of mean," I say quietly.

"Sor-*ry*," she says. "I thought you didn't like her anymore."

"I just miss her," I confess. It's got to be the understatement of the year.

She turns to look out the window, and I know I've upset her. "I'm sorry," I say. "It's just that—I thought she was a good friend, you know? And *fun*—they all were."

"So I guess 'good friends' tell everyone all your secrets now?"

"I mean, sure, part of me wants to throttle her, but you know Delia—you *know* she thought she was helping. You used to be best friends with her too. You know how sweet she really is."

"*Sweet*? Gag," Brynne says. "I'd still be mad if I were you."

"Yeah, but still," I say. "I was always afraid that no one would like me if they knew the truth about what a freak I am—you know, a weird mom, therapy, that kind of thing. But you know everything about me now, and you still like me. And it turns out they've *all* known that stuff about me for a while, and it never bothered any of them."

"What. A. Revelation," she says flatly, and crosses her arms over her chest. The bus squeals to a stop. Her stop. She gets up and pulls her backpack on. "I'll call you later," she grumbles. Then she gets off the bus behind Carolyn and Tamberlin. The bus pulls away, but I turn to watch them. Carolyn and Tamberlin walk together, talking with their hands and laughing with their whole bodies. Brynne walks about twenty feet behind them, with her face toward the ground.

Brynne's already called by the time I get home. Corny tells me. I sigh. I don't really want to call her back after the way she acted on the bus. As it turns out I don't have to, because a little while later she calls again.

"I wasn't sure your grandma would remember to tell you I called," she says.

"Oh, she did." I don't tell her that Corny told me *Brianna* called. Or that I wasn't sure I should call her back at all.

"Anyway, have you written a love letter to Delia yet?"

"You think that would work?" I say, only half-kidding.

"I can't believe you. Someone screws you over like that and you still want to be friends?"

"But we were *best* friends," I say.

"So? And now *we're* best friends. You don't need her."

"I just really do miss Delia. And Mandy and Phoebe and even Joey!"

"Phoebe," she says. "What a joke. That whole thing is just ridiculous."

"What whole thing?" I ask.

"That thing with Brant. I know it was mean, but I really didn't think it would work out."

"Brynne, what are you talking about?"

She sighs. "I totally dared him to do it. To ask her to the Fall Ball. Then he was supposed to dump her the night before. I told him I'd dump Danny and go with him if he did." She makes a sound like *ugh*. "Oh yeah, like *that* worked out."

I'm surprised at how much something like this can hurt, even when it's not done to you. "Why would you do that?"

"I don't know. I guess it was kind of fun to see how far he'd go." She sighs again. "What an idiot I am. I never thought he'd like, totally go for her." She mimics Brant in a girly, high-pitched voice: "*Oooh, she's just so exotic. She's so beautiful!*"

Exotic! *Exotic?* I mean, *wow.* "So he really *does* like her?"

"Well, they went to the dance together, didn't they? And that part? Was no joke."

I'm in shock at how everything—and I mean *everything*—seems to be turned on its head.

Right now, the pressure inside my chest is rising. Brynne's acting sort of crazy—and is it any wonder? I'm starting to think her crazy gene has already kicked in. Maybe mine has too, and maybe I'm too whacked to even know it. "I have to go," I say.

But she starts apologizing again. "Olivia, I'm sorry. I really am. But it worked out for them both, didn't it? Don't be mad, okay?" Her voice cracks, which gets me. I *so* wish I didn't feel sorry for her. The flossing in my head is accomplishing nothing—yet again.

"Brynne—" I start. I take a deep breath. I miss my friends, and enough is enough. "I really do think we need to—"

"SHUT UP! I HEARD YOU!!!!" she screams. Her brother, I remember. "Crap. I gotta go. I guess I'll see you tomorrow. Like always."

But I'm ready for always to stop right now.

I pick up the phone and make a call.

"Dad?" I collapse in the front hall, near the old corded phone. The floor creaks. Oomlot's toenails click against the wood as he comes to find me. Then he lowers himself next to me, as if collapsing in the hall is the thing to do. I snuggle up next to him and run my hand down his back. I will be absolutely covered in yellow-white dog hair when—and if—I ever get up.

"Hey, Liv. What's up? I'm just sitting here with Grey watching *Law & Order*." Then he says in this really creepy high voice, "Me like the assistant D.A."

"What was *that*?"

"Oh, that was Grey," he says. "She's gotten to be a big fan."

Oh, dear God, no. He sounds like he's losing it a little, too. He laughs out loud at himself.

"Dad, you do know that's not normal, right?" I try to laugh with him but I end up in tears.

"Liv? You okay?"

Oomlot sniffs my face as I cry, like he's trying to figure me out. I bury my hand in his soft fur. "Is that offer still open? The one where you said I could move back home?"

He's quiet for a second. "Well, yeah. If that's really what you want. But honestly, it doesn't really sound like it is." Then he asks, with doubt in his voice, "*Is* it?"

Oomlot looks like he's finally given up trying to diagnose me (*Is she sick? Is she mad? Is she hurt? Will she feed me?*) and lays his head in my lap with a sigh. I console myself by rubbing his velvety ear, and he starts the loud breathing of dog purrs. I can't imagine leaving him.

Through the screen door, I see Corny outside. She's watering the lawn, and the dogs are playing chicken with the stream of water. Queso approaches the water, then scurries off to hide under the massive Ferrill. Tess runs back and forth as elegant as a deer. Bella lies on the grass, rolling from side to side, daring Corny to soak her. No, I can't imagine leaving any one of them— Corny *or* the dogs.

"What's going on, Liv?"

So I tell him what's gone on, minus, of course, the training part. Or the Mom part. I just tell him that Delia betrayed me, and I lost all my friends and started hanging out with Brynne. But now I want all my old friends back.

"Okay, well, I'm not a girl. And I'm not thirteen. But I don't get why you can't all be friends."

"Stop talking like a guidance counselor," I tell him. "Things like that just don't happen."

"Nothing happens if you don't make it happen. You think a house builds itself?"

"Now you're talking like a carpenter."

"So I should know what I'm talking about, right?" he says. "Don't you think you could talk to Delia and them, you know, straighten this whole thing out? Sounds like you've already forgiven them."

"I don't know if I have or not," I tell him.

The truth is, I'm not even sure I really know what forgiving *is*. It's not forgetting. It's not pretending it didn't happen. Clearly, I only know what it's *not*. I wish there was some sort of manual on forgiveness, like there is on dog training.

"Look, you don't have to tell me the exact details of this betrayal, or anything you don't want to," my dad says. I feel a rush of love for him. "But answer me this. Are you still mad at them?"

"Mad?" I ask. "No, not really. I know Delia was trying to look out for me. The rest of them—well, they just kind of went along with Delia's stupid plan."

"Sounds like she meant well."

"Yeah, she did. They all did," I say. "And it almost doesn't even matter anymore. I just want them back."

"Well, then," he says. "Sounds like you've forgiven her."

"Really? You think?"

231

I have to wonder, all this talk about forgiveness—it's a concept right up there with holy stuff and saints and angels and all those other things that seem so out of reach. But my dad makes it sound so simple.

"Hey, I've done my fair share of forgiving. I know these things. Just because you love someone doesn't make them perfect."

He's talking about my mother. The air seems to thicken around me. But thankfully, before I start to choke on it, he says, "Liv?"

Breathe in. "Yeah?"

Outside, the dogs bark and Corny's laugh rings out. Someone must have gotten drenched.

"You know . . ." I hear a smile in his voice. "I may have some bad news soon, okay?"

It makes me smile too, just a little bit. Bad news means his job in Valleyhead might be drying up. Bad news means he may be moving here soon. Bad news is good news. Which I guess is normal when your world is completely upside down.

45.

Hounded

IT'S WEDNESDAY. I decide I'm going to straighten everything out before lunch. Maybe my dad is actually right.

But that never happens. What happens is that on the way to lunch, Brynne takes my arm and rushes me down the corridor, around the corner to the dark, dead-end hall where the janitor keeps her stuff. She goes to a door, wiggles the handle, and pushes me in. Through another little door is a couch with a staticky TV tuned to a Spanish soap opera.

"Look. Janitor's closet. Our lunch spot from now on," she says, beaming.

My heart starts fluttering. I think about Delia and Mandy and Joey and even Phoebe, and how the only thing I want right now is my old spot at the lunch table with them. But all I can say is, "Why don't they lock the door?"

She frowns. "It's broken," she says, narrowing her eyes, and I find myself wondering if she had anything to do with that.

"Isn't this Mrs. Vittle's room? Where is she?"

"*Duh.* Lunch duty," Brynne says. She sighs. "Will you please just stop worrying so much? We'll have fun. No one's going to find us here." Which only serves to make me a little more worried.

Before I can tell her that I haven't brought lunch today, she opens her backpack and lays a couple of packages on the crate used as a makeshift coffee table: peanut butter crackers, a tube of Pringles, a crushed bag of Fritos, and some packets of fruit chews. "Have whatever you want, but I brought these especially for you." She holds up a package of M&M's.

There's something so incredibly sad about it all—the sense of desperation under all those snacks laid out on the table, the tiny room—that keeps me from just standing up and walking away. So I grab some M&M's and let her turn up the volume on the TV, and we both watch like we completely understand Spanish. But all I'm really understanding is that everything feels broken and I don't know how to piece it back together.

Later, Corny and I go to see Kisses. I have grand plans to take her out into the backyard today; we're *that* close. But when I set the stones out on the lawn, she stops at the first one—two stones back from where we left off. The more I try to coax her out, the less she seems willing. By the end of the session, she's retreated to the patio. It's hard not to feel lame.

On the way home, Corny tells me we'll try again soon. She talks about how we saved Bella from wood and that soon we'll save Loomis from bikes, and maybe even sooner we'll save Kisses from those terrible blades of grass.

I guess I don't look too convinced.

"Look, Olivia, I know it's frustrating. Sometimes, with dogs like Kisses, you take one step forward and two steps back."

Which pretty much explains everything happening in my life now. Every single little thing.

La Vida del Perro

IT'S ONLY BEEN about eight weeks since I hatched my evil plan, and so much has changed. It's clear who the alpha dogs are. First of all, now everyone is going around with marker on their lips. Our old lunch table is full of people like Morgan Askren and Erin Monroe and whoever else is lucky enough to get there first. Brant has a regular seat, and it's right next to Phoebe's. The Bored Game Club has swelled in membership, and now *two* teachers sit in the back of the room, one of whom, rumor has it, is a game specialist, hired *specifically* for that purpose. The biggest trend in school is having your own personal place-marker. Kids are bringing in everything from Barbie heads to bottle caps to house keys to mark their spot in Monopoly or Sorry! or whatever they're playing at the time. Having a place-marker means having a place in the popular crowd. The *popular* crowd. *My* old crowd.

It is time.

It's Friday, we're in our secret lunchroom, and I'm practically starting to *think* in Spanish. I guess even a couple of days of *La Vida Rica* will do that to you, especially if your brain is thirteen and still spongelike. I am on my third pack of M&M's when I finally get the nerve to bring it up.

"Brynne?"

"Hmmm?" I watch the chewing in her temples and feel a rush of overwhelming guilt. I've totally and utterly ruined the life of a regular eating, breathing, chewing, feeling human being.

"Don't you ever think we should, I don't know, get back out there?"

"Out *where*?"

"I mean, maybe make some friends?"

She shakes her head. "I like it here," she says. "Want another?" She tries to hand me another pack of M&M's.

"No thanks," I say quickly. She kind of shrugs and sits back again to stare at the TV, setting her foot up on the crate next to the buffet of snack food.

"I miss it," I say.

She holds a hand out, signaling me to be quiet. Her eyes get big and her chewing stops. "*Oh. Em. Gee*," she says through a full mouth. "No way he's going back to her!"

I take a breath and watch. Normally this would be enough to throw me off track—let's face it, these things do tend to suck you right in, language barrier or not. When it's clear that, yes, Ismael is begging Consuelo for her *corazón*, and that Consuelo isn't sure it's hers to give anymore, a tampon commercial comes on, and I say it again. Only more in the *telenovela* way.

"I just can't do this anymore."

Brynne crinkles up her forehead, trying to make it into a joke. "Well, I don't know what you have against Ismael and Consuelo, but we can find something else to watch."

"I mean I can't be your only friend, Brynne," I say, and try not to think about the fact that it was my own engineering that made it this way.

I'm kind of hoping that her pride will kick in, that she'll deny that I'm her only friend and tell me that she's been voted most popular since third grade—even if those elections were strongly discouraged by faculty and school administration and are in no way considered "official"—but instead she says, in a very breaking-heart way, "Why not?"

I guess she realizes how very *un*popular she sounds, because she says, "God, Olivia, what happened to me?" She laughs unhappily. "God, I sound like such a loser."

"But you're not, Brynne. You're the Most Popular Girl in School," I say, as if the title stays with you for life—like it does for U.S. presidents and alcoholics. My voice is so awkward, so useless.

"*Was*," she corrects me, stabbingly. "*Used* to be." She starts to cry. I'm a little worried Mrs. Vittle will hear us. Or worse, the hundreds of kids we go to school with, thus cementing our new-found reputation as pond scum.

"People used to want to be my friend," she continues, wetly. She snorts. "God, what happened?"

"I really don't know," I lie. Bald-faced.

"I'm such a joke. I wish I could just drop out of the elections. I don't even care if I get an F in Social Studies now."

The guilt is gnawing through my heart.

"Brynne—"

"And now you don't even want to be friends with me! *You!*"

It's tunneling through my spleen.

I swallow and say, "It's not that I don't want us to be friends. I like you, Brynne, I really do. I just don't want to be your *only* friend."

Now it's making its way up my esophagus.

She looks at me like I've just slapped her or something, and says, "I would love to have things back to normal. You keep asking me that, and *yes*, I would love that! But I don't know how to make that happen! I feel so . . . so worthless."

It's pushing its way up my throat. I'm afraid I'm about to get sick.

"Brynne," I say, swallowing hard to fight the rising lump of guilt and M&M's down. "There's something I have to tell you."

47.

Doghouse

"ON *PURPOSE*?!"

Brynne is so mad, her stringy neck cords are showing. Her hands are in fists at her sides, and her head nearly hits the low ceiling of the room. The fourth period bell has already rung, and we are officially taking our middle school careers into our own hands. Not only are we cutting class, but we have trespassed on off-limits school property—not even for the first time.

"Well, kind of," I have to admit. I try to keep my voice calm and reasonable, even a little apologetic. "We were tired of being dorks. And tired of you guys all picking on us—we were sick of it."

"So you just—you just trained everyone to hate me? You just outright *ruined my life*?"

I say a little prayer that she'll understand. As if some kind of special magic will happen and she'll turn to me and say, *I'm sorry I drove you to that point. And training the whole school? Now, that's clever.* "Brynne, I'm sorry. I just meant to, maybe, take you down a notch or two."

"Congratulations!" she yells, her eyes bulging. "You succeeded! Satisfied?" Little splashes of spittle come out with her *C*'s and *S*'s.

"I'm really, really sorry," I say. And I am. And for a fleeting second I feel relieved to finally be telling the truth.

"Will you stop it with your sorries?" she yells again. "I don't accept your apology!"

"Look. Maybe I can fix it," I say, hoping that I can, although I haven't worked that out yet. "I'll do everything in my power to make it better."

"*You*—" She jabs her pointer finger into my shoulder. "You have no power anymore! If you did, you wouldn't be in *here*, with me." And then she leaves, slamming the little door so hard that a super-duty-sized broom clangs loudly to the floor.

I sit back down on the couch, curling into a little ball. My head seems to be exploding with thoughts that all confirm that what Brynne just said is true. Absolutely true. I'm about the most powerless person in school right now. And the sad thing is that I've dug the biggest hole—and have no idea how to get Brynne out of it. Or myself, for that matter.

And now it's even deeper, because Mrs. Vittle just walked in.

Tears are pooling in my eyes faster than I can blink them away. For the last twenty minutes or so, I've been sitting in "isolation," on a plastic chair in a room outside the assistant principal's office. There are no windows, no plants, no cheery posters of cats hanging upside down that read HANG IN THERE. Not even a food-pyramid poster. Nothing to look at but the PTA newsletter, which refers to the upcoming bingo night and other things for good kids and not delinquents like me.

And then a voice calls me. "Miss Albert," it says. I look up to see an angry face framed with a high, tight hairline and bun that seems to be a living example of the word "severe." My case has been fast-tracked right up past assistant-to-the-assistant principal, Mrs. Forester, and even past assistant principal, Mrs. Greve. I'm now face-to-face with Mrs. Vander-Pecker.

"Your grandmother's on her way in," she says. "In the meantime, you can explain to me what's going on."

My head is so full I feel like it could burst, and my words are trapped somewhere near my trachea.

"You started this year as an A student, but lately you've been getting C's and D's on your assignments. You're no longer taking part in"—she shuffles papers—"the Board Game Club." Jeez. Middle school is so Big Brother. "And now you're cutting class and watching TV in the janitor's lounge?"

I try to breathe in through my tight throat. Then I try Brynne's line—the line she used with her mother. Not that I want to, but I'm truly desperate. "I'm going through something." My voice is all warped from trying not to cry. Mortifying.

Now she leans back and gives me a look that would be saying "bullcrap," if it could indeed say that without breaking school rules.

"I'm sorry. This is a difficult age," I say. I've heard every adult say this at least once, so it's something she can't argue with.

She sighs with disappointment and looks back to my folder—my life on paper—tapping her pen across her orange-lipsticked mouth. Someone should really tell her that orange brings out the yellow in her teeth. Of course, now is not a good time to give her any helpful advice.

She puts the file down and looks at me. "You're obviously a good student—normally, that is. You've never had any behavioral problems before. It's rare when a decent student suddenly earns a suspension."

All of a sudden my heart is pounding in weird places, like my ears. "You mean," I say, as my armpits begin to feel prickly and moist. "You mean detention."

She blinks. "No, I mean suspension." I'm sure I go white. She continues. "Trespassing. Truancy. These are very serious offenses."

"But *suspension*?" I ask, the frustration ripping out of me. "What about Brynne?"

"She'll be seen to. It's not for you and me to discuss." She wheezes out a long exhale. "But let me ask you, Olivia. I never expected to see you in my office in this way. What happened?"

"It all started," I say, knowing how ridiculous this will sound. "It all started with ketchup."

"Okay, I've had enough," she says, nostrils flaring.

I feel faint. I'm only half aware of Corny coming in, saying little, signing papers, and hustling me to the pickup. "Sorry," I murmur to her. She doesn't say a word to me about it, doesn't ask me to explain.

Instead she tells me she's scheduled an emergency session with Moncherie. Which I guess is good, because I really need to warn her.

Whelped

"I'VE GOT SOMETHING to tell you," I say to Moncherie, before I even sit down.

For a minute she looks worried. Then she sighs. "Olivia," she says, shaking her head. "You do this every time. You always have something you've just got to tell me, and it's usually so you can avoid talking about your mother, isn't it?"

"It's not that," I say, and shake my head, which feels like it is swelling. My eyes are bulging with tears. My nose is filling with snot. My throat is squeezing shut. I am sure that my head is about to explode.

From the way Moncherie is looking at me, I could be right.

"You have to stop the training," I tell her.

"What are you *talking* about?"

"You're using dog training on men, aren't you?"

"Why would—" she starts slowly.

"Didn't you cancel my last appointment because you had a date?"

244

"What?" Her mouth opens and doesn't shut. Her left eye squints, making her right eye look monstrously large in comparison.

"I don't think you can use this training on humans. It backfires!"

"Olivia?"

I can't stop. "You'll lose everything you ever cared about."

And then my head does explode, leaving a wet, soppy, snotty, Niagara Falls in its place. Moncherie hands me a box of Kleenex and then, when I use the last one, a roll of very thin toilet paper, and I don't know how much time goes by while I leak and ooze and otherwise deconstruct.

Finally, after the explosion slows to a trickle, Moncherie says, "First, let's get this straight. I'm not using dog training on men. Is that clear?"

"But you wanted to know the steps," I whine. "And then when you canceled our appointment, I just thought—" My sentence dries up. I'm starting to feel really embarrassed. "Well, then, why *did* you cancel our appointment?"

"It wasn't for a date," she says. "It was—look, never mind. We're here to talk about *you*, Olivia. What's going on?"

Bathroom walls. Bathroom walls, my heads says to my lips—my old rule. *Don't tell her anything you wouldn't want written on the bathroom walls.* But my lips win.

I tell her how Delia betrayed me. And how all my friends were part of it.

Which takes us to the issue I've been trying to avoid all along.

The issue of my mother.

Moncherie leans forward in her chair. "So you're saying Delia

245

betrayed you because she said something about your mother's, well, problem, to Brynne. Do you have any idea why she would have done this?"

I shrug. "She said she was trying to get Brynne to stop teasing me. But she told all of our friends way before then—they all knew!"

She sits back, taking a long breath. "I can see why you're disappointed in Delia. You trusted her enough to tell her about your mother, and I know how carefully you guard that. You don't like to talk about it even with *me*."

I start to feel a bit understood, and it makes me cry a little more.

"But, Olivia, why *do* you guard it so carefully? What bothers you so much about your mother's situation?"

Okay, so I guess I'm not that understood. I squirm. "People judge you. It's embarrassing."

"Like someone in your family having cancer, maybe?"

"Cancer's a *disease*."

"So is what your mom has, Olivia. It's called mental illness. *Illness*. You really think your mom *chose* her depression?"

"No," I breathe. I feel a headache coming on. At least I *hope* it's just a headache. "But she did choose to just leave me. How's that supposed to make me feel?"

She pauses. "How *does* it make you feel?"

For a second, I don't say anything. The butt-end part of my brain has been opened. The trunk has been unlocked. And this time, there's nothing I can do to stop it. "Unacceptable. Unwanted. Unloved." I look up at her. "Un-everything!"

"Sometimes people do pretty drastic things, but not for the

reasons we think. Have you been reading any of her letters?"

"Not really."

"I seriously think you should. People with mental illness can get better, and she's trying to do that right now."

For a second, I feel an inch better. But then she says something again.

"Mental illness is not a choice."

Oh, jeez. Well, crap, then.

"Olivia? What's the matter?" Moncherie's smile has left her face. Now she looks worried.

"Well, if it's not a choice—"

Her eyebrows draw together and she nods slowly, like she's trying to coax the words out of me.

It works. "Then *what*? What's that mean for me?"

She turns her head slightly to the side. "I'm not understanding the question."

"Hello? The crazy gene? You and I *both* know I've got it. And now you're saying there's no choice—that I'm going to go crazy, whether I like it or not."

"The *crazy gene*?" she asks, looking at me as if it's already taken over.

"I don't know what it's really called, but you know what I'm talking about," I say, flustered. "My mom and I are related. We even look alike, everyone who knew her tells me that."

"Ooh," Moncherie says. "Well, think about it. You know how when you ride down Route 39 you see all those subdivisions? Those houses that look exactly alike from the outside?"

I stare at her blankly.

"Well, they may be the same model, let's say a Dorchester, and the same exact floor plan, you know, a center-hall colonial—they may even be the same colors on the outside—but on the inside, they're all so different. There could be two houses right next to each other, but inside it could feel like two different worlds!"

She smiles at me and blinks.

Do I have to even say this? I guess I do. "But we're not houses. My mom and I, like, share the same genes. The same, you know, DNA."

She seems to think about this for a second. "Okay, let's see. What color are your mother's eyes?"

I open my mouth to answer and then realize I'm stumped. I can't remember my mother's eyes at all.

Moncherie seems to realize this, and steps back in. "Your dad—well, I only met him one time, but he's got brown eyes. I mean, if I remember correctly," she says. She cocks her head and looks toward the ceiling. "Well, maybe *chestnut* is a better way to describe them. They're very—*rich*." She even sighs. Then she quickly looks at me and turns a little pink.

Um, does she have a crush? *Ew.* "They're brown," I say with a flattened voice.

"Right, right. And yours are green."

Well, okay, not just *any* green, but that's okay. I'm still trying to remember my mother's eyes—what color are they?

"So not everything is passed along the way you think it is. Genes are more complicated than that. Even identical twins have differences." The glint in her own brown eyes is just twinkling like crazy.

The timer dings. She has this satisfied look on her face, like she just ate a really good meal. No doubt she'll be drawing a hefty check mark on her notepad after *this* session. "Don't worry. You're not destined to go crazy," she says smiling. "Even though you can act a little nutty sometimes."

I think I smile a little too.

On the way home, sitting next to Corny and watching Queso act absolutely thrilled to be riding in a car, I remember something.

My mother's eyes. They're blue. A gray-blue.

Which is nothing like Caribbean green. Nothing at all.

The Omega Dog

WELL, YOU'D THINK all that emotional stuff would be over. But the next morning, Saturday, I'm sitting on my bed, petting Oomlot, when I feel the weight in my chest start to rise again. It nearly chokes me as it climbs up my neck and starts pressing on my temples and streaming from my eyes. And once it starts pouring out, it becomes impossible to stop. I'm crying—sobbing, really—so loud that Corny hears me from downstairs and comes up.

"Olivia?"

I can't answer. She comes into my room, trailed by Queso, who is acting rightfully concerned in that wide-eyed dog way. Corny hands me a box of tissues from my dresser and sits down on my bed. I don't know how much time passes, but I become aware of the fact that she's been petting my head. I curl up to Oomlot, who sighs deeply, as if he's merely tolerating me. I don't blame him. Even *he* can probably sense I'm a complete Marcie.

"Want to tell me what's going on?" Corny asks, in this sweet and calm voice.

I confess it all. I tell her about how the plan got started. I

250

tell her about how people reacted, how I felt like I was in total control, and how we brought down Brynne. I tell her about Delia, and how she told everyone about my mother—my secret— and what happened after that. I tell her how much I miss my friends. And how I'd do anything just to have them back, if I only knew how.

She is shaking her head with wonder, and looking like all the anger from yesterday has drained right out of her. "Olivia," she sighs, her voice heavy.

"I'm really sorry about the training," I say. But the words fall short of what I feel. Those words work when you bump into someone in the hallway. But they don't exactly work when you've just ruined your life and someone else's.

"I know you are." She raises her eyebrows. "But have you told Briana how sorry you are?"

"*Brynne*, you mean. And I tried," I tell her, and pick at my cuticle. I can feel her still looking at me. "Okay, I'll try harder."

I hear her sigh. "You know, you can't treat the world like a . . ." She looks around the room and spots Queso. "Like a Chihuahua." Queso looks at her like she not only understands English but agrees completely, and jumps into Corny's lap. "And what's going on with you and Delia?"

"She tried to apologize, but I wouldn't listen. I just hadn't for-given her yet."

"Must be the stubborn hound in you." She smiles. "But you have now?"

"Yeah, I think so," I say, remembering the conversation I had with my dad. "But I just don't even know what to do next."

Corny looks me in the eye. "You know all the steps you've been going through to train people?"

I nod.

"Well, here's my advice. Do the opposite. Forget about being an alpha dog." I don't bother telling her that it's safe to say that that's been long forgotten. "Step one. Call her. Apologize. Listen to her. Be humble. It's not about being right. It's about making things right." She gives me a hug and says, "Just start right now."

"What's step two?"

"Do step one all over again. This time, with Brianne."

"Brynne."

"Whatever. You know I'm terrible with names. All I know her as is the nice, little pretty girl who liked my cooking."

And I really want to believe that underneath it all, that's exactly who Brynne is.

50.

The Pack

DELIA ANSWERS the phone. "Hey," I say. I squeeze Oomlot in closer to me. I really need his support.

"Olivia?" She makes my name a question.

"Yeah. It's me."

She's quiet, so I just jump in with everything I should have said two weeks ago, my heart pumping wildly. "Look, Delia, I'm sorry. I was mad at you for telling everyone about my mother, but I understand why you did it, even though it was dumb. And I was mad at all of them for just knowing, I guess. But I don't really think you're a bad friend. I actually think you're the best one I've ever had." Then I take a breath and add, "I miss you."

And then she says she'll have to call me back, but in a way that makes me sure she never, ever will.

Five minutes later—when I'm well into planning a future with only an eighth-grade education because I never want to go back to school, *ever*—she *does* call back. I break out everywhere in a sweat of relief. I make a line through where I've written "professional poop scooper."

"Sorry," she says. "It's just—I miss you too, but I'm still a little mad. I mean, I'm sorry that I said anything to Brynne—or to anyone. That was wrong, I know. But then you just totally ignored me and blew us all off."

"I know—I was mad at all of you. You, especially. But I'm sorry too, I'm *really* sorry."

She breathes out loudly. "I am too, Liv. I'm sorry." Then, "I heard you got suspended."

"You heard? *Already?*"

"Yeah. Actually, I heard that you got caught shoplifting and were put in handcuffs and hauled off to jail. Oh, and did you know you drink whiskey too?"

I laugh. "I do?"

"Yeah. Apparently you were drunk on it. And you threw up in the police car."

A snort comes out of my nose, which makes Delia laugh too.

"I hope you defended my honor," I joke.

"You know, this time? I just kept my mouth shut. I probably should have just done that before."

"It's okay. I mean, I was really mad, but you know what? It's really okay. I mean, it's kind of a relief, actually, not to have to keep a stupid lie going."

"But no one in the Bored Game Club is *not* going to be your friend because your mom's in a—one of those centers."

"I guess I know that now. I was just scared of being a perma-freak. You know, like tainted somehow."

"Even if you were a perma-freak, we'd still love you."

I smile. "I honestly think that's the sweetest thing anyone's ever said to me."

"No it's not. This is: I've been admiring your glossy hair

254

for quite some time now," she says.

I'm aware of the strange sensation of my lungs fluttering, and my stomach quivering, and my throat shaking, before I realize I'm laughing hard. For the first time in a long time. "You're right. *That* is. Thank you. I guess that's one thing I have Brynne to thank for."

"What's going on with Brynne anyway?"

"She found out about the training—I had to tell her. The guilt was killing me."

"Is she mad?"

"That's an understatement. She's livid. I'm a little scared."

"Well, you really should try to straighten things out with her. Especially with the elections coming up. Not that I really think she can do anything to get things off track at this point, but just because we don't need any surprises."

"I will," I promise. "But Dee, I'm not so sure the whole plan was a great idea. I think we really wrecked her life."

"Oh, I don't know," Delia says. "I think everything worked out like it should. Didn't this whole thing bring out the good side of her? I mean, you got to know her pretty well. What do *you* think?"

I push aside the thoughts of Angry, Spittling, Janitor-Closet Brynne and try to delve into the memories of Travel-Scrabbling Brynne. Dog-Loving Brynne. Sweatpant-Wearing Brynne. BFF-Wanting Brynne. "Yeah, she can be really nice," I agree.

"See?" Delia says. "Besides, someone's going to be the alpha dog in any situation. Wouldn't you rather have it be us?"

"You're right," I sigh. "God, I've missed you, Dee!"

"I miss you too, you know? Fall Ball would have been so much more fun if you were there."

My heart starts to feel warm and glowy. I ask, "How was it anyway?"

"Oh. It was okay, I guess."

"So you did go with Danny?"

"Ugh. Don't remind me," she says. "You know how Brynne used to say he had fart breath?"

"Yeah."

"Well, it's actually true."

I laugh. Probably too much. I'm just so relieved to be talking with her. Then I ask, "How about Phoebe and Brant?"

"Oh." Delia giggles. "Actually, I think Brant's a little mad. Phoebe ended up spending the whole night talking to Joey."

"No. *Way.*"

"Yep," she says. "Remember how weird he used to get when she brought up Brant? We're thinking it was pure jealousy."

I laugh. I mean, *wow.* I start to open my mouth to tell her what Brynne had said about that date, how it was a dare, and then I decide I've done enough harm. I need to leave happiness alone.

"Um, Olivia," Delia says carefully. "Look, everyone's still kind of upset. They think you overreacted and then pretty much just abandoned them. But I'll talk to them, okay?"

Then she tells me she better go, she's got a bunch of campaign stuff to do for the final push. I tell her I have to go, too—I've got to make that phone call to Brynne. But when I do, her phone just goes straight to voice mail.

It's her happy voice, which makes me feel worse. "It's Brynne! Leave me a message!"

So I do. "Hey, Brynne. It's Olivia. I'm really sorry. Call me."

I know she won't. I guess I'll have to straighten things out my first day back. I tell myself that it will all be okay. I just wish I was more convincing.

51.

Leashed

MY SUSPENSION IS only for two days, but I never want to have it again. It's not like a day off. During my sentence, Corny gives me work—scooping poop out in the field and gathering dog hair. The poop, of course, I throw away, but Corny insists I rake the dog hair into large clumps so the birds can grab it by the beakful and line their nests with it. Also, not only do I still have to do schoolwork and homework, but my teachers have given me special assignments that I'm supposed to use to prove that I understand everything they did in class. Which is not easy when you haven't been in class. It's just a ton of reading without the benefit of some honor roll student raising a hand and asking the question that you've been secretly wondering yourself.

I mean, I hate school and all, but suspension is *way* worse.

Corny tells me we're going to go see Kisses, which requires a little prep work on my part. I make myself look in the mirror and practice looking confident, like in the old days when I was first learning how to train. I tell myself that I'm good enough, that I'm smart enough, and so what if I've just made a few mistakes? (Okay, a few really horrible ones.) But no matter what I do, I feel like the victim of some bad self-esteem seminar—like one with dancing, life-size puppets that sing songs about cloudy days and sunshine and pretend it's okay that some of us are dumb and/or ugly. Or stink.

In sixth grade, after one of those assemblies (featuring a puppet *playing a ukulele*), this girl named Lizzie Buchholz, who suffered from some mysterious odor problem we named *bathabus neglectus*, decided it was okay to wear the same pair of red-and-blue-striped kneesocks to school every day. Because a loser puppet told her she was fine the way she was.

You couldn't really blame her. It actually makes sense. Because, really, if you're fine the way you are, why should you try to change anything? Grades, attitude. Food-chain status. Or, like in Lizzie's case, hygiene.

But I guess this is where low self-esteem comes in handy. Because at this very moment, all the puppets and ukuleles and ribbon dancers in the world couldn't convince me that I'm okay. And this is actually a really, really good thing. Because I seriously need to get my butt in gear. Starting now.

Corny stares at me with an amused but puzzled smile as I get into the passenger seat of her pickup. "You certainly look"—she pauses—"ready, I guess is the word. I wasn't sure you'd be up for it, but this is a nice surprise."

Especially since my last two days have been so crappy. Literally. "We have the sod?" I ask, although I'm hoping we won't need it.

"Right in back," she says, pointing her chin toward the bed of the truck.

"Treats?"

She picks up a biscuit-filled plastic bag next to her and shakes it for me. Then she looks at the bag, makes a *hmmm* sound, and takes one out for herself. She bites into it. "Hungry?" she asks, offering the bag to me.

I guide her hand away and pretend to stick my finger down my throat to gag myself. It's only a slight exaggeration.

She shakes her head. "One of these days you'll have to try one. They're actually quite good."

"I'll take your word for it," I say. I take a deep breath. I may get used to bagging poop. I may get used to psychotic dogs. But I will never get used to my grandmother's bizarre food habits, no matter how human-friendly she claims her biscuits to be. Blech.

"Well, Kisses certainly eats them up," she says.

"Kisses probably eats her own vomit," I point out. Not that I've seen her do it, but I'm sure she would. Most dogs do that kind of thing.

"Oh, Olivia, that's disgusting," she says, like eating a dog biscuit *isn't*. My face cracks into a smile, and I'm starting to feel my mood lift.

That is, until I get out of the truck and find that Kisses has not just taken one step back, or two. She has apparently been walking backward for a while now and has wound up in a world where "human" is standard lunch fare and is served on platters, between buns, and in buckets. Her head is low, her body is crouched, and she is oozing out a low, suspicious warning growl like a small but incredibly powerful motor.

For a second I think about getting back into the truck. But then I have a flashback to Lizzie's putrid socks. Do I really want to be fine with the way I am at this very moment, scared to death of a tiny hairless dog that's afraid of grass?

I do not.

I notice Kisses's trembling back leg. Although she howls, I can see she's frightened. I take a second to correct my body language and let the stench of my own fear waft away. She howls again, lurches forward, but steps right back. I avoid her eyes and stand my ground. Before she can spring forward again, I clap my hands, just once. It distracts her, and she jumps backward. I step forward. She howls but steps back. I take another step in her direction. Her howl turns into a whine, and she turns and runs toward the house, away from me.

"I'm sorry," Mr. Dewey says. "She was doing so well, but lately . . ." His voice trails off.

"Don't worry. So she's had a little bit of a slip. We can make up for lost time," Corny says. I hope she's right. And not just in the case of Kisses.

After almost two hours of doing everything we'd done in the weeks before, Kisses finally agrees to go back on the sod, and after several reward biscuits, seems almost happy about it. I nearly cry tears of relief. Kisses also agrees to step out on the stones that I put out on the lawn. But she still seems to think that she'd be risking her life to let one foot step away from the stone. So we're basically back to where we left off.

You'd think I'd be disappointed, but I'm not. At all. It's not going to be today, but I know we'll get there. Kisses will make peace with the lawn sometime soon. I can see her running in the grass, lying in the sun, even wriggling around on her back the way some dogs do when they look like they're scratching away an itch and having a thrilling time doing it.

And if some ukulele-strumming puppet told me, right here, right now, that I'm fine just the way I am, I might actually, just a little bit, believe it.

52.

How to Beg (Forgiveness)

IT'S WEDNESDAY, my first day back from my sentence.

The bus slows to a stop in front of my driveway like a cranky old lady—wheezing, groaning, creaking, and generally making me feel like I'm making its day a little harder. I step on board and the bus charges off, and I almost take a tumble into Tamberlin Ziff, who screams loudly and then enjoys all the eyes on her.

"Sorry," I mumble, although she's not really the one I need to apologize to. That person's sitting in a seat alone, about seven rows back.

But as I get closer, Brynne gives me a quick look. Then her face hardens and she lifts her backpack from the floor, placing it on the empty part of the seat next to her. I stop at her row.

"Brynne?"

She doesn't look at me.

"Brynne," I say a little louder.

She glances up at me again, with the same hard look. Then I realize she's listening to an iPod. She turns up the volume and looks away.

"Sit down!" the driver yells in the same voice she used to use on the barkers. I find an empty seat. And then I'm back to reading *Car and Driver* over the shoulder of Little Kid. It may not be a glory seat, but it's actually strangely comfortable. One little piece of my old life is back.

I go to my locker and look around. Maria, who's standing less than a foot away from me at her own locker, doesn't even glance in my direction. "Hi," I say to her.

"Hi," she bleats, avoiding my eyes.

I smell my armpit just in case. It would almost be a relief to reek and have something to blame everything on, other than my own stupid self, but all I smell is the shower-fresh scent of Teen Spirit.

And then I see Mandy. Our eyes meet, and she freezes like she's in a bit of a panic. I refuse to let her get away, and luckily she's petrified by shock and the awkwardness of the situation.

"Hi," I say. I smile. Not too confidently, since I have to show that I'm humble.

"Hi." She smiles back. It's a little shaky, but it's still a smile.

All around us, people are rushing by, greeting her as they do.

So I just say, "I want to help on the campaign."

She laughs a little. "Well, elections are two days away."

"I know. I'm sorry I haven't been around for a while." My words sound too lame for how I really feel, so I say, "I'm just sorry about everything, period."

"Yeah, well . . ." She shrugs. She looks down at her shoes. They're clogs. "Well, if you hadn't made me run for president, I never would have done it." She looks back up at me.

I smile. I miss her so much, clogs and all. And *yes*, she *is* the kind of person who can pull it off.

"Can I come back to the Bored Game Club?"

She gets kind of squirmy. "I don't know. Probably not today, okay? Let me talk to Phoebe and Joey first. Half the school's been coming to the club, so we've been pretty swamped." But she looks at me sympathetically. That's the thing about Mandy. She may play at being tough, but at heart she's like Wonder bread. "But soon, okay?"

I reach forward to hug her. She stumbles backward a bit and then leans in for a squeeze. When I let go, she gives an uncomfortable laugh. "Okay, I'll see you soon. And by the way?"

"Yes?"

"Nice hair." She smiles. "I mean it."

With Tucked Tail

"YOU KNOW," I hear a voice say on Thursday morning. A nice voice. A voice that makes my insides feel especially warm and gooey. "You can always vote for me."

I look up from my locker. It's Caleb and we're alone and I've forgotten how to breathe. I wonder where his entourage is, but I can't ask since I've also forgotten how to speak.

He gives me a slow smile. So slow it's like slow motion. Or maybe that's just how it seems to me since I seem to be savoring it the same way I savor white chocolate truffles. Then he walks away, and I realize that my upper lip has broken out into a sweat. Since when is this even possible? I dab my lip with my sleeve and for the duration of exactly one (very powerful) heartbeat, I find myself thinking that maybe I *will* vote for him.

But of course I come to my senses.

Because thirty seconds later, I sense a presence behind me. I turn around. It's Delia. She gives me a little smile and says hi.

"Hi!" I'm way too excited to see her.

"I'll save you a spot at lunch today, okay?"

I become aware of the fact that my mouth is hanging open and that my eyes are dry from not blinking. "Really?" I ask.

"Seriously, Liv," Delia says. "Where would we be without you?"

She kind of laughs a little and walks away, and I feel weird and light and like smiling or singing. It's so strange to me, this feeling, that I forget that there's a word for it. *Happy*.

Delia's straddled her butt across two seat circles, so when I tap her on the shoulder she looks up and scoots over. "Thanks," I say to her. "Hi," I say to everyone else. And I do mean "everyone else" because there's not only Phoebe and Joey and Mandy, but a couple of others, like Brant and Erin Monroe and even Morgan Askren. And of course Peyton Randall. Who have all obviously been prepped for—and have probably been forced to approve—my presence. It makes me a little angry, since I was there way before any of them, but I brush it off. I've got my friends back, and that matters more than anything else right now.

Delia offers me a Tater Tot, which I take out of appreciation, although I'm too nervous to taste.

I wait for everyone to talk. They're way too quiet, and it's making me aware of my chewing noises. I'm actually secretly hoping that Joey will burp or fart or pick his nose, but he's turned into Mr. Manners.

Phoebe gives me a prim smile when I look at her, like it's a little painful to do even though she's been doing a lot more smiling lately. And laughing too. I mean, I've seen her in the hallways and watched her across the cafeteria. Mandy is eyeing my pizza, so I hold it out to her. She smiles at me, rips off the pepperonis, and pops them into her mouth. And when Peyton crinkles up her snooty little nose and says to her, "When did you start eating nitrites?" and Mandy looks over at me and rolls her eyes, I feel tons better.

"Will you read my speech?" Mandy asks me after lunch.

"Uh, *yeah*," I say, since it's the most ridiculous question ever. "I'd love to."

She hands me a stapled stack of paper and gives me a nervous smile. "I can't believe it's tomorrow."

"I really think you're going to win."

"What about Caleb?" she asks, looking a little pained. "People *love* him."

"Yeah, but they love you more," I say. "Come on, didn't I hear that the Bored Game Club has gotten so packed that the school's going to host a Pictionary-thon in the spring? And that two girls got detention for a fight they had over a Chuck E. Cheese coin?"

She nods. "Yeah, we were trying to play Monopoly, but they both wanted to use it for their game piece."

"See?" I smile at her even though I still feel a little unsteady about it all. It's not Supercandidate Caleb I'm worried about—it's Brynne. Obviously, she's not going to win, but there are still things like rafters to be concerned about, and things that could be rigged to fall from them and onto people on the stage, like, say, Mandy.

But maybe, *hopefully*, I'm just being paranoid. Honestly, the only thing Brynne's been guilty of lately is ignoring me completely.

In fact, I hardly even see her. She eats lunch in the library, and she's moved seats away from me in class. I'm sure she would have already given up on the campaign if she didn't desperately need that extra credit. To be honest, it's actually pretty understandable that she wants nothing to do with me. I don't even think I can blame her. I might as well just deal with it.

And anyway, I've also learned that because of past incidents, the ballots will be strictly controlled by Mrs. Vander-Pecker, and that the stage will be well secured before and during the speeches. I've also made Mandy promise to check all doors and hallways before entering them, and to walk with a buddy, even if that buddy is Dawn Lane. She keeps telling me to relax. I'm trying.

I read the speech and it's good. It's great, in fact. It nearly erases my worries. In it, Mandy talks about how we're all entitled to our little piece of power. Even *I* felt wonderful and valuable after reading her speech. And not only that, but she's promising to ban the things that we all hate, like family-life education and especially Sleeterball.

That night, I call her and tell her that if I wasn't already sold, this would sell me. She seems happy to hear it.

And then I tell myself that it's too late for anything to mess this up. And I find it almost believable.

Almost.

54.

Speak

FRIDAY MORNING STARTS a little drizzly, which I don't take as a bad sign. And it's good that I don't waste any worries, because by the time first period is over, the sun has come out.

Mandy was too excited to eat breakfast, so in between first and second period we're all crowded around her, coaxing her into eating a Luna bar so she won't pass out up there onstage.

"I'm not sure I can eat right now," Mandy tells us.

"Well, there's still lunch," Delia says.

"What, are you crazy? She can't eat lunch," Phoebe says.

"Yeah, she'll spew," Joey agrees. "Come on, try it. It's s'mores flavored," he says. "These are better than Twinkies."

I look at him like he's lost his mind. It's then that I realize he's also lost a little weight. I mean, he's still no, well, Caleb Austin, but he's looking less like the kid on *Family Guy*.

She takes a bite of the Luna bar and chews, and we all cheer a little. "One more bite," Delia says. "You've got to keep up your strength."

Then we hear, in the high-pitched yell of Corinne d'Abo,

"Forecast calls for—" She is trotting down the hall in her blue unitard, leading a string of Spiritleaders. She turns her ear toward the front and cups a white-gloved hand behind it. "Come on, Frosties! Let's do this right!" she says again, only louder and higher, "FORECAST CALLS FOR—"

"What"—Mandy says, looking confused. But before she can finish with—"on God's green earth?" Corinne points at Mandy and screams, "That's right! Come on, all you Frosties. Like she said. *FORECAST CALLS FOR—*"

Now people around us chant, *"What!"* while we scoot toward a reinforced passageway.

Corinne is absolutely delighted. She circles her hands in the air, signaling for the crowd to be louder. "I can't *hear* you! *FORE-CAST CALLS FOR—*"

"WHAT?" Total pack mentality is in play.

"FORECAST CALLS FOR FLURRIES!" Corinne cries, her voice screeching. Then she and the Spiritleaders twirl gracelessly down the hallway, white-gloved jazz hands knocking into white-gloved jazz hands. It's clumsy, sure, and there are a few falls, but there seem to be no open wounds.

"They've tamed out without Brynne," Mandy notices.

"They're still dangerous," Phoebe says.

"Yeah, but once Mandy's in office," I remind them, "they're so *over.*"

I think I feel Caleb's presence in my knees even before I see him, like I've developed some type of radar. "Ready for today?" he asks, like a grown-up might. He smiles at Mandy but shoots me a fleeting glance that quickens my pulse just a little.

"She's ready, all right," Delia says protectively.

"Want a bite?" Mandy asks, showing him the Luna bar.

"Delia says it'll keep your strength up."

"No thanks," he says. "I'm feeling strong enough already."

"Good luck," I say, but he's already turned away. I'm not sure he heard me, which is okay because I'm not sure I meant it. Well, okay, maybe I do, just a little, as long his luck's not better than ours. I mean, I hope he comes in second. Even a *close* second would be fine with me.

Once he's gone, Mandy gives us a look of panic.

"Don't worry about him," Phoebe says.

I catch of glimpse of Brynne over Joey's shoulder. She's watching the last Spiritleader disappear down the hall. If she would just talk to me, look at me, maybe I would feel better about things. But then I remind myself, she kept the secret about my mother. She also covered for her former friends when they pulled the Trash Bag Day prank on her. And I try to shake the concerns out of my head because I'm just being silly.

I'm sure I am.

Long before the other kids are let in, the campaign staffs are allowed to claim their seats in the auditorium. I am sitting between Delia (I'm so happy, I have to fight the urge to grab and hold her hand) and Joey. Phoebe sits on the other side of Joey, analyzing our choice of seats, wondering if we should move for the fourth time.

"Calm down, Pheebo," Joey says. It's his new name for her. I'm not quite sure when that started, or why, since Mandy's still Mandy and Delia's still Delia. He only today started addressing me by my name again, instead of *that woman*. We are seated in the center of the third row, which two minutes ago Phoebe declared was the perfect visual and cheering distance from the stage. "I'm not moving again."

"I wish we could go backstage," Delia says. "I hope she's not getting sick."

But then Mandy peeks out from stage left. She spots us, smiles and waves, and I feel much better. We all wave back. Joey yells, "Go Mandy!" and Phoebe joins in, even doing that *WOOT WOOT* thing, which is really weird coming from her.

Caleb's co–campaign managers, Carson and Ryan, turn and nod at us with blank expressions, the way rude people do when they don't want to be accused of being unfriendly. This professionalism is just nerve-racking. Poor Dawn Lane doesn't have a campaign staff. And Brynne's consists solely of Mrs. Ardensburg, the Teen Life teacher.

Then it's like a dam burst. Kids start flooding in, bringing waves of sound with them, and filling in seats all around us. Phoebe has tried to reserve the seat next to her, just for "breathing room," she says, but Peyton Randall sits down like it's reserved for her. Phoebe looks at us and secretly rolls her eyes. I thought maybe she'd been saving the seat for Brant, but when Joey taps her gently on the knee and whispers something, I think maybe not. Things have changed a little—okay, *a lot*—since I've been away.

Now Delia grabs and squeezes my hand. I squeeze back and we turn to each other and smile, and I sit there and think about how good it feels to have my best friend back.

"Everything's going to be okay, isn't it?" I ask her. It's not that I think she's psychic or anything, but her reassurance is pretty powerful to me.

She leans in closer to me. "Look," she says. "I love you and all, and I don't mean this in a bad way, but will you please *shut up* and stop worrying?"

Then she laughs. I feel my heart swell a little, and I laugh too.

And then Mrs. Vander-Pecker calls the event to order.

"Ladies and gentlepeople," she says, over the noise of the room full of middle schoolers. "Ladies and *GENTLEPEOPLE!*" Her voice gets louder in an attempt to make ours lower. By the time it actually works, her eyes are bulging, her neck looks like a tree root, her face is the color of a beet, and I think everyone has finally shut up just so they can study the curiosity up there behind the podium.

"*Thank* you," she says finally, but not sounding at all grateful. "Today I am happy to introduce our four candidates for school president. They have all worked very hard to get here, and I hope that you will give them the respect they deserve. First, I offer you Dawn Lane."

There's clapping, and then Dawn appears onstage, dressed a little like an American Girl doll. She is wearing a white puffy blouse under a denim vest, with a matching denim skirt. It looks like that fake denim fabric people cover pillows and couches with. I think she just blew it.

"Hi, everyone," she says. "My name is Dawn Lane. I am an honor roll student—well, most days." She pauses and looks around the audience with a smile, like she's waiting for a laugh. When it doesn't happen, Mrs. Vander-Pecker lets loose with a clearly made-up one. "And head of the Future Financiers of America. But I'm not rich—yet." She pauses again. It's excruciating. Another forced laugh by Mrs. V-P.

She keeps talking, but I turn to Delia and wince. She winces back.

"I don't know if I can take this," Joey says, his face twisted in pain. "It hurts."

Then, cutting through the discomfort is the sound of a recorder. Through my fingers I see Dawn playing the instrument, eyes closed, face angled toward the heavens. She makes her way through a screechy sequence of notes, stops, and after we all breathe, says, "Wait. I messed up." And then starts it all over again.

When she stops for the final time, she says, "And I hope you'll all remember that one when you go to the polls this afternoon. Thank you."

"What was it supposed to be?" Delia's able to whisper this to me above the (very tame) clapping. Up onstage, Dawn bows.

"I don't know. It sounded a little like 'Three Blind Mice,'" I whisper back.

Joey laughs. "'Three Blind Mice'? We're supposed to remember *that* when we go to the polls?"

Phoebe mulls it over. "I think it was 'Beat It.' An homage to Michael Jackson, perhaps?"

Peyton leans forward. "'We Are the Champions,'" she announces.

"*Ooooh*," we all say in unison.

Mrs. Vander-Pecker appears onstage again. "Thank you, Dawn. I think everyone appreciates a good tune. What a pick-me-up!" She claps again, which means that we all have to also. "Next, I'm happy to present Mandy Champlain."

This time the clapping intensifies. It gets louder as Mandy walks out onstage. Much louder. There are whistles and hoots and people yelling, "Go Mandy!" Joey knocks his voice down about an octave and probably yells the loudest. Phoebe beams over at him and his man-voice.

I'm just hoping Mandy's checking the rafters. I can't help it.

"Wow, thank you," she says. "I wish I had a song, but unfortunately you're going to have to settle for just me." People laugh and clap, like it's incredibly funny, just because they like her. I can't believe it. I'm thrilled. "And I'm not so sure a dance would win your vote," she says, to more laughter. "The thing is, I don't have a gimmick. I can't promise you a song or dance, or even soda machines in the cafeteria, for that matter. Or cool P.E. uniforms, which I know is important. But what I can promise you is a real person." She tries to continue, but the clapping and cheering is way too loud. She smiles until it quiets. "A few weeks ago, the thought of getting up here in front of all of you—and actually getting votes—was just a dream. But it was a dream I wanted to go for. Not for fame and fortune, although that would be nice, but for one reason: I wanted each person in this school to have a voice."

A couple of people stand and start chanting "Mandy! Mandy!"

"No matter how weird you may be or how weird the rumors about you are." (A few laughs and snorts.) "No matter how smart or dumb you secretly think you are." (A few nervous ripples of laughter, some fidgety rustling.) "No matter how hot or not everyone else thinks you are." (Audience squirms noticeably, more nervous laughter, one throat-clearing.) "No matter if you're a dweeb or someone like, say, class president." (She smiles. Everyone laughs.) "Every single person." (She pauses.) "In this godforsaken school." (Audience hoots in agreement.) "Has something. To say." (Audience claps and whistles.)

"If elected, I will make sure that each one of you has someone to say it to. And I will make one-hundred-percent sure that your voice is heard. Because, as we all know . . ." (She pauses and looks around.) "YOU are the most important part of Hubert C. Frost Middle School, and it's finally time you were given that respect."

I don't think there are many times in a middle school auditorium when a crowd goes wild without some type of illegal activity going on, but this is one of those rare moments. People cheer. People stand. And everyone claps.

And by the time Mrs. Vander-Pecker gets everyone calmed down enough to introduce Brynne, I say good-bye to all my worries.

And that's when it happens.

55.

Mad Dog

WE SETTLE DOWN and sit back in our seats, though our moods are somewhere near the ceiling. I feel relief, like I've just taken my last exam of the school year or something. You don't know what you've earned yet, but the most trying part is behind you.

From behind the podium, Brynne opens her mouth.

And laughs.

A lot.

Everyone is looking at her like she's crazy, and I grow still as a rock, with fear. She laughs more.

"You want to know what's so funny?" she asks the audience. No one says a word. Throughout the auditorium, mouths gape open but remain completely silent. "What we just heard from my opponent. That was—well, there's no better word for it—*hysterical*." I'm starting to feel a little queasy, and my stomach makes a gurgling sound that I'm sure *everyone* hears, because the room's as quiet as a tomb. Brynne has everyone's attention. Mrs. Vander-Pecker clears her throat, and it echoes throughout the auditorium. "Mandy Champlain says she has no gimmick! Well, that right there was a

277

'song and dance' if I've ever seen one," she says, making air quotes not just with her fingers but with her entire hands.

I can't move.

"Do you want to know why you like her so much?" Someone yells "Go, Mandy" in the audience, but it sounds defensive and forced. "You like her and all her little friends because you've been *trained* to. Trained like *dogs*. You've been rewarded with candy and staplers, and you've been treated like common house pets. The truth is, you couldn't possibly like these cretins if you hadn't been *trained* to."

She clasps her hands and looks around confidently. Then she says, "Lights, please."

I can't exhale.

The lights dim. The theater screen whirs and lowers. Brynne opens a laptop, and an image appears on the screen. "This, in fact, is my opponent just a few months ago." It's a photo of Mandy. Her hair is sprayed gray. Her lips are shockingly black. There's even some accidental black Sharpie on her front tooth. There's a gleaming yellow pustule over her eyebrow, where her piercing sometimes is. And she's flipping off the camera. The audience takes in a collective breath of air. Delia's nails drive into the back of my knuckles.

"You know, she's gone through two campaign managers," Brynne says. "You might remember *her* first." A photo of me pops up. Well, of me and my butt, with the gigantic ketchup stain spread across my irregular-sized khakis. I hear a few people suck in their breath at the sight, and other people in the audience start to shift and murmur. I am both mortified and paralyzed.

"But *that* one left to pursue her true calling." And then another photo appears on the screen. It's me again, this time a picture taken at my house—something she must have snapped that weekend she stayed with me. In the background, Bella is squatting in a round-back position. In the foreground, I'm wearing a pair of Corny's overalls and I'm bending over, scooping turds into a bag. Squeals of disgust ring out.

"And then there was campaign manager number two," she says, all snippily. A close-up of the surface of the moon pops up. Or at least that's what it appears to be. "Oh, gosh, I'm so sorry about that," Brynne says to the crowd. "You shouldn't have had to see that. Not so soon after lunch." The photo zooms out, revealing a cheek, a pair of root-beer-colored eyes. The zoom-out continues until you can see Delia's face, turned toward the side, and her hand, obviously raised as a shield to the camera. The crowd *ewws* and moans.

"Oh, Holy Mother," I hear Delia say, in a strained whisper. I might as well just die right now.

"This isn't right," Joey says, just in time for his rather large body to pop up on screen. He's looks like he weighs about twelve hundred pounds, and he's stuffing Funyuns into his mouth with his fist. His eyes are closed as if it is the most meaningful and enjoyable moment of his life. You can hear the roar of people starting to talk and laugh.

"*Nice*," someone in the row in front of us says in a voice dripping with sarcasm.

"And last, but not—well, does it even matter at this point?" Brynne seethes. And up pops Phoebe, looking a little like a troll, but much, much paler. She's staring adoringly at Brant, who appears to be completely oblivious to her. Her hand is grabbing the seat of her pants like she's trying to adjust a wedgie. A laugh circles the room.

The lights come back on. Everyone is looking around the room—looking for *us*. "It's funny to me that this group of people, who I can't *legally* call losers from the stage like this, is running this entire school. Are you all going to let yourselves be treated like dogs?"

Mrs. Vander-Pecker appears onstage, grasps Brynne by the shoulders, and they disappear behind the curtain. The noise of the crowd starts to swarm, getting louder by the second.

Delia releases my hand. "I thought you were going to fix things with her."

"I tried," I manage to stiffly whisper back.

Phoebe looks at me with eyes rimmed with red. She jumps out of her seat, and Joey starts to follow, but Mrs. V-P reappears onstage and does the thing with her neck again. "Everyone, *sit down!* And be quiet! We still have another candidate to hear out, and *no* one will leave this room until we do. He has been *incredibly* patient, and I ask—rather, I *demand!*—that you be just as patient with him." She throws out a flustered hand. "Caleb. Austin."

Caleb floats onstage and stands there looking out at us like he's God or something. And then he claps once. Then twice. Then after a third time, he breaks into a crescendo of applause.

"Wow. That was great. Just *fantastic*," he says. "Thanks, Brynne. *Very* entertaining."

He puts his fists on his hips and shakes his head, looking amused.

"That's gotta be a first," he says. "I mean, don't get me wrong. Some people will do anything for a vote. I'm sure that happens all the time. But to accuse us all of being dumb? Of being trained like dogs? I know I'm not a dog; what about you?"

The crowd begins to murmur.

"Look, be honest with me. Tell me you want my vote. But don't—*please* don't—insult me!"

People start to clap. Someone throws a balled-up piece of notebook paper across the auditorium and yells, "Fetch!" The crowd laughs loudly.

Caleb laughs too, and looks relaxed and amused. "So why aren't you all just tripping over yourselves to catch that? I mean, come on, aren't you all *good dogs*?"

The laughing and hooting rolls across the aisles like waves. Each wave makes it louder.

"Sit!" he calls out. "Oh, see," he says teasingly, "maybe she's right. You're all sitting." With that, the crowd begins to stand, and to cheer. "Hold on," he calls out. "Bad dogs! I said sit!" More people stand. The cheering gets louder.

The claps and cheers have reached a deafening level, like a 3-D, stadium-seating version of the applause that Mandy got, which seemed so fabulously loud at the time. People are barking, yelping, and literally howling.

Caleb smiles. Over the excitement, he shouts, "Shall we move on?"

"Speech!" someone yells out.

And so he launches into it. He *does* promise soda machines in the cafeteria and better P.E. uniforms. He even mentions getting a pool built, but I don't think anyone's really listening. They're having too much fun.

They've just found their pack leader.

56.

Down Dog

WELL.

The good news, I guess, is that Brynne *does* get in trouble. Not as much as she would have if her mom hadn't made a case about her "going through some adjustments," but still, trouble. She gets sentenced to in-school suspension, where she has to spend three days with the kid who broke his ankle when he hijacked the clinic's wheelchair and rode it headfirst down the stairs in a botched attempt to simulate a thrill ride, and the kid who fractured his nose when an encyclopedia he threw at a library window bounced right back at him.

And then there's some weird news. Some really weird news.

It happens a week after the election fiasco. I'm on my way to seventh period when I hear, gushed over the loudspeaker by an overly cheerful voice, "Ol*i*via *Al*bert and Brynne *Shawn*son. *Please* report to the guidance office! Olivia. *Al*bert. Brynne. *Shawn*son. *Thank* you!"

I stop in my tracks, and Little Kid bounces off my backside. I shuffle to the side and ready myself to head back down the hall toward guidance. And then I see her—Brynne—coming from the opposite end of the hall. We make eye contact and hold the stare. It's like we're heading toward a duel.

She makes it to the office first and quickly goes in, not bothering to hold the door for me.

"Good after*noon*, ladies!" It's Ms. Underwood, the guidance counselor, behind the musical voice. She smiles, displaying a friendly little gap between her two front teeth. "Just have a seat, please!" She motions to the only two chairs in the room, which, despite the vast space around them, are attached together just below the seat.

Brynne avoids my eyes and sits down, no questions asked.

"Um," I say, inching closer to Ms. Underwood's desk. I keep my voice low. "I was just wondering—why are we here?"

"Oh!" she sings out, surprised. "I thought you already knew. Peer mediation. The two of you are going to have a little chat with Carolyn. She should be here any moment."

Carolyn Quim.

Brynne looks up with a panicked expression.

"Oh, but, I didn't know—" Brynne starts stammering. "Is Carolyn really qualified? I mean, she gossips."

"Oh, sweetie, don't worry," Mrs. Underwood says. "She took an oath. *Con-fi-den-ti-al-ity*," she says, her voice working its way up an octave.

Dear God. This could be awful.

Or.

Maybe not. Maybe I will exercise my mad forgiving skills. Maybe I will take the high road. Maybe I can harness the power of Carolyn's gossip and right this horrible wrong.

"Oh, looky-look!" Ms. Underwood says. "Here she is now!"

Carolyn walks in. Brynne's jaw clenches again.

Mrs. Underwood shoos us all off to the conference room.

I try to soften the tension by complimenting Carolyn on her clogs. Yes, *clogs*. But it doesn't work.

"So," Carolyn says. "What are we here to talk about?" She looks at Brynne, but Brynne stares down at the table.

I'm pretty sure the school just wants us to make peace so there are no more crimes like ketchup harassments or slide-show assaults. So I say, "I'll start. I'm sorry, Brynne."

Carolyn holds up her hand. "Wait, *wait*! Jeez, let me get my handbook out." She pulls the book out of her backpack, scans a page, and says, "Okay, Brynne, your turn."

Brynne still says nothing.

"Oh my God. *Seriously*?" Carolyn says to her.

"It's okay," I say, very maturely. "She's probably still mad at me. I wasn't exactly a good friend to her."

"Your turn," Carolyn says to Brynne. "Again."

"Well, she's right about that," Brynne says, quietly. "She *wasn't* a good friend. She was just using me."

"But I—"

Carolyn whips her head around. "Wow, really? It's not your turn yet, Olivia. You've already gone *twice*!"

"I *was* done talking," Brynne says.

Carolyn leans her head back and sighs. "Okay, maybe you should say 'over' or something, just so I know."

Brynne still won't look at me. "Okay. Over."

Carolyn turns to me. "Olivia? What do you have to say to that?"

"I was just going to say that I did really like her. Over."

Carolyn looks confused but turns to Brynne. "She says she

really liked you." Then I hear her clear her throat with a little grunt. Her cue. "To each her own, I guess."

"I heard."

Carolyn says, "So, over?"

"No, not *over*!" Brynne raises her voice. "I still have a question. If you liked me so much, why did you ruin my life? OVER!"

"I didn't mean to ruin your life, but you know what? I liked you a whole lot better after I did. I'm sorry! And I'm not even mad about what you did up onstage anymore—"

"Really?" Carolyn interrupts. "'Cause seriously? I'd be pissed."

I continue. "I just know that I hurt you pretty bad, and I wish you would just forgive me. Over."

Brynne finally looks at me. "You act like that's so easy to do," she says through a stiff jaw and with little slits of eyes.

I find that it's not always easy to have patience with someone who talks to you with a stiff jaw and slitty little eyes, and I start to stumble off the high road. "Brynne, you know what? You used to be pretty awful to me, if you remember!"

Carolyn interjects. "She didn't say 'over.' Neither one of you are saying 'over' anymore. Do you want to get mediated or not?!"

Despite the fact that I'm getting annoyed, I know I need to do this. "Look, the truth is that we haven't always liked each other, but I wish we had. You're nice and smart and funny when you want to be. And I screwed up. And I'm sorry. Over." There. Now let *that* get around the school. I hope Carolyn's not taking her peer mediator confidentiality oath too seriously—this is one of those times when I'm actually hoping the gossip will fly.

Brynne turns her stare back to the table.

Carolyn consults her handbook. "So, okay. Brynne, do you accept this apology?"

Brynne shrugs. "Fine. But it doesn't mean we have to be friends."

"Excellent!" Carolyn says. "Okay, so you're supposed to apologize, too."

Brynne leans back and crosses her arms over her chest. "Sorry," she says, narrowing her eyes at me.

Carolyn looks back down at her handbook. "So I guess we have a resolution, right?"

"Yes," Brynne says. "Yes, we do." And then she glares at me and says, maybe a little too pointedly. "*Over.*"

Okay, then.

"Oh my God, really?" Carolyn jumps back in. "You're going to be like that? I don't get you, Brynne. Why the heck did you even re—"

She stops talking. We both see it happen. Brynne's face starts to melt.

Well, not actually melt, but that's what it looks like. Her eyebrows, her eyes, her mouth—everything starts to slide downhill in slow motion. Her forehead moves like high tide, taking up more than its fair share of face space. Her mouth forms a downward oval. It takes me a minute to realize it, but she's crying.

Crying.

Not the angry, splattery type of cry that she had on the day of my confession, but a deep, mournful one. You know those whale sounds you hear on those shows on Animal Planet? Well, if you were anywhere near water, that's exactly what you'd think you were hearing.

Carolyn softens, her eyes round and worried. Over the sobs, she whispers to me, "You think I should touch her?"

"Um, maybe?" Brynne's sadness is pulling me in, but I, too, feel completely helpless.

Carolyn clears her throat. "There, there," she says loudly, patting Brynne's shoulder.

Brynne shakes Carolyn's hand off, puts her forearms on the table and places her wet face on them.

"You know," Carolyn says, slowly scooting her chair back. "I—I'm thinking you guys need a minute. I'm just . . ." She sticks her thumb out and motions it over her shoulder. "Gonna go, then." She gathers her handbook and papers and speed-walks out of the room.

I get up and go around to Brynne's side of the table. I sit down next to her. "I'm so sorry, Brynne. I really did, you know, like you."

She sits up. She takes a deep breath. Her arms lift. My hands instinctively fly to protect my neck. Her arms wrap around me. Her face burrows into my shoulder. "I—I—I liked—" Snort. Sniffle. Hiccup. "I liked—" Gasp. Snort. "You. Too. A. Lot." It takes her about twenty minutes to get it out, and by the time she does, the shoulder of my shirt is soaked. Which is kind of *ew*, but still, a small price to pay for a truce.

Finally, her cries subside and she sits up straight. She doesn't look at me as she dabs at her face and blows her nose. "Okay, so there's that," she says with a little laugh. "We probably should go before they kick us out of here. Two more minutes and we'll officially be loitering."

I surprise myself with a nose-laugh. Now who's *ew*?

"You should probably go before that happens," she says. She gives me a half smile.

"What about you?" I ask. "Are you okay?"

"I'll be fine," she says, still sniffling a little. "Look, I just need a minute alone, okay?"

"You sure?" I ask. I don't know how I feel. I mean, I *did* like her. And despite all that's happened between us, maybe I still kind of do.

"Yeah."

I get up to leave. I'm almost to the door when she calls my name. I turn around.

"I really *am* sorry," she says, without meeting my eyes. "For the mean things I've done. Sometimes I just don't know how else to act. And for my campaign speech. I was just, you know, in a really bad place. I mean, I thought we *had* something, and then—" Her voice starts to warp a little. "Anyway, that's really all I wanted to say. That's why I requested peer mediation."

Wait. My mouth drops open.

"*You* requested this meeting?" I'm honestly baffled. And sort of touched by it all, too.

"I know. Dorky thing to do and all, but—" She shrugs, still avoiding my eyes. "I didn't know how to do this. You know, I've never apologized to anyone before. Without being forced to, I mean."

I open my mouth to say something—maybe to thank her. She holds up her hand. "No, you know what, Olivia? Don't say anything else, okay? It was just supposed to be an apology—not a conversation."

It's Brynne, all right. And despite the edge in her words, I'm kind of relieved. Nobody can say I killed her spirit. It suffered a little damage, but it's far from dead.

57.

Heeling

ON SUNDAY AFTERNOON, I'm in the kitchen washing dishes when there's a knock on the door. Oomlot breaks out with a bark that makes him sound mean, and races to the foyer. Queso follows, yapping. I wipe my hands on a dish towel and walk down the hall toward the front door. Through the screen, I see Moncherie crouched on the porch, rubbing the belly of Ferrill, our hopeless guard dog.

"Mon—" I start to say her name and remember I can't pronounce it without sounding like I'm practically choking on phlegm. "Hi?" I ask, rather than say. "You want to come in?"

"Actually, I think you should come out here," she says, smiling.

"Uh. Okay?" I toss the dish towel over the banister and step out onto the porch. Oomlot squeezes past me, eager to get outside. And then I see why.

"Isn't she beautiful?" Moncherie gushes.

I think my gasp is loud enough for her to hear. The strangest-looking dog I've ever seen—and I'm being polite here—is sitting in the backseat of Moncherie's car. The dog's eyes are so droopy and wide-set that it looks almost fishlike; its coat looks like a used Brillo pad; its ears are ragged and crooked. An unidentified object dangles from its mouth.

"Her name"—Moncherie pauses, beaming—"is *Olivia*."

A laugh escapes me. "Are you serious?"

"Well, yes, I'm serious. You're the whole reason I adopted her—all your cute dog stories got me wanting one. You know she came from a hoarder? She was one of one hundred and twenty-six dogs. But you wouldn't know it—she just seems so *wonderful*."

Before I can say anything, Moncherie takes a deep breath and her smile wears away a little. "Look, I've got some other news." She sighs and shifts her weight in her Minnie Mouse–style pumps. "Remember that day I had to cancel our appointment?"

I nod, reddening, remembering how I accused her of dog-training a man when it's clear now that it really *was* a dog she was interested in.

"Well, I was actually on a job interview. And, guess what? I got the job!" She pulls her shoulders back and straightens up her posture. "You're looking at the next Harold and Harold representative. I'm going to be a *real estate agent!*"

"Like, sell houses?" My forehead stiffens. I'm not sure why I feel sad, but I do, just a little.

"Exactly!" she says, then studies me. "You okay?"

"Yeah." I laugh nervously.

"Olivia, what's up?" She looks concerned.

"I think I want to tell you something." I swallow. "Can I still do that?"

"Sure," she says, her forehead crinkling. "Is this about—"

I nod. "My mom."

She takes my hand and we sit down on the steps of the porch, and I tell her about something I've done. How I read one of my mother's letters. And how she told me she missed me. And so I read the next one. And she said she was feeling better. And then I read the last one. And she said she was sorry. And then I did something I hadn't done in an even longer time. I tell Moncherie how I wrote back.

And how I told my mom that I forgave her, now that I know what that really means.

She squeezes my hand. "Oh, I'm so proud of you, Olivia! Doesn't it feel great?"

"Like rainbows and unicorns," I joke. But it does feel good.

She laughs and wraps her arms around me. I can't help but laugh and hug her back.

"Now, look," she says. "I want you to promise me one thing."

"Okay. What?"

"That you'll never use dog training on a person again."

"I already told you I wouldn't."

"No, I mean really promise me. Say it with me," she starts. "*Moncherie*," she leads me, with that horrible faux French accent. I just keep smiling. "Come on, Olivia, you have to say it. *Moncherie* . . ."

I take a deep breath. "*Moncherie* . . ." I butcher her name.

"No," she says, "Open your throat. *Moncherie* . . ."

So I do it. I open my throat and say her name like I'm going to hock a lugie. I am burning with embarrassment, but she looks almost proud.

"I will never use dog training on a person again," she coaches me.

"I will never use dog training on a person again," I repeat.

She looks pleased. I recover and ask, "So—is that it? Am I ever going to see you again?"

"Well, I'm hoping maybe Olivia and I could stop by sometime and take you for ice cream or something. What do you think? I mean, you'd have to ask Corny. Or your dad. He's still moving up here, right?" She looks a little too hopeful.

"In the spring," I say. It's the latest bit of news I've gotten. He says it's for sure.

"Spring, huh? Well, just give me a call." She takes my hand, turns it over, and writes a number on my palm. "That's my cell. Just call me, okay?"

I tell her I will. And I mean it.

She turns to leave, and I follow her off the porch. "What's that in Olivia's mouth?"

"Oh, yeah!" Moncherie's face lights up. "Can you believe it? She came with her own Lindsay Lohan doll! Isn't that cute?"

I step toward the car. Olivia the Dog eyes me suspiciously. In her mouth she holds the naked doll by the torso. One of the doll's arms is raised overhead, as if trying to flag down help. The other arm is missing—just gone. Short red-brown stubs of hair sprout from most of the head. On its face is a pink-lipsticked smirk.

Oomlot follows us down from the porch. He jumps his front paws up on the car and sniffs the doll. Olivia the Dog starts to growl. *Uh-oh.*

"Oh, Olivia," Moncherie says to her. "You just stop that. That's rude!" She turns to me and smiles, almost proudly. "She just loves Lindsay."

I haven't had much experience with dogs obsessed with

Lindsay Lohan. At least not yet. I smile—I may be hearing from Moncherie sooner than she thinks.

She reaches in to give me a hug. "I really enjoyed working with you, you know that?" She sighs, releasing me from the hug, but holding on to my shoulder. "I hope you got something out of our little talks."

"Oh, I did," I tell her, and watch as she brightens a little. And I'm sure I *did* get something out of our talks. Maybe it wasn't exactly therapy the way those weird old bearded guys like Freud would have wanted it, but whatever it was, it definitely opened my eyes.

Which are, I remind myself, totally Caribbean green.

58.

A Girl's Best Friends

"*SMELT* IS NOT a word," Phoebe yells out.

"It is too! Look it up," Joey tells her. "He who *smelt* it dealt it."

"It's a type of fish," Peyton Randall says from across the room, where she and Erin Monroe are playing Trivial Pursuit.

"Yeah, that too," Joey says, and laughs.

"Joey," Phoebe whines. "Sometimes I wonder about you." But then she laughs—yes, it's almost becoming a normal thing for her—and looks at him from the corner of her eye. It's a little uncomfortable to watch.

In the month since the election, Phoebe and Joey have been getting along rather well. Too well. Delia nudges me, and we laugh to ourselves, even though it's a little creepy.

"What's funny?" Phoebe asks. Her eyes flash at us. Then she turns bright pink and quickly tries to change the subject. "Who's next? Where's Mandy, anyway?"

"With Mister *Presidente*," I say. After Caleb was elected, he chose Mandy as his vice president. In my rich and growing fantasy life, he's done this to get closer to me.

"She's really been spending a lot of time with him," Phoebe says, her voice all syrupy with suspicion.

"They're going over the results of their poll with Vander-Pecker," I say quickly. "It's just *business*."

"Hmmm," Phoebe says.

She may be getting on my nerves a little now, but I take a deep breath and remind myself of what life was like without her. Without *them*. And I'm glad all of that's getting further and further behind us.

"It's not like they're going out or anything," I say.

She looks at me, eyebrows raised. "No one said they were." Now *she* looks amused, and *I'm* turning red.

Just as she says that, Mandy and Caleb walk into the room. "That was *productive*," Mandy says, and smirks, settling into the seat next to me that I had been secretly saving for Caleb.

He turns a different chair around and sits behind both of us. Mandy continues. "I think just about everyone we asked for ideas for improvement said they wanted better-looking teachers. And I had to go report that to Vander-Pecker."

Ms. Greenwood stirs. We all gasp. I wish it wasn't so easy to forget that she's in the room.

It's my turn to read out the list of words I found in our Boggle round. One of them is "done," but I'm nervous because I can practically feel Caleb's sweet peppermint breath on the back of my neck. I can't focus, and I end up saying it with a long O, like "Doan."

"*Doan?*" Delia says. "What's a *doan?*"

"I'm not sure," I say, puzzled by my own find.

Then Mandy peeks over my shoulder. "That's *done*, genius. Like finished."

Everyone laughs. Now I wish I hadn't worn my glossy hair in a ponytail, because despite the joyous breeze of Caleb's mint-breath, I'm sure my neck is flame red.

The door opens again. We all look up to see Brynne. My breath becomes stuck in my lungs.

"Hey," she says. She looks right at me and gives me a sideways smile. "Can I—? I mean, I brought Clue."

My friends and I had discussed this, after our reunion. We knew all her friendships had dissolved, and her campaign speech didn't win her any votes. We knew that one day she'd be here, wanting to move on, wanting to have some friends.

Mandy thought it might be good karma to let her in the club. Delia thought it might be the right thing to do. Joey thought it might be good for games that require partners. And after some persuasion, Phoebe, being Phoebe, decided it could be a good investment. "I suppose in a year or so," she said, "everyone will have forgotten about eighth grade, and she'll probably be even prettier. Which could rub off on the rest of us."

And me, well, I learned that underneath the bark and the bite is just a girl. One who wants to be accepted, just like me— just like any one of us. One who wants to play board games and eat M&M's and cuddle puppies. And, oh yeah, go out with Ryan Stoles. But I'm keeping that to myself. I owe at least *that* to her.

"Hey," Mandy says to her. "Come on in."

Brynne walks in and sits down in the space next to Phoebe, who wiggles her chair aside—in the direction of Joey—to make room for her.

This might not exactly be pack-leader mentality, but maybe there are times when everyone just needs to be a part of the pack.

Acknowledgments

MANY THANKS TO:

Casper, for being my (irresistibly cute) muse. And to Friends of Homeless Animals, for letting us adopt him.

Kylie and Stew, for making my life richer, funnier, and more meaningful. And for giving me time, space, love, and lots of karate moves.

Michele Nesmith, for helping me survive middle school and all things beyond. This is "our" book.

Lois Nason and Uschi Schueller, for your boundless friendship and constant support.

Mom and Dad, for taking away the TV when I was six (I know, right?) and surrounding me with books. You did say one day I'd thank you. You were right.

My agent, Holly Root, for picking me out of the slush, polishing me up, and making my dream come true.

My editor, Abby Ranger, for limitless (though well-tested) supplies of patience, kindness, encouragement, and talent. I could quote from a song involving wind and wings and heroes and such things, and while it would all be applicable, it might get awkward. Many thanks also to Laura Schreiber for her keen eye and great editorial insight, and to Marci Senders for her creative genius. If you really can judge a book by its cover, I hope to live up to it.

Also thanks to Hailey Slaton, Debra Ginsberg, Erika Robuck, and Michael Neff for various and sundry great things that went toward helping me complete this book.

And if you're reading this? I especially thank you. You'll always be Best in Show in my eyes. Because there wouldn't be a show without you.